# A SPECIAL BLEND OF MURDER

## CAT CHANDLER

FIVE SISTERS PUBLISHING

Cover Art: carrie@cheekycovers.com

Content/Edit Services: Behest Indie Novelist Services

❀ Created with Vellum

*For my wonderful, bright and beautiful daughter, Erin*

# FOREWORD

To My Readers:

This book originally published in July, 2017, just a few months before the devastating wildfires that struck the Northern California Wine Country. The book is set in that same wine country, in a fictional town with a unique history. Unfortunately, the original name of the town was "Arson". Given the events in October of 2017, I didn't feel that was any longer appropriate for a town set in that area. With this re-release, the town now has a new name and a new backstory, while the rest of the story is substantially the same. If you purchased the original version, with the same name and title, then you have already read this book and Book 2 in the series. Book 3 will be out in March, 2018.

*Cat Chandler*

# 1

Nicki Connors stopped and set her steel bucket filled with gardening tools at her feet. She placed her hands on the small of her back and lightly pushed inward, stretching her spine while she waited for her friend and landlady to finish looking over their newly created flower bed.

"The petunias should go over there." Maxie Edwards pointed a perfectly manicured nail, polished to a high gloss in a color called Pink Bliss, at a small, empty spot of ground to her right. From the top of her silver hair to the toes of her expensive, backless sandals, the older woman looked ready to attend any high society, afternoon garden party. She certainly didn't look as if she'd be doing the gardening herself.

*Being overdressed to muck in the dirt isn't a detail that would ever bother Maxie,* Nicki thought fondly. She consulted the schematic Mason, Maxie's husband and a retired police chief, had left for the two women to follow. Although Mason Edwards had traded his title of "Chief" for that of "Master Gardener", he still expected his orders to be followed to a "T". Something Nicki was sure she respected a great deal more than the retired chief's wife did. So she wasn't even a little surprised when there were no petunias listed in the spot where Maxie was pointing.

"Um. I think Mason wants the petunias on the other side of the bed." Nicki held out the hand-drawn plan. Her generous mouth twitched upward at the corners when Maxie waved the paper away without so much as a glance.

"My Mason is a genius in the garden, but he doesn't know everything," Maxie said. She always referred to her husband of twenty years as "my Mason", and now everyone who knew them had turned it into the ex-chief's name, running the words together and always referring to him as "myMason". Even Nicki.

"I don't know, Maxie. Your husband is very particular about his plants."

Maxie laughed. "He can putter about and arrange the entire landscaping around the house to his heart's desire, but the artist colony is my project. And I want the petunias planted here."

"Okay," Nicki said without any further argument. After all, she was extremely grateful to be part of Maxie's "artist colony". It was a group of six townhouses clustered along a circular drive built on the far end of the Edward's property. Maxie only rented them to writers, or in the case of Nicki's close-as-a-sister friend, Jenna Lindstrom, to people who helped writers. Jenna was a computer whiz, and Maxie was thrilled to have someone nearby who could set up and maintain her website. So was Nicki. Without Jenna's help, there would be no website for the petite writer to blog from.

Nicki sighed as she dug into the dirt. She loved living in the wine country. Maxie's mini-estate was just west of the town of Soldoff, and not far from its much bigger and better-known neighbor, Sonoma. It was the perfect place for her. She only wished the reason she'd moved here was for a new adventure rather than to escape from bad memories.

Nicki had landed on the Pacific Coast three years ago because she'd needed to get out of New York City and start fresh somewhere else. Anywhere else. She still loved the Big Apple, and always would. She grew up there, went to college and culinary school there, and had been carving out a good career in its big city dining scene.

But her mother was also murdered there.

Julie Connors lost her life within steps of her top floor, rent-controlled apartment. Her body left lying beside her front door for her daughter to discover several hours later when Nicki had stopped by because her Mom hadn't kept their lunch date.

Six months after she'd buried her mother, who'd raised her alone since Nicki was five years old, she'd still been numb and been dragging herself into work every day. Until one night she'd arrived home to find her roommate, Jenna, randomly tossing both of their things into boxes.

Confused and astounded, Nicki had stood in their postage-stamp-sized living room in the apartment they'd shared, with her mouth open and eyes as big as saucers while Jenna had casually told her they were following Alex, their other former roommate, to California. Enough was enough. They needed to get away, and that's what they were going to do.

So just ten days later, Nicki had found herself standing on Fisherman's Wharf, gazing across a beautiful sparkling bay, and admiring the world-famous Golden Gate Bridge gleaming in the distance.

Once the move was made, she'd started writing freelance pieces for magazines about the food and leisure life in the wine country of Sonoma, as well as starting a blog of her own. And to supplement her income, she'd also begun penning spy novels. Her every-girl's-dream secret agent, Tyrone Blackstone, had steadily gained a solid following.

Fueled by her modest but growing success, Nicki began including write-ups in her blog about the wineries she loved to visit. To her happy amazement, Matt, the owner and editor of *Food & Wine Online*, had proclaimed her a natural wine enthusiast and critic, which prompted her to spend many of her spare hours reading up on the finer points of winemaking and, more importantly to her, wine tasting.

"... and I loved the article you wrote on Todos Winery," Maxie said.

Nicki blinked as she realized her landlady was talking to her.

"Um... Todos? Yes, I did an article for Matt's magazine on Todos."

"I know, dear," Maxie chuckled. "That's what I said. I enjoyed reading about Todos through your eyes. And I'm sure Bill was thrilled."

Nicki smiled. Bill Stacy was the owner of Todos Winery. He was definitely a cowboy who'd taken to growing grapes, and Nicki liked him very much. "He's a nice man."

"Yes, he is. So is that very attractive deputy, Danny Findley. Who, by the way, has a huge crush on you."

When Nicki rolled her eyes, Maxie put her hands on her hips.

"I have it from a solid source. Of course, half the men in town have a crush on you."

With her honey-blond hair, expressive hazel eyes, and perfect curves packed into a five-foot- two-inch frame, Nicki had not only inherited her late mother's beauty, but also her only parent's disinterest in anyone who never bothered to look beyond it. Which is why she glanced over at Maxie and shrugged.

"I've met most of the men in Soldoff, and I'm fairly sure a respectable number of them aren't interested in women at all," Nicki said.

"That may be true, but Danny certainly is," Maxie insisted. "He's a nice young man with a very solid future in the police department. And those aren't easy things to find in a potential husband these days."

"Young being the operative word. I'm at least eight years older than he is. What is he? Twenty-three?"

"He's twenty-six, dear. Five years isn't that big of an age difference."

With the last of the petunias planted, Nicki hoped their placement wouldn't gain her the eternal wrath of myMason. She put her trowel into her bucket and stood up.

"I have a boyfriend, Maxie," she reminded the older woman. "There's no need for you to play matchmaker."

"Until he puts a ring on your finger, of course there is," Maxie said before jumping to another topic. "How do you like your new domain?" Maxie had the entire kitchen in Nicki's townhouse renovated, with the last cupboard handle finally installed just that morning.

"It's wonderful," Nicki declared. "I feel like I'm trespassing in someone else's house every time I walk into it. I love it!"

"I'm so glad." Her landlady looked across the expanse of lawn and waved. "Speaking of doing something criminal, here comes my Mason with Chief Turnlow.

Nicki swiveled around and lifted a hand to shade her eyes. The two men were slowly walking in their direction, with the new police chief doing most of the talking. He was a big man, with thinning hair and blue eyes which could quickly transform into a laser-sharp gaze.

After picking up her bucket, Nicki took a big, comically exaggerated step away from Maxie.

"I don't want to be anywhere near you when your husband sees where you told me to put the petunias."

"That's all right, dear. I'm sure I can talk him out of any bad mood over such a minor transgression." Maxie paused and smiled as the two men came within earshot.

Mason Edwards was only an inch or so taller than his wife, with gray hair and a matching mustache in the same shade. He had a lean build he kept trim by doing the gardening all over their large property, as well as looking after a good piece of the public areas in town. It saved the local councilmen from having to budget any money to keep the central square mowed and attractively landscaped for the hordes of tourists that descended on Soldoff every weekend.

"Hello, dear." Maxie gave her husband a peck on the cheek.

Just as Nicki had feared, he immediately looked over at the petunias then frowned at his wife. "I guess we'll be discussing this later."

"Of course." Maxie smiled at the big man standing next to Mason. "Good afternoon, Chief Turnlow. I hope everything is calm in Soldoff today."

The chief's eyes crinkled at the corners. "It is, Maxie. Just a speeder or two racing through town on their way to Sonoma." He looked over at Nicki and nodded. "Hello, Nicki."

"Hi, Chief. Soldoff must be a bit tame after Los Angeles," she commented. Chief Turnlow had spent twenty years in the LAPD homicide department. Nicki liked him, and even occasionally wished he'd been the one assigned to her mother's case. Maybe then it wouldn't have gone cold.

"Peace and quiet can be a good thing," the chief replied.

Nicki couldn't have agreed more.

## 2

Nicki was dropping wide-cut noodles into a pot of boiling water, and congratulating herself over the fact her back wasn't stiff after all the flower planting activities from the day before, when a familiar voice echoed down the front hallway.

"Hello? Anyone home? Your door's unlocked."

Rolling her eyes, Nicki paused for the second it took for the front door to hit the side of its frame with a loud bang.

Jenna never closed anything quietly. Even when she, Nicki and Alex had pooled their resources and shared a just-starting-out-on-their-own, very compact, New York apartment, Jenna had slammed doors. Alex was sure it came from Jenna growing up on her family's farm. Their techno-whiz friend had been more accustomed to barn doors than those found in apartments or townhouses. And Jenna's habit hadn't changed, even after the three friends had left their little apartment behind and headed west.

The smacking sound of flip-flops against wood floors grew louder as Jenna approached the kitchen. With a quick grin, Nicki ruffled her hair into a messy-looking array of uncombed strands

before grabbing a spatula from a container on the counter. She
threw a handy dish towel over the cutting board in front of her
and started beating her spatula onto the towel just as Jenna
appeared in the doorway.

"Are you serious?" Her friend laughed, brushing away a stray
lock of thick hair that was naturally kinked into tight waves. She'd
gathered most of the unruly, dark mass into a band at the nape of
her neck. From there it fell in a riot of tangles, tumbling halfway
down her back. "You're expecting me to believe you've worked
yourself to the bone over preparing our lunch, and now you're
actually abusing one of your precious, gourmet ingredients by
pounding it into smithereens beneath that dish cloth?"

Nicki shrugged and stopped beating the poor towel. "You
never know what disturbing cooking habits I've picked up lately.
After all, this *is* California, the land of all things strange and
unusual."

"We're out in the middle of practically nowhere, surrounded
by vineyards, and we're on a first name basis with every single
soul in this town. You can't believe we'll run into someone or
something more strange and unusual than the average lunatic in
the Big Apple? And what is that supposed to be, anyway? Food
abuse by spatula? Really?" Jenna rolled her eyes.

"You computer geeks are such logical souls," Nicki said with a
shake of her head.

"And you artistic types always take the most dramatic spin on
everything, even preparing food," Jenna shot back.

Both women grinned at each other before closing the
distance between them for a quick hug. Nicki grabbed Jenna's
arm and pulled her over to the large island dominating the
center of the kitchen. The self-proclaimed geek's big brown eyes
were magnified even larger behind the lenses of her oversized
glasses. Her gaze darted around the room and she let out a low
whistle.

"The ren-o turned out really beautiful."

"It did, didn't it?" Nicki's smile grew wider. With its brand new, marble-covered island, deep farm sink and gleaming stainless-steel appliances complete with a six-burner, gas stove, the kitchen was her favorite room in the house. Gone were the days of keeping her wine in a tiny, worn-out refrigerator more suited to a college dormitory. Now she had the most modern, temperature-controlled wine cooler available.

There was no doubt about it. This was her dream kitchen. And just as she'd told Maxie, she couldn't believe it was hers to cook in whenever she pleased. Nicki always clapped her hands in glee every time she walked into it. A job she loved, a kitchen to die for — her new life in California suited her just fine. She even adored the small town she was now calling home. So far away and so very different from the huge city of high-rise buildings and subways where she'd grown up.

Soldoff was only a few miles from the much more famous wine town of Sonoma, but had a unique charm of its own. The odd, hodgepodge style of the buildings clustered around the town's central square drew enough visitors on any given weekend to double the number of permanent residents, and during an art or wine festival, that number grew into the thousands. But even then, the town barely rated a dot on any road map of a State used to counting its population in the millions.

What Nicki liked the most though, was Soldoff's quirky history.

Her adopted home gained its name after its founder bid farewell to the town and moved back East, where he promptly started selling land plots in the golden State of California, most of which were already owned by his former neighbors. It was a toss-up of who was more surprised, the newcomers with a fancy, hand-written deed in their hands, or the owners who were already living there. It took several years, and a few fistfights, to straighten it all out. But along the way the town became known as the place that had been "sold off", and over time, the name stuck.

Fortunately for the residents, that was the last raucous incident in the town's history.

*That is,* Nicki thought, *if you didn't count the annual Double Cross Festival.* The rowdy celebration of the event that gave Soldoff its name attracted dozens of famous artists and winemakers, along with thousands of tourists who came to mix, mingle and gawk at them.

"The Candy Couple certainly went all out for you," Jenna said, using the local nickname for Maxie and Mason. Their original nickname of M&M had changed to accommodate Maxie's declaration that it was likely a copyright infringement on the chocolate treat sold in every grocery store. With that proclamation, the laid-back, agreeable town residents switched over to *Candy Couple.*

"Don't call them that," Nicki chided. "They've been nothing but kind—especially Maxie renting both of us a duplex at half the going rate."

"She rented your half of the duplex for half price because you joined her Ladies in Writing Society, and from what I saw yesterday out my window, plant petunias for her. And she rented the other half to me for the same, excellent price because I put up her website," Jenna said. "Which isn't worth the break in my rent since Maxie insists on poking around in the admin screens and changing the codes on the plug-ins. Besides, they both call themselves the Candy Couple. So does the rest of the town. Why shouldn't we do the same?"

Nicki had to concede Jenna's point. Their mutual landlady never seemed to mind the nickname, and Maxie was notorious for fooling around on her website, leaving havoc in her wake.

"What did Maxie do now?"

"This time she tried to change the entire theme and launched one that didn't fit the layout at all." Jenna leaned her head back and closed her eyes.

"Well, okay. Whatever you said sounds horrifying." Nicki bit

her lip to keep from laughing. She did her best to appear innocent when Jenna shot her a narrowed-eye look. "What?"

"I'm compelled to mention you also have a website, and a
growing blog which pays your rent and lets you buy the fancy
food you love to cook, and I love to eat. It wouldn't hurt to learn
how to keep your site in running order. I mean, what will you do
if something happens to me?"

"I suppose if you collapsed from an overdose of excessive
consumption of hamburgers, I'd have to hire someone else,"
Nicki said.

"Who would cost you a small fortune."

Sliding onto a tall stool, Jenna set the paper bag she was
carrying on the kitchen island and leaned an elbow on its
smooth, marble top. She grinned at her friend. "My neck was
hurting from searching for you down there."

Nicki stepped back and put both hands on her hips. "That's
right Jenna Lindstrom. Whenever you hit a wall in an argument,
you try to distract me by making fun of my height."

Jenna took a loud, deep sniff of the fragrant aroma hanging in
the air. "You may be small in stature, but you cook like a giant. Is
that your famous homemade chicken soup?" At Nicki's nod,
Jenna glanced over at the heavy mixer stand at the end of the
counter with a pasta-making attachment on top. "And you made
the noodles yourself?"

Nicki picked up the large pot and carried it to the sink to
drain the contents into a strainer she'd placed there. "Of course."
Then pointed at the bag in front of Jenna. "And if my soup is so
world- famous, why did you bring that?"

"Strictly as a supplement. I'll wither away on that skimpy,
healthy diet you and Alex always rave about," Jenna sniffed. "You
know I love your soup, but I'd be starving again in a couple of
hours if that's all I ate. Speaking of which, you'd better hurry it
along. Alex should be calling at any moment for our catch-up
session."

"Right you are."

Nicki grabbed two serving bowls from a shelf beside the stove and gently slid her cooked, homemade noodles into their bottoms. With the efficiency of long hours spent in a kitchen, she ladled in the broth before sprinkling fresh, chopped parsley on top. Nicki carried one bowl over to Jenna before retrieving the second one for herself, along with a plate.

She snorted in exasperation when her friend reached into her paper bag and plopped a large, greasy hamburger onto the plate.

Shaking her head, Nicki picked-up her cell phone on the first ring. After a quick, "hang on" to the caller, she hit the speaker button and dropped the phone into a small stand on the counter.

"Perfect timing, Alex. Jenna's about to chomp into one of her grease burgers from Eddie's Diner to go with the delicious lunch I slaved over the entire morning."

Nicki tilted her head and wrinkled her nose at the glare Jenna sent her way before picking up her spoon and dipping it into the steaming bowl in front of her.

"Nicki made soup. I can't live on soup," Jenna complained.

"Nicki's soup is a main course all by itself." Alex's voice floated out from the cell phone. "And right now, I'd kill for it. I'd even kill for a greasy burger."

"Did you have to settle for the hospital cafeteria food again?" Nicki asked.

"I'm one-hundred percent certain I'm looking at the same salad I ate for dinner last night."

"Were you called in?"

While Nicki's voice was full of sympathy, Jenna simply shrugged.

"Well, you knew the hours when you decided on emergency medicine," Jenna said. "If you'd gone with psychiatry like you were thinking about when you started med school, you could have kept more human hours."

Alex laughed. "Pot calling the kettle black there, Jenna. Back in New York you were always up and working when I dragged myself home from my rotation, no matter what hour it was. And I doubt that's changed much."

"The only one of us who keeps anything resembling reasonable hours is me." Nicki didn't bother to hide the touch of smugness in her tone. "The writing and blogging life does have its advantages."

"Uh huh," both her friends echoed in unison, making Nicki laugh.

"Unless you have a deadline to meet," Alex put in.

"Well, there is that," Nicki agreed.

"Or you're trying to get in extra time with Tyrone Blackstone, the ultimate spy." Jenna winked at her friend who calmly continued to enjoy her soup.

"He is pretty dreamy and steamy when he isn't on a mission shooting people. The absolutely perfect guy," Alex said.

"Dreamy and steamy? I'm definitely using that in the next book blurb." Nicki grinned, delighted with the catchy phrase.

"Isn't any man perfect when he's a figment of your imagination?" Jenna asked. "But Tyrone *is* one of my favorite characters. Interesting what gets conjured up in of that mind of yours, Nicki Connors."

"Ignore her, Alex. So, what have you been up to?" Nicki asked. She wiggled in her chair to settle in more comfortably. She loved the easy rhythm of their friendship, especially during these cozy chats.

"Okay. But you first," Alex said. "I need to swallow at least two bites of this incredibly wilted salad from the cafeteria."

"After a long night at my desk, I sent the last of my articles to Matt. This morning he sent a return email asking for a conference call." Nicki glanced at her watch. "In less than an hour. After which, I'm hoping for three, uninterrupted days to finish writing Tyrone's latest adventure and get it ready to send to my proofreader."

Jenna clapped her hands. "That's great."

Nicki did a slight bow before turning her gaze to the phone. "What about you, Alex? How's that hunky fiancé of yours?"

"Ty is fine, and I'll let him know your new book is almost done. He likes to be forewarned of your publishing dates, so he can hide from the other guys in the firehouse."

"I keep telling him, the hero's name is Tyrone, not Tyler. Why does he always think I'm writing about him?"

"Because he's a guy, and they all think they're dreamy and steamy." Alex's tone was so matter-of-fact her audience of two nodded in agreement.

After a moment Nicki grinned and glanced over at Jenna, who looked as if she was fighting to hold in her laughter.

Since he was a fireman, Ty assumed women in general saw him as a hunk, even if the idea made him flush with irritation whenever one of his fiancée's friends teased him about it. But Nicki knew the honest, protective fireman had already figured out that to love Alex meant he had to put up with all of them. They were a package deal.

"Your turn, Alex."

With her usual enthusiasm for all things healthy, Alex briefly described her still very sketchy wedding plans before launching into an excited explanation of her latest exercise regimen which she fully intended to rope Nicki into.

"It seems to me you find that exercise routine more interesting than planning your wedding," Jenna said around a mouthful of burger.

"True words," Alex conceded. "A quick ceremony at city hall would work for me, but Ty and my mother want a wedding."

"And on that note, I guess it's my turn," Jenna laughed. She immediately related a hilarious story involving an engagement and wedding site she'd designed for the bridezilla to outdo all bridezillas.

Time flew by until the distinctive clang of the alarm on Alex's watch sounded through the speaker. The doctor's sigh was loud and clear across the cell phone.

"I have to get back. We're monitoring a chest pain patient and I want to look in on him. I wish we weren't so far apart so we could have our catch-ups in person."

"It's only forty minutes from here to Santa Rosa," Nicki said. "Why don't we plan on driving over tomorrow?"

"Alex has three days off next week and is coming here since Tyler's on duty at the firehouse," Jenna reminded her. She pointed to the far wall. "Stop using that paper calendar and go to the electronic one on your phone so you can keep everything straight." She raised her voice before adding, "both of you."

"And you need to stop eating so many burgers so your arteries won't clog, and you end up in the ER," Alex replied.

"And I have that conference call with Matt in ten minutes," Nicki said with a glance at her watch. "We'll see you next week, then. Okay, Alex?"

"Oops, just got a page. Talk later."

The phone went dead. Nicki reached over and tapped the hang-up button while Jenna gathered up her now empty bowl and plate and headed over to the sink.

"I have to go, too. I need to straighten out Maxie's website, and then put the finishing touches on another one for a new client who wants to go live on Friday."

Jenna set her dishes in the sink and turned toward Nicki, her eyebrows raised behind her glasses. "How is Matt, by the way?"

"He's fine." Nicki gave her friend a puzzled look. "Why?"

Jenna shrugged. "Just wondered. I know you write articles for his online magazine, but he spends a lot of time on the phone with you."

"Don't start, Jenna. He's the owner and editor of the magazine, and I'm only one of the many freelance writers he assigns articles to. Nothing more than that. Besides, I have a boyfriend. Remember?"

"If you say so. But if Matt spent as much time talking to all his writers as he does with you, he wouldn't be able to do much else."

Before Nicki could come up with a solid counter-argument, her cell phone rang again.

"And he always calls right on the dot. I'd say he has a crush on you." Jenna gave an exaggerated blink of her eyes. "I'll see you later."

With no other choice but to answer the call, Nicki stuck her tongue out at the tall, dark-haired woman grinning back at her. With a last wave, Jenna disappeared into the hallway. Nicki pressed the *answer* button before putting the phone on speaker.

"Hang on a minute, Matt." A second later the front door rattled as it was slammed shut.

"I gather Jenna just left?" Matt asked.

"Yes." A little self-conscious over Jenna's observations, Nicki put on her best professional voice and got right to business. "I emailed the last two articles this morning. I'm sure you haven't had time to read them yet, but..."

"I have," Matt interrupted. "They're fine. I'd be happy to discuss them in more detail, but unfortunately, I'm short on time today. Nicki, I need to discuss another assignment with you."

She relaxed. He sounded all business and nothing more. Jenna was crazy.

"What do you have in mind? I'll be free later this week."

"Well, I know you're looking forward to working on your novel, but I need a wine event covered, and it's happening right in your neighborhood."

Curious, Nicki walked over to the calendar Jenna hated, and that she kept on the cork board next to the refrigerator. She always noted the local wine and food events on it, as well as any scheduled in the various wine regions around Soldoff. She saw nothing going on in the next four days that might draw Matt's interest.

As if he could see what she was doing, Matt answered her unspoken question.

"It's a private event. Not publicized. The magazine got the invitation over a month ago, but I didn't intend to send anyone."

Nicki turned away from her calendar, picked up her phone and headed for her comfortable office where she kept her laptop. "Oh? Why not?"

"Because it's being hosted by Holland Winery in honor of their head winemaker."

"Okay."

"I like Jim Holland," Matt continued. "But his winemaker is George Lanciere, and his ego is way out of line. Especially for a guy who hasn't produced a single, notable limited blend of his own in ten years that's worth writing about. The wines he's produced for Holland have been solid, but not spectacular. And his mouth is so big, he's lucky someone hasn't killed him."

She could hear the scowl in Matt's voice. Which was totally out of character. "If you don't think much of Mr. Lanciere, why are you interested in this event?"

His first response to her question was a heavy sigh. "There's a rumor going around that he's unveiling a new blend to rival the Holland chardonnay which made the winery, and George, famous a decade ago."

Even though he'd piqued her interest, Nicki kept quiet. She knew Matt well enough to stay silent and wait until he'd worked through his thoughts in his own way.

"The guy can drop dead and take his latest creation with him as far as I'm concerned. But as editor of *Food & Wine Online*, I can't ignore this."

"How solid are the rumors about this special new blend?" she asked. Nicki had heard the gossip about Holland's head wine-maker, and none of it was very flattering. But she'd never met the man.

"Solid enough for me to confirm them last night with Geri

Gant, the assistant winemaker. When the announcement showed up on their website this morning, I called Jim Holland and accepted the invitation. They're expecting you to be there tomorrow."

Nicki couldn't quite stifle her groan of protest. "Tomorrow?"

"Holland Winery is only a fifteen-minute drive from you, isn't it? I know there's a tasting room off the main square in Soldoff, but the unveiling is strictly a winery event. Is there another conflict in your schedule? Aside from your novel writing time? I know that's important to you, and I'm sorry to have to ask, but I'd appreciate it if you could cover this event for me. That is, for the magazine."

Acutely aware of how much Matt had helped her freelance writing career get off the ground when she'd first moved to California, Nicki could not say "no" to him. Sighing to herself, she bid a silent goodbye to at least one of her free days to pen "the end" to her novel. She'd be getting a lot less sleep over the next few days if she agreed to cover the event, write the article, and still meet the deadline for her book.

"Email me the details. I'm happy to attend and give you a write-up on whatever happens at the event."

"You won't be thanking me after you meet George Lanciere. I'll owe you a big favor for this one."

# 3

The next morning Nicki pulled into the parking lot of Holland Winery right at 10 a.m. She wasn't surprised by how many cars were already lined up in the generous space despite a large sign on the driveway's entrance proclaiming that the tasting room was closed to the public. The lucky invited guests usually came and went throughout any private event, but were apparently ignoring that usual practice for this one.

George Lanciere had posted an announcement, all in capital letters, onto the winery's website just that morning, stating the limited number of available tastings of his special blend would be scattered throughout the event. Which Nicki took as a warning to arrive early and stay for the entire thing. She'd read the marketing hype about the mysterious new blend while she was sipping a cup of coffee and nibbling around the edges of an organic whole-wheat bagel.

Now as she gingerly picked her way between the oversized trucks and SUVs in the parking lot, Nicki steered her compact car straight for the outer edge. There was no problem finding an empty space near the production buildings. With a resigned sigh, Nicki flipped the ignition key of her nine-year-old Toyota to the off position, grimacing when the little car shuddered for a full five seconds before the engine finally stopped running. Her mechanic had proclaimed that at 250,000 miles, it was past time to put the pitiful thing out of its misery.

But Nicki's bank account didn't share his sentiment. She was still making payments for her mother's funeral and her own subsequent move across the country. She couldn't stretch her wildly fluctuating writing income to make a car payment too. The steady freelance work of supplying articles to Matt's very popular e-magazine went a long way toward easing her tight budget. So did her new series of novels. But the payments from *Food & Wine Online* outdid her books and her blog, which was why she was sitting in the parking lot of Holland Winery instead of lounging about her home office in pajamas, writing the last three chapters of her latest novel.

As much as Nicki wanted to barricade herself inside her comfortable townhouse and finish the manuscript, she simply couldn't. Not only for the sake of her budget, but because she really did owe Matt.

Flipping down the car's visor to reveal a tiny mirror, Nicki turned her face both ways to get a good look at her reflection, even though she couldn't see much more than her eyes staring back at her. Thinking she should have used a tad more than the bare hint of make-up she usually wore, Nicki settled for a philo-sophical shrug. She wasn't here to impress anyone. She only needed to meet George Lanciere during his self-proclaimed finest hour, be sure to sneak at least a taste of his new blend, and then high-tail it back to the townhouse. Hopefully this whole detour from writing her novel would only take a couple of hours — three at the most.

Feeling more cheerful over the prospect of quickly putting this assignment to bed, Nicki fished lip gloss out of her purse and made a rapid, targeted swipe across her mouth.

"All right-y then. First Matt's article about Mr. I'm-so-important Lanciere's big announcement, then a fast break for home after getting the reaction of a few of the people this winemaker will allow to taste his creation," Nicki said out loud before swinging the car door open. She stepped out and took a quick glance around.

The tasting room and adjoining parking lot were built on a slight rise, offering a beautiful view of the surrounding vineyard. Nicki smiled. She never tired of looking at rows of neat vines radiating out from the central spoke of a winery. It was always photo-worthy to her, even in late September after the grape harvest.

The crunch of footsteps against crushed rock broke the quiet moment of peace. A woman hurried up the ramp leading from an outbuilding to the parking lot. Recognizing her, Nicki raised a hand in greeting.

"Hey, Geri!"

The assistant winemaker halted in her tracks as her head snapped up and her eyes darted around the lot. At first her gaze passed right over Nicki.

Used to going unnoticed, largely thanks to her height, Nicki belatedly remembered she'd decided to wear flat sandals instead of the three-inch wedges she was usually in the habit of wearing.

"I'll be lucky if I cross anyone's line of vision at this grand unveiling," she muttered to herself before waving a hand back and forth to catch Geri's attention. It took a few waves, and a slight jump up which did nothing for her dignity, before the assistant winemaker finally spotted her and changed directions.

Nicki studied the solidly built woman striding across the parking lot. Geri always wore the same unadorned white shirt with the winery logo on the front pocket, black pants and sensible black shoes sporting thick rubber soles. If the middle-aged assistant intended to fade into the background, then the outfit was definitely a huge success. From Nicki's observations on prior encounters with Geri, that's usually what happened. No one noticed the assistant winemaker.

But today Geri spruced it up by trading the black pants for a stark black skirt that fell halfway between her knees and calves. At least Nicki assumed she meant to dress up for the event and wasn't deliberately trying to look like a nun. With her short dark hair and downcast eyes, the only thing missing was the headpiece.

Nicki wrinkled her nose at the catty thought. Geri didn't deserve that. It wasn't easy being a female winemaker, even an assistant one, in the mostly male profession. Feeling guilty, Nicki made a mental note to mention the assistant's name in her article. With that resolution filed in the back of her mind, she put on a smile and waited for Geri to cross the distance between them.

"I hope I'm not too late for the big unveiling," Nicki said once the woman had come close enough that she didn't have to shout.

Geri still halted a good six feet away.

"No, no. I'm sure Mr. Lanciere will serve his newest blend later." Geri's eyes continued to dart about as her lips twitched just a smidgeon upward into a stingy smile. "Are you here for your own blog or for *Food & Wine Online*?

"I wasn't lucky enough to receive a personal invitation to a George Lanciere private event," Nicki said. "The magazine sent me."

Geri's only response was to clasp her hands in front of her and keep her feet firmly planted.

Determined to be friendly, Nicki ignored the physical distance Geri was doing her best to keep between them and walked forward. "Shall we go inside? I don't want to disappoint my editor."

Nicki tilted her head toward the tasting room, mildly surprised when Geri turned and walked beside her instead of following three steps behind. But apparently walking together didn't mean talking together. When Geri remained silent, Nicki tried again.

"Is the winemaker going to give his assistant her proper due for helping with the crush and blending this year?" Nicki asked, using the common terms for the annual grape harvest.

When Geri only gave a hard snort, Nicki sent her a sideways glance. "I take it that's not George Lanciere's style?"

"No. It isn't."

"Well, maybe for his special blend, then." Nicki forced a hint of cheerfulness into her voice. If the constantly busy gossip mill in the wine community was to be believed, poor Geri would be lucky to receive an approving nod from George Lanciere, much less a whole sentence of praise.

Geri turned her head just enough to stare at Nicki. "Why would you say that?"

"Since you help with the crush and the blend for the Holland brands, I assumed you helped with a Lanciere private production, too."

"I most certainly did not help *him* put up his special blend."

"Oh. Well, it's not important. How did production go this year?" Surprised by the intensity of her denial, Nicki deftly changed the subject. She relaxed when Geri's smile grew as the assistant launched into a technical discussion of the recent crush.

Since Nicki was familiar with the basic process, she only listened with half an ear, murmuring politely whenever Geri paused and took a breath. Thankful the assistant's lecture on how to make the perfect wine was cut short when they reached the tall double doors leading into the tasting room, Nicki stepped inside, eager to get the assignment started and finished.

The inviting space boasted a long, stand-up bar at the far end, with a generous number of high tables randomly scattered around the room. Just as the large gaggle of cars in the parking lot promised, the place was packed.

Nicki stood on her toes, trying to locate a friendly face. She was familiar with many of the winemakers and winery owners in the area, and already knew Jim Holland, the owner of the winery that also bore his name. Not only had she written about Holland Winery several times in her blog, it was one of the first stops she, Alex and Jenna had made when they'd explored the countryside around their new home.

"This is the wrong water. Go back and bring a bottle from my private refrigerator and be quick about it."

The angry command snapped through the air in a half-French, half-New Jersey accent, and was loud enough to be heard over the raised mix of voices in the room. The din quieted as heads swiveled, looking for the source of the outburst.

"Hey," Nicki couldn't stifle a startled yelp when Geri latched onto her arm and quickly moved through the crowd, pulling her reluctant captive along with her. Not wanting to make a scene by digging her heels in, Nicki smiled at the people they passed, trying to nod pleasantly and act as if everything was just dandy and fine while being dragged across the room.

Geri skidded to an abrupt stop at a table surrounded by a group of men. They turned together to stare at the two women.

Nicki brushed hair out of her face and narrowed her eyes on Geri, watching the color bloom on the taciturn woman's cheeks as her lips clamped into a tight thin line. The assistant wine-maker stepped between the frozen-in-place waiter and the man glaring at him, effectively blocking any further verbal abuse of the young server.

From the pleading look Geri tossed at her, Nicki realized the older woman was trying to protect one of her staff and needed some help. Deciding a distraction away from the young waiter was definitely in order, Nicki took a quick glance around the table before turning her smile on a huge man with his round belly hanging over a wide, leather belt.

Jim Holland stood a good foot over Nicki's head. He sported a solid build and thick brown hair shot through with wide streaks of gray. His dark-brown eyes took on a sparkle, accompanied by a warm smile and slight bow, as he held out his hand.

"It's nice to see you again, Nicki. You're looking wonderful."

Always delighted with the gracious, old-world charm that somehow seemed at odds with the bear of a man, Nicki shook his hand and grinned back. "Thank you. You're looking fine too. This is a wonderful event you've put together."

"It's an event, all right. But wonderful? Kind of hard to tell yet."

Nicki turned and smiled at the tall dark-haired man with the silver buckle on his belt and sporting a well-worn, dusty cowboy hat, who had suddenly come up behind her. "Hello, Mr. Stacy. How are things over at Todos?"

"My winery is doing just fine. The crush went well, so the blends from this year's production should be excellent."

"*I* think we will have *good* blends," the short, rotund man who'd yelled at the young waiter snapped out.

"I'm sure Todos's wine will be excellent," Nicki said, hoping to lessen the impact of the glare Bill Stacy fixed on the man who Nicki concluded must be George Lanciere, the head winemaker at both Holland Winery and Todos.

But it was obvious she may as well have saved her breath when George puffed his chest out and wagged a finger right under her nose.

"Todos wine will be good, but *not* excellent. Again, Monsieur Stacy does not buy the best grapes from the coast for an excellent blend. So, the wine will not be excellent."

Nicki took a long step back to avoid being poked, and to gain some distance from the stench of nicotine clinging to George Lanciere like an invisible fog. The man had either recently jumped through a campfire, or had a very serious smoking habit.

She cocked her head to one side and raised an eyebrow, but prudently kept her mouth shut. Apparently she was getting that first-hand experience of the nasty arrogance Matt had warned her about. Nicki drew in a deep breath and silently studied the sneering winemaker. His thinning hair and thick lips topped by a pencil-thin mustache added to a picture of rock-solid arrogance.

She couldn't believe he'd take such a back-handed slap at one of his employers, and at a public event, no less. It wouldn't surprise her if Bill Stacy took a swing at the arrogant, puffed-up man.

"Could be a whole list of other things besides the grapes," Bill cut in, showing admirable restraint despite his clenched fist. But he gave the shorter Lanciere such a hard stare, the men around Nicki straightened their backs and bounced quick glances between the winery owner and his head winemaker.

A dark red crept up George's neck. "What are you saying? That my skill is inferior?"

"I guess we'll have the answer to that after we get a taste of this new blend of yours."

With his dark eyes smoldering, George turned his attention to Nicki. Setting his feet apart, he put his hands on his hips and narrowed his gaze. "Who are you?"

Jim stepped over and wrapped a heavy arm around her shoulder. "This is Miss Connors, George. She writes a great blog about our little area and what we have to offer."

"A blog?" George's lip curled upward as his eyes shifted to Jim. Before he could open his mouth and say something Nicki was dead sure would be ridiculously insulting, Geri gave the man a light tap on his shoulder. The assistant jumped backwards when the winemaker whirled around to face her.

"Um," she stammered, her wide-eyed stare going to Nicki and then immediately down to the floor. "Matt Dillon sent Nicki here."

George's eyes lost their smolder and took on a speculative-looking gleam before he hid it behind a casual shrug. "Ah. The man named after a cowboy on TV. *Gunfire*?"

"*Gunsmoke*," Nicki corrected. "His mother was a big fan. Matt's also the owner of *Food & Wine Online,* which is why I'm here. And for my own blog, of course."

"Nicki is a friend of Matt's." Jim spoke each word slowly, his narrow-eyed gaze never leaving George Lanciere's face. "And my personal guest here today as well. It's never a good idea to offend the press, and rude to insult a lady, so mind your manners." The winemaker's jaw visibly tightened but he gave an abrupt nod and kept his mouth shut. Jim returned the nod before smiling at the little group in general.

"The wait for your big unveiling is putting everyone on edge. Why don't you get started?"

George shot Nicki one last, sideways glance before bending at the waist in an exaggerated bow. "Of course." Straightening, he clicked his heels, did a stiff-backed about-face, and marched off toward the back of the tasting room.

Bill Stacy picked up his glass and raised it over his head in a silent salute before dropping it back down. He took a deep sip of the lightly amber-colored liquid. Setting the glass carefully on the table, he watched the winemaker disappear through the doorway behind the tasting bar.

"This should be interesting."

# 4

Nicki searched for something to say to break the uncomfortable silence. Turning toward the only man at the table she didn't recognize, she gave him a broad smile.

"I'm Nicki Connors."

The youngish-looking, sandy-haired man dressed in a neatly pressed, denim shirt and close-fitting, khaki-colored pants, nodded his head and returned her smile before his gaze went back to darting around the room. The hands holding his wine glass were noticeably shaking.

"I'm Jeremy Brennan and I'm happy to meet you, Nicki. I'm a fan of your blog. Especially liked the piece on that new winery up the coast."

"Bon Vin?" Nicki asked. At his nod, she laughed. "The owner is one-of-a-kind. She said she wasn't much on fancy names so called the place exactly what it is, 'Good Wine'. And since she uses only French oak barrels, she translated the name into French."

"Well, that's a lot less expensive than hiring a marketing

company to come up with a name." Jeremy's mouth drooped slightly at the corners as he looked down at his shoes.

His pose reminded Nicki so much of Geri, she wondered if the two of them might be a good match. She made another mental note to mention the possibility to Maxie. At least it would give her landlady someone else to focus on besides Nicki.

Bill Stacy shifted his stance to face the younger man. "You paid hard money to a marketing company, and the best they could come up with is Trax? You should ask for a refund, Brennan."

Jeremy's back stiffened and his eyes narrowed on Bill's face. "It brings up images of a journey."

"It brings up images of a railroad," Bill snorted.

Nicki let out a deep sigh. Something was firmly stuck under Bill's skin. Something or someone, she silently corrected. But whether or not his bad mood was caused by George's nasty remarks, the man seemed determined to take it out on the very tailored, and clearly on edge, Jeremy.

"I like the name," she declared before Jeremy said anything to set Bill off even more. "I think I'll have to take a trip out your way soon."

For the first time since their introduction the young winery owner smiled. He followed that by leaning so far forward Nicki thought he meant to kiss her. Luckily there was a table between them.

"Any time. You should come to the launch event."

Jim reached over and gave Jeremy a firm slap on the back, taking the younger man by surprise. The big man winked at Nicki when the force had Jeremy bending completely over until his nose touched the top of the table. Bill made a fast grab for his glass and lifted it out of harm's way, shaking his head at both men.

Seemingly unfazed by the near disaster of tall, stemmed

glasses crashing to the stone floor, Jim grabbed the back of Jeremy's shirt and hauled him upright.

"Sorry, son. Only meant to congratulate you."

Putting two and two together, Nicki raised an eyebrow in astonishment. "*Trax* is sponsoring the new Lanciere label?"

"Let me go." Jeremy twisted around and glared at their host whose large hand was still latched onto a fistful of shirt.

Jim gave another short apology while Nicki once again stepped in to keep the peace.

"I didn't know George Lanciere was *your* head winemaker too."

"He isn't. At least not yet." Jeremy's voice took on an unhappy note to match his sudden frown, and his gaze was once again on his shoes. "But he will be. We're still in negotiations over that point."

Bill let out a short laugh before pinning Jeremy with a hard, direct stare. "Be sure he doesn't 'negotiate' you right out of your own winery."

"He's not as bad as you're making him out to be," Jim said. "There's plenty of room for everyone to play in this ball field. George knows that."

"He's done both of us a poor turn on more than one occasion, and you know *that* too." Bill pointed to the now-silent Jeremy. "If you want to help this young hotshot, you'll tell him to be careful and watch his back. George doesn't play by any rules but his own anymore, and he doesn't care who he steps on to get what he wants."

"Anymore?" Nicki asked, despite the fact she'd just told herself to stay out of this argument. But as usual, her curiosity got the better of her. "Did he used to play by the rules?"

Bill's dark eyes met hers for a moment before turning away. "I liked him better when he was plain old George Lancer. Before he hit it big with that last private blend of his and decided to become more French."

"More French?" Nicki sent a confused look around the table.

Jim laughed. "He changed his name from Lancer to Lanciere, claiming he'd decided to go back to the original spelling."

"Along with the change in his name came an inflated ego and a whole list of demands." Bill's voice was flat and hard. "We all allow our staff to put up their own private blends if they're willing to pay for the grapes and barrels, but he had the barrels written in as part of his pay. Including a stipulation that we had to supply him with only French oak barrels out of our own pockets."

"Instead of American oak?" Nicki asked.

Jim lifted his hands in the air in an age-old helpless gesture. "Most of us use both for our wineries, but the American oak is cheaper. His demands forced us to buy more barrels of the expensive kind."

"Now he's claiming he has some old vines a long-lost relative shipped him from France," Jeremy put in, the sour note in his voice accompanied by a confirming nod when the others turned to stare at him. "Says he planted them a while ago on his own secret patch of land and used the grapes in this new blend of his."

"And he also seems to have developed a very bad French accent," Nicki said absently, not even aware she'd said it out loud until all three men laughed.

"Noticed that, did you?" Jim grinned at her.

She sheepishly smiled back at him. "Hard not to. He sounds like a comical imitation of one of the chefs at my culinary school who *was* from France."

"French oak, French name, French accent and now French vines. Maybe he needs to take an extended trip back to his imaginary homeland and get it straight in his head," Bill muttered.

"Well, he'll be out soon with this new wine of his, and we'll see what tale he'll be telling then," Jim pointed out. "While we're waiting, did any of you catch the game last night? It was a good one."

"Not that good. We lost."

Nicki continued to smile and tuned them out. She'd discovered long ago when the conversation drifted to sports, which she never watched, that it was better not to say a word.

As the game rehash grew more intense, Nicki slipped away without drawing a single glance from any of the men. Which suited her just fine. She needed to mix and mingle a bit and gather some color, and maybe a tantalizing hint of gossip and rumor, to put into the article for Matt. She certainly couldn't send him a write-up on George's amazing transformation to all things French, then conclude with a few heated opinions on last night's game.

Having little to do but wait for the man to make his grand entrance with his new blend, Nicki steadily worked her way around the entire room. She politely greeted acquaintances and gained introductions to several winery owners in the area. When her cheeks began to hurt from smiling so much, she consoled herself with the tried and true adage that *who* you knew in the wine business was almost as important as *what* you knew about them. Something her perpetually absent boyfriend, Rob, repeated loudly and often.

And what she knew right now was that the Holland, Todos and soon-to-be Trax head winemaker was universally disliked in the close-knit wine community, and today he was taking his own, sweet time to present his new blend. Nicki gave her wristwatch a quick glance and frowned. George had disappeared through the rear door more than an hour ago.

Wishfully thinking how much she'd love to skip the whole, unveiling, Nicki wandered over to the bar and smiled at Geri. The assistant winemaker was busy pouring tasting glasses of Holland's newest release to groups of guests leaning against the counter's long length. After a few minutes she reached Nicki, wearing the pasted-on, stiff smile she'd given everyone standing at the bar.

"What can I pour for you? We're offering a good variety of chardonnays and several wonderful reds as well."

Nicki politely shook her head. "Nothing at the moment, thanks. I just finished a glass from Charlie Freeman's place, and it still needs to settle a bit."

To her great astonishment Geri's shoulders relaxed and her eyes even warmed up.

"If you had a glass of one of Charlie's wines, I suggest you stay near the ladies' room."

When Nicki laughed, Geri's cheeks bloomed red.

"Please don't get me wrong. I love Charlie. Really, I do. But he's made the same bad wine for at least twenty years, and never fails to bring it to all the growers' tastings."

"I understand having a glass of his wine without gagging is a kind of initiation test for newcomers to the area," Nicki's hazel eyes lit with amusement.

"It most certainly is," Geri replied with a quiet chuckle. "And if you accept one whenever he offers it, that's a sure sign you mean to stick around for a while."

"Well then, I'm going to be a permanent resident. He's such a sweet old guy, I could never turn down a glass of his wine," Nicki declared. Geri graced her with a genuine smile as if she approved of the notion.

But Geri's lighter mood didn't last long. When she glanced behind Nicki, the assistant's smile instantly fell into a frown. "Oh no. Here comes Jim and he doesn't look happy."

The big man easily made his way through the crowd, heading straight toward them. *Geri is right*, Nicki thought, taking in Jim's lowered brows and pursed lips. He wasn't happy at all.

"George needs to get on with this tasting of his," he stated, wasting no time in getting to the heart of his annoyance. "The owners are tired of hanging around and they're starting to leave. I'm not going to have him embarrass me if he's back in his aging room sulking about who-knows-what."

He glanced around and Nicki followed the direction of his gaze just in time to see three people push out the big doors and turn left, presumably heading to the parking lot.

Jim turned back to Geri and growled. "Go find him. I'll make an announcement that we're going to hurry him along."

"I need a short break to take care of some personal business. Maybe someone else...."

Geri trailed off when the owner spun around and headed back through the crowd. Nicki glanced over at Geri, who was wringing her hands while her lip visibly quivered. It was obvious the woman didn't want to go find the head winemaker and deliver Jim's message. Thinking the odious little man must have treated his assistant very badly, Nicki took her elbows off the bar and sat up straight.

"I'll go with you. If George throws a fit, you can make a run for it. I'll keep him trapped in his room until you can bring reinforcements."

At Geri's raised eyebrows, Nicki grinned. "I may be small, but I grew up in New York City. I've had enough defense classes to bring any man here to his knees."

Geri surprised her again when she nodded her agreement and motioned for Nicki to follow her. Together they went through the door behind the bar and slipped out of sight.

"Does George live on the property?" When Geri gave her a sideways glance, Nicki shrugged. "Jim mentioned he might be in his private room."

"Jim gave George a room to age his own wine. He always keeps it locked, although anyone could get the key since Jim keeps it hanging on a hook in his office."

With nothing else to say, Nicki followed along behind Geri in silence. It was only a minute or two before Geri turned right and headed down a wide hallway, finally stopping in front of a solid, wooden door that was standing half open. When the assistant halted in the doorway, Nicki stood on her toes and peeked over her shoulder. Not able to get much of a view, Nicki stepped around the silent woman and shoved the door completely open.

"George? Are you in here? It's Nicki Connors and Geri." With the assistant winemaker practically breathing down her neck, Nicki took several steps into the room. "George?"

An audible gasp behind her had Nicki turning around. She raised a questioning eyebrow at Geri whose shocked stare snapped over to Nicki's face and stayed there.

Puzzled, Nicki turned back around, her gaze sweeping across the interior of George Lanciere's private space. It didn't take long to spot the feet and ankles sticking out from behind the edge of a row of barrels. She rushed over, only to skid to a stop at the sight of the winemaker lying sprawled, face down on the stone floor, in a pool of something with such a strong stench that Nicki quickly pressed her hand over her nose and mouth. There was a trickle of blood seeping out from beneath George's head, and a wineglass was smashed into jagged shards that splayed outward from his motionless form.

A sudden, sharp pain shot up Nicki's arm when Geri's fingernails dug deep into her bare skin. She winced when the assistant clamped down even harder, but managed to rise on her toes and crane her neck forward to get a better look at George. Seeing an unblinking, protruding eye, Nicki's stomach lurched violently. Pressing her hands to her midsection, she took deep, slow breaths until the sick feeling subsided into the background.

When she was sure her stomach was going to behave, at least for the moment, Nicki held her breath. She shook off Geri's hand and stepped forward to kneel beside the unnaturally still body. She gently laid a hand on his back, counting her own breaths and waiting through the fifth one before closing her eyes. There was no movement beneath her fingertips.

Covering her mouth again, she rose to her feet and faced Geri while she reached into her jacket pocket and pulled out her cell phone. "Do you have your cell phone with you?"

Geri's breath came in such jerky, fast bursts, Nicki sincerely hoped the woman didn't faint on her. "Use your cell phone and call Jim." When all she got was a blank stare, Nicki reached out and gave Geri's shoulder a hard shake. "Call Jim. I'm calling 9-1-1."

Nicki kept her own cell to her ear and her stare on the assistant as she fumbled for her phone, her hands shaking so badly she barely managed to tap out the winery owner's number. At least Nicki hoped that's who Geri was calling.

"9-1-1. What's your emergency?"

"There's been a terrible accident at Holland Winery."

## 5

"I didn't expect to see you again so soon, Nicki."

Chief Turnlow carefully lowered his solid weight into the only other rickety chair in the small room that was across the hall from where George lay dead on the floor. Nicki wasn't having much luck blocking out the low murmur of voices and the scuffle of feet drifting across the hall as the emergency crew went about the grim business of removing the body. Each sound conjured up a vivid picture of the scene in her mind, so she hunched her shoulders and fought the urge to put her hands up against her ears.

Her excellent imagination wasn't doing her any favors right now.

"Are you able to answer a couple of questions now, or do you need to lie down for a few minutes?"

Nicki stiffened her spine and raised her chin a notch. She was not going to fall apart the way the assistant winemaker had. The last time she'd seen the plainly dressed woman, Geri was sobbing loudly with her face buried in Jim's shoulder while he quickly guided her out of the room. So by default, Nicki was elected to stay behind with the deceased George and wait for the police. Luckily, she didn't have to wait long.

"I'm as fine as I can be under the circumstances, Chief," Nicki folded her hands in her lap to keep them still. "Are you sure George is dead?" She winced at the ridiculous question, but she couldn't think of anything else to say.

"As a doornail," the chief confirmed. "Can you tell me what happened?"

Her mouth opened and then shut again. Looking straight at the chief, she shrugged. "I don't know."

At his raised eyebrow, she shrugged again. "Geri and I went into the room and he was lying on the floor."

"Did you touch or move anything?"

"No." Nicki shook her head and took a deep breath. "Just his back."

Chief Turnlow's eyebrow rose a notch higher. "His back?"

"I put my hand on his back to check if he was breathing."

"Was that before or after you called 9-1-1?"

Nicki's nose wrinkled and her eyes narrowed as she thought it over. "Before."

"Hmm..." The chair creaked out a warning as the chief leaned back, crossed his arms over his large chest, and studied Nicki in silence.

She didn't like that little humming noise he was making one bit, and showed it by glaring at him. "I wasn't checking to make sure he was dead before I called 9-1-1, Chief Turnlow. So you can stop giving me that look as though I just became your primary suspect."

He chuckled and sat up straight, uncrossing his arms and placing his hands on his knees. "Probably should have known I couldn't intimidate a New York City girl. And as far as you being a suspect, I don't think you are. Unless, of course, I find out you went missing during the tasting." He slanted his head to one side and smiled. "Did you?"

"I didn't even go to the ladies' room," Nicki declared. She relaxed when his chuckle grew into a short laugh.

"Well then, having cleared up the matter of your whereabouts, why don't you tell me how it happened to be *you* who found the body?"

"Jim asked Geri to find Mr. Lanciere. He'd been gone a long time, and everyone was waiting to try his new blend."

"Lancer," the chief said as he took out a small notebook and a stub of a pencil.

"What?"

"The name on his driver's license is George Lancer."

Nicki ducked her head and bit her lip to keep from smiling. Somehow that didn't seem very respectful to the dead-as-a-door-nail winemaker. "So, I guess he isn't French after all?"

The chief barely lifted his shoulders in a small shrug, his gaze staying on his notebook. "Don't know if he's French or not. I'm just saying the name on his driver's license says George Lancer." He flipped over a page before raising his head to smile at her. "If Jim asked Geri to locate Mr. Lancer, why did you find the body?"

"Geri didn't want to go alone." Nicki sighed. "George wasn't always a nice man."

The lawman nodded. "So I've heard. Then Geri asked you to come along?"

"Not exactly. When she looked upset by Jim's order, I offered to come along and she agreed." Nicki's eyes narrowed. "We came to his private aging room, opened the door and there he was. I put a hand on his back to see if he was breathing, then told Geri to call Jim, and I called 9-1-1. There's nothing more to tell than that."

"What did you do while you were waiting for help to arrive?"

Nicki gave a snort to go along with her annoyed stare. "We didn't *do* anything. We stepped away and waited. Jim was there after I finished counting the bottles and glasses on the tray but before I got around to all the stones on the wall."

He did a few more scribbles in his notebook. "How many bottles and glasses did you see?"

"You didn't count them yourself?" Nicki asked, then sighed when the chief remained silent and smiled at her. "Four bottles, one uncorked, and three glasses,"

"Why were you counting the stones in the wall?"

Now she was the one to cross her arms and give him a bland stare. "The situation didn't lend itself to clever conversation. Besides, Geri was sobbing, and I'd already counted all the rings in the barrelhead in front of us, so I moved on to the stones in the wall. Which I kept counting while Jim took Geri away and left me there alone with the bottles, the barrels and a dead body."

The chief reached over and patted her knee with one large, beefy hand. "I'm sorry you found the body, and I don't think you killed him. The fact is, it's unlikely anyone killed him. He probably had a heart attack. I understand he was a heavy smoker, and he didn't have the look of an exercise nut. But that'll be for the coroner to decide." He paused and tapped his little notebook. "I'm just trying to sort out who arrived at the scene and in what order. I take it after you and Geri Gant found the body, Jim was the next person to arrive?"

---

AN HOUR later Nicki walked into her townhouse, giving the front door a hard shove behind her. Not bothering to check if it had latched shut, she dropped her purse onto the floor instead of the hallway table and headed straight back to the sanctuary of her kitchen.

Pausing by the center island, she leaned against it for a moment, braced her hands on its top and closed her eyes. The picture of George Lancer's dead body instantly appeared in her mind, causing her eyes to snap open again. Taking several deep breaths, she focused her gaze on the far wall.

"I am strong and at peace." She tried another deep inhale and then exhale. "I am strong and at peace." Breathe in, breathe out. "I am strong and at peace."

She continued for several minutes, without much luck in getting her nerves to settle down, before finally giving up.

"Time to try something else," she muttered. Stepping around the island she headed straight for her pantry. In times of crisis there was nothing better than her last-resort, sure-fire cure for any ill. Thankfully she always kept it on hand, despite Alex's frown whenever she caught sight of it in the pantry.

For better organization, and certainly not to hide anything, Nicki had decided to move her stash to the very back shelf, care-fully resting it behind a flour canister. Her hand latched onto the bag and dragged it out into the open. Turning, she marched out of the pantry, snatching up the container filled with potato chips that she always kept behind the small bucket of individually wrapped rice cakes.

She was perched on a stool at the center island when the front door slammed shut, followed by the sound of footsteps running down the hallway.

*I guess the door didn't latch after all,* she thought without too much concern.

"Nicki? Where are you? Your door was wide open."

"In the kitchen, Jenna." Nicki licked the salt from a chip off her fingers just as Jenna burst through the doorway, her mass of curly black hair bouncing wildly around her face.

"Oh sugar!" Jenna's eyes took in the container of chips before moving over to the pile of chocolate-covered peanuts mounded up in front of her friend. "It was as bad as all that?" She leaped across the room to bury Nicki in a hug.

"It was. But I'm feeling steadier now." Nicki held a chip up high and batting away the mass of dark hair swirling about her face. "Jenna, you need to step back before you smother me with that mane of yours."

"I don't care," Jenna declared. "I can't believe you're going through this whole thing again."

Nicki managed to use her free hand to get a grip on Jenna's shoulder and push her away. "I'm fine. It wasn't like finding mom." Nicki paused for a moment and took a deep breath, determined to keep calm. Feeling her friend tremble, Nicki tugged on Jenna's arm until the tall woman collapsed onto the adjacent stool.

"Try the breathing exercises we learned in that meditation class," Nicki said as she shoved half the pile of chocolate peanuts over toward Jenna. "If that doesn't work, try these. I'll get a bigger bowl for the chips."

Hopping off her stool, Nicki walked over to the cupboard housing her dishes and came back with a large serving bowl. She unceremoniously dumped the entire container of chips into it. "The meditation didn't work for me, so I decided to go with Plan B."

Jenna nodded her understanding and reached for a chocolate-covered peanut with one hand and a chip with the other. Neither woman said a word for several minutes as they popped chocolate and potato chips into their mouths.

*The universal cure for all things*, Nicki thought, taking one last chip before shoving the nearly empty bowl to the other side of the counter. Jenna followed suit with the few pieces of chocolate remaining in the much-depleted pile in front of her.

"Now that we're both calm, I want you to tell me everything. Who was he? Maxie said it was probably a heart attack," Jenna said.

"Ah. I should have known Maxie would hear all about it almost the instant it happened." A ghost of a smile played around Nicki's lips. Before she had a chance to explain the strange events at Holland Winery, the distinct sound of a door opening echoed down the hallway.

"I need to get an automatic lock," Nicki muttered before raising her voice. "We're in here, Maxie."

She looked over at Jenna who rolled her eyes.

"Our landlady never feels the need to ring the doorbell at my place either," Jenna groused.

"I told her she didn't have to," Nicki confessed.

"Well *I* certainly didn't tell her any such thing," Jenna said with a glance at the doorway. As the click-click of heels drew closer, she crossed her arms and tapped her foot.

Maxie walked into the kitchen, her platinum-blond hair perfectly styled, and her make-up applied with an expert hand. The landlady's dark blue eyes went straight to Nicki with lightning speed.

"There you are. And it looks like you're none the worse for wear. I came as soon as I decided you'd had enough time to drive home from Jim's winery." She closed the gap and reached out to pat Nicki on the shoulder before turning and raising her eyebrows at Jenna. "Well, how is she? Oh, never mind. I'll just check for myself."

The older woman stepped up to give Nicki a long hug which the younger woman immediately returned with real affection. Nicki genuinely adored her unique landlady.

"I see you've found the best cure for a difficult day," Maxie said with a glance at the candy and chips as she stepped back. "I keep a large stash of chocolate in my kitchen cupboard if you ever run out."

Jenna laughed. "So do I."

"As do most of the women I know," Maxie put in with a wink. "Now, tell me what happened? Paul was a bit vague when he called."

"Paul Turnlow? The police chief?" Jenna asked. "He called you from the crime scene?"

"Now, dear," Maxie said with a gentle touch to Jenna's shoulder. "He doesn't believe it's a crime scene. He seemed very sure the poor man passed peacefully from a heart attack."

Nicki recalled the picture of George lying sprawled out, his forehead bleeding, probably from the force of his head hitting the concrete floor, and his eyes wide open, staring blindly at the shards of glass all around him. Whatever had happened, it certainly had not occurred peacefully.

"What did the chief tell you?" she asked.

"That George was preparing his new blend for the grand tasting and had a heart attack, and you and Geri found him." Maxie paused for a moment and smiled. "He called and asked me to let him know that you made it home all right."

"That was very thoughtful of him," Nicki said even as her forehead wrinkled in thought.

After a long, drawn-out moment of silence, Jenna snapped her fingers in front of her friend's face. "Earth to Nicki. What are you thinking so hard about?"

"Did Chief Turnlow say anything else? Like he was busy gathering evidence, or questioning everyone who was there?" Nicki asked.

"No, he did not. Should he have been?" Maxie tilted her head to one side and studied her tenant and fellow writer. "Why don't we start at the beginning? I thought you had plans to barricade yourself in your office and finish your novel. How did you end up at the Holland wine tasting?"

"Matt. He asked me to cover it for the magazine."

Maxie gave Nicki's hand a quick pat. "And I'm sure he'll pay you very well for it. He's such a nice young man. Don't you think so?"

"We all think so," Jenna said with a touch of impatience. "Well, go on. What happened once you got there?"

For the next ten minutes Nicki obligingly recounted the whole story, starting with encountering Geri in the parking lot, and ending with feeling no movement under the hand she placed on George Lancer's back. When she'd finished, she gratefully accepted the glass of water Maxie set down in front of her. She took a big gulp, then smiled her thanks at her landlady.

"And he reeked of a weird smell."

The other two women exchanged a look before turning back to Nicki.

"Weird? In what way?" Jenna asked.

Nicki closed her eyes and inhaled, deliberately bringing the scene and the smell into her mind. "It was a kind of cross between a bad fish odor and a cigarette, overlaid with cherry."

"He was a very heavy smoker, dear," Maxie pointed out. "And the smell was probably even more pronounced after he died." She nodded at the inquiring look Nicki sent her. "Paul said he'd also thrown up, so it could be that's what you were smelling, because maybe he did eat some cherries and fish? Winemakers can be a little odd."

Nicki pursed her lips. "Then he must have inhaled a carton of cigarettes and a whole bushel of cherries, it was that strong an odor. I almost gagged on it."

Jenna leaned forward and stared at her friend from behind the large, round lenses of her eyeglasses. "What are you saying?"

Nicki took a deep breath and turned to face both women. "I hope the chief collected evidence because I don't know what he died from, but it wasn't a heart attack."

The complete silence following her pronouncement wasn't exactly what Nicki was looking for, but at least they hadn't laughed at her. She took it as a sign that she didn't sound completely crazy.

"Nicki, dear, you aren't one of those doctors who examine dead people, whatever they're called." Maxie lowered her voice to a soothing tone. "I'm sure Chief Turnlow will send poor George to the larger department in Santa Rosa to look into all those medical things. That's what my Mason always did.

"Let it go, Nicki," Jenna said quietly. "The odds are it's just like the chief told you. This George person probably died of a heart attack, or stroke, or something else perfectly explainable. And if he didn't, it's a matter for the police. You've had enough murder in your life."

## 6

Two days later Nicki sat at the glass-top desk she'd bought less than a month ago as a thirty-first birthday present for herself, and stared at the wide screen of her computer. The document in front of her proclaimed it to be chapter twenty-eight. If she could just get this one done, there would only be two chapters left to complete. Yep. That's all she had to do. Get this one done. But no words came to her. For the last hour and a half all she'd written was "Chapter Twenty-Eight".

Nicki sighed and shoved a lock of hair behind her ear. It was the first time her intrepid hero, Tyrone Blackstone, had completely eluded her. It was very unlike him. She glanced over at the timer next to her desk. She had a good thirty minutes left in her morning writing session. Right about now she'd hoped to be penning her way toward the words, "The End", before throwing together a quick, but hopefully delicious, lunch to kick off Alex's arrival for a girls-only weekend. But in the last few days all she'd managed to write was "Chapter Twenty-Eight".

"Pathetic, Connors. Really pathetic." Considering the blank screen for a long moment, Nicki finally closed her eyes and brought up a mental picture of the last scene she'd written. It was a tried and true trick she used whenever she was stuck. Seeing the scene in her mind usually led her to what happened next in the story. Behind her shuttered eyes she visualized it, right down to the glint of moonlight off the gun her hero was holding in his left hand.

There he was, Tyrone Blackstone, hunk and spy extraordinaire, pressed flat against the wall leading into the alley, his broad shoulders and hard-muscled chest tense over what might be around the corner. With the ease and grace of a panther on the hunt, he rounded the corner then slowly swept his gun across the narrow opening, his eagle-eyed gaze taking in the whole scene at once.

Nicki relaxed and let her imagination go as her super-spy peered into the dim alley. The narrow walls were made of stone, and barrels were scattered all over the interior. At the far end lay a sprawled-out body, surrounded by a sea of glass and...

Nicki's eyes snapped open. It seemed her imagination had deserted her along with her favorite hero. There wasn't anything fictional about *that* scene. All it needed was a tray crowded with full wine bottles and empty glasses to make the picture complete. It was bad enough that same mental picture was causing her to lose sleep at night, now it was preventing her from getting any work done. And it didn't take a session with a therapist to know why.

Nicki bit her lip as she considered the problem. Jenna was right. With the trauma of losing her mother, she'd had enough unsolved murders in her life. Hadn't she moved three thousand miles to put it behind her? But she could hardly keep doing that. Another three thousand miles and she'd end up on a raft in the middle of the Pacific Ocean. So what could she do?

Solve the murder.

Nicki's eyes opened wide at the thought that came out of nowhere.

*How do you propose to do that, Connors?* She silently shook her head. *You know why Mom was killed. You may not know who, but you know why—for her money and the big diamond ring she wore. You have no idea why George Lancer was killed, aside from the fact no one liked him.*

Puzzling over it, Nicki started to push back from her desk when a noise from her computer told her there was an incoming call on Skype. She glanced at the screen and smiled. Up popped Matt's picture next to the icon of a ringing headset. She quickly clicked on his image. Within moments he was smiling back at her from the screen. With his thick wave of dark hair dipping over his forehead, slightly angular features, and large, black-rimmed glasses, he really was kind of cute in a nerdy, where's-Waldo sort of way.

"Hey, Matt." Nicki smiled at her editor who was obviously sitting in his very disorderly office in Kansas City. She had no idea how he ever found anything in the piles-on-top-of-piles, which had his desk completely surrounded by mountains of paper. "How's the weather?"

"About twenty degrees colder than it is where you are." Matt grinned. "And before you ask again, I live here because it's the center of the country, and I can get anywhere in the USA in three and a half hours."

"Except Alaska and Hawaii," they said in unison.

"Great minds think alike." Matt winked. Nicki laughed at the pleased look on his face.

"How are you?" she asked.

Matt's grin turned down at the corners as he leaned closer until his face filled the entire monitor. "I think I'm supposed to be asking *you* that question. I just got back into the office and Jane gave me your message."

Jane was Matt's very scary, and super-efficient, admin assistant, whom Nicki had the unnerving experience of meeting in person exactly once. The stick-thin admin, with her crisply pleated blouse and deadly sharp stare, reminded Nicki of an old-time teacher in a private school for wayward girls. All she lacked was a long yardstick for rapping some unsuspecting knuckles. Jane always had Nicki secretly thanking whomever it was that had invented email so there was no need to actually talk to the woman.

"Why didn't you shoot me your email instead of sending it to Jane?"

Matt's sharp tone took Nicki aback. "I knew you were away on business. I just assumed Jane would be sorting through what you needed to see and what could wait."

"I told her to send all your messages to me immediately," Matt mumbled.

"I'm sorry?" Nicki wasn't quite sure she'd heard that right. Send him all her messages immediately?

"Not important." Matt leaned back in his chair, propping his elbows on the armrests. "What happened? Your email said you couldn't turn in the story about Lanciere because he was murdered?"

Nicki felt the instant rise of heat in her cheeks, but did her best to sound nonchalant. "Oh? Did I use that word? I honestly don't remember. And his name is Lancer. It turns out he wasn't French at all."

"Don't change the subject, Nicki," Matt said. "I put a call into the police department and the deputy said George Lanciere, Lancer or whatever his real name was, died of a heart attack at the tasting.

"You called the police department?" Nicki was astonished. "Why didn't you just wait and ask me?"

"Why did you say he was murdered?" Matt shot back. "Was that deputy stonewalling the press, or do you know something he doesn't know?"

"*Food & Wine Online* is hardly *The New York Times*, Matt," Nicki observed with a roll of her eyes. She fought a smile when

Matt's frown grew as he ran a hand through his unruly, wavy dark hair until pieces of it stood straight up from his forehead.

Nicki thought he looked ridiculous. And adorable.

"We're an electronic medium with a sizeable audience. That's good enough. And stop trying to distract me. 'Heart attack' and 'murder' aren't words you mix up by mistake. What's going on, Nicki? You may as well tell me, or I'll just call Maxie, Jenna or Alex until one of them spills the beans."

"There aren't any beans to spill," Nicki insisted. "So there's no need to call all around town. Let's just say the police have their conclusions, and I have my suspicions."

Matt leaned into the screen once more. "How about you keep talking and tell me exactly what happened?"

Because she really was dying to tell Matt everything, Nicki didn't utter a peep of protest before launching into a detailed description of the entire day George Lancer died, from the time she pulled her not-so-reliable Toyota into the Holland parking lot, until Jenna's pronouncement about too much murder in her life.

Matt didn't make a sound for what seemed like an eternity. Absolutely positive he was going to tell her she was crazy, she let out a deep sigh and slumped back in her chair.

"All right, go ahead."

Matt raised one eyebrow. "Go ahead and what?"

"Go ahead and tell me what you think."

"I think Maxie had a good point about you not being a medical examiner," Matt said.

Nicki shrugged. "Okay. I can agree with that."

"And you won't know what happened until the medical examiner declares the official cause of death, so you'll just have to wait."

"I hate it when you're so calm and reasonable," Nicki complained and slouched further into her chair. She wouldn't find anything out for days, maybe weeks, and even then, only if myMason agreed to ask the current chief for the findings. There was also the small matter that somewhere in the middle of her retelling of the events to Matt, she'd made up her mind. George Lancer *was* murdered, and she was going to find out who killed him.

A big drawn-out sigh came loud and clear through the speakers on her computer.

"I know that look, Nicki Connors. You aren't going to let this go, are you?"

Nicki wiggled her way to sitting up straight in her desk chair and gave Matt a cheeky smile. "No, I'm not."

After another loud sigh, Matt took off his glasses and rubbed his eyes. "All right. Then let's start with motive."

"*Let's*, as in you'll help?"

"Do I have a choice?" At Nicki's laugh, Matt's mouth twitched at the corners. "Motive, Sherlock Connors. Why would someone kill George Lancer? Aside from the fact he was a royal pain and had an inflated opinion of himself."

"That might be enough," Nicki said. "Except you could say the same about half the winemakers here. Half the winery owners, too, for that matter." Nicki reflected on the idea for a second. "Well, maybe less than half of the owners. They're generally a pretty good lot."

"So, it would have to be something else besides being a jerk," Matt said.

"What do you know about George?" Nicki asked.

Matt put his hands out, palms up. "Not much more than what I've already told you. Aside from a dislikable personality, his big claim to fame was a special and very limited blend he put out under his own name ten years ago. Jim Holland gave him his break by sponsoring it under the winery's brand."

"Hm." Nicki's eyes narrowed in speculation. "George was having the first tasting of his new blend at Holland Winery, but he was going to bring his label out under some kind of agreement with Trax."

"How do you know that?" Matt's eyebrows drew together. "Lanciere, oh sorry, I mean Lancer. Did Lancer tell you that?"

Nicki shook her head. "No. Jeremy Brennan, the owner of Trax, told me that."

"Haven't had the pleasure of meeting him, but I've seen his picture. Nice-looking guy."

She glanced over at the screen and Matt's frown. "Oh. Yes. I suppose he is if you like the preppy type. Hang on a sec, I need to find a pen." When she triumphantly held one up after rummaging about for a full minute, Matt smiled at her.

"I'd be happy to use any resource *Food & Wine Online* has, or any personal one I have for that matter, but you'll probably learn more just by asking Maxie. She pretty much has the line on everyone in the wine business in Sonoma county."

Thinking that really was an excellent suggestion, Nicki grinned. "I'm sure if I asked she'd be happy to lend a hand in the investigation. So will Alex and Jenna."

"Lord help us all," Matt said, half under his breath.

Nicki ignored him and glanced at the clock at the bottom of the screen instead. "Speaking of needing Divine help, Alex will be here in less than an hour and I need to have lunch ready for her and Jenna, so I'd better get the fries ready to go."

That announcement was met with a bark of laughter from her editor-in-chief.

"Fries will make Jenna happy, but not Alex. You're in for a long lecture if you serve the good doctor even a homemade version of fast food."

"Not this time," Nicki corrected. "I'm making zucchini fries. And they're baked."

"So now Alex is happy and Jenna is not," Matt said.

"They'll be accompanied by a very nice, fairly lean, ground beef hamburger, with all the fixings. Since Alex is in love with my zucchini fries and Jenna with my special burger mix, they'll both be ecstatic." Nicki nodded.

Matt gave her a long, steady look. "So, you aren't preparing a lunch but a bribe to get them to go along with this whole, let's-track-down-a-killer scheme of yours."

Nicki saw the small tic in the sudden tightening of Matt's jawline and knew he wasn't happy. The last thing she wanted was her editor giving her an ultimatum that she give-up the investigation, or he wouldn't assign her any more work for his magazine.

"Like you said, there probably wasn't a murder," she responded and threw in a generous smile for good measure. "We'll probably be skulking around for no reason at all."

"That's only if you can bribe your friends into it. Otherwise I know you, and you'll just go out on your own. Which I don't like one bit, Nicki Connors."

"I don't need to bribe my friends, Matthew Dillon," Nicki echoed back before giving him her most angelic smile.

He let out another loud sigh before his shoulders finally relaxed and he winked at her. "Maxie likes chocolate candy. The ones with the soft centers. Thought I'd throw it out there. You never know when you might need that kind of random information."

She clicked off on his laughter and grinned at the now-blank screen as she dug her cell phone out of her jacket pocket. Matt really did know her well.

Punching in a number, she waited just a single ring before Alex's crisp "Hello?" sounded in her ear.

"Alex, I need you to make a stop on your way here. Can you pick up a box of chocolates? The kind with the soft centers."

## 7

"These zucchini fries are so good, I might just forgive you for the grease burger and having me pick up that candy." Alex brushed the overly long bangs out of her eyes and tucked them behind an ear. Her deep brown hair was cut short on one side and into a neat, wedge shape on the other, giving her what Nicki always referred to as a very fashionable, chic look, and Alex happily declared as "maintenance free". Her wide, blue eyes glanced over at Jenna, perched on the stool next to her. They were nibbling on the last of their lunch as they waited for Maxie who'd happily told them she would be available to drop by about the time they were ready for dessert.

"Is that your second hamburger today? Because I'm sure you had one for breakfast."

"Did not," Jenna replied. "I had a wheat bagel and a glass of orange juice so I could enjoy my lunch without any guilt whatsoever. And I intend to reward myself with a piece of that candy. Maybe even several pieces."

"That I bought under extreme protest." Alex's gaze switched over to Nicki. "Speaking of which, why did you want me to pick up chocolates with creamy centers? I know your taste runs to chocolate-covered peanuts."

"Which she happily indulged in a few days ago. Along with a whole bowl of potato chips," Jenna said.

"Half a bowl." Nicki's generous lips thinned and she put her hands on her hips as she glared at Jenna. "You ate the other half. And why are you ratting me out?"

"Sympathy eating," Jenna said with a shrug. "You were upset."

"How much of those peanuts and chips did you eat?" Alex demanded.

"You'd eat chocolate peanuts too if you found a dead body," Nicki shot back.

Alex's frown relaxed when she looked over at Jenna and nodded. "She has a point there. What was your excuse? And don't say 'sympathy eating'."

"Don't need one. I'm not a pound overweight and as healthy as a horse, as the saying goes," Jenna said. "Besides, I'm enjoying every bit of my lunch, at least until Nicki tells us why she's bribing us."

"That *is* the only reason she ever makes zucchini fries," Alex agreed.

Both women turned to stare at Nicki, who made a show of rolling her eyes before giving up the pretense and holding her hands up in surrender. "Okay. I confess. I need your help in solving George Lancer's murder."

Both her friends sat straight up, identical frowns on their faces.

"How do you know he was murdered? And why do *you* have to solve it?" Jenna asked.

Alex stayed silent, but Nicki could tell by the intense gleam in her eyes that she was turning something over in her mind.

"You-hoo? Am I too early?" Maxie called out from the hallway. She appeared in the kitchen doorway before Nicki had a chance to answer her.

"Dr. Alex," the older woman beamed at Nicki's friend. "How nice to see you again. And Jenna is here, too. That must mean you ladies are up to something. I'm so delighted to be invited in on the plot."

"Nicki doesn't believe that winemaker died of a heart attack. She thinks he was murdered," Jenna stated, completely glossing over the usual exchange to polite greetings.

Maxie raised her perfectly shaped eyebrows at her tenant as she settled herself onto one of the stools at the kitchen counter. "You still think so? How intriguing. Being a writer, I'm sure you have an instinct for that sort of thing. Are you going on a gut feeling?"

"I'm just positive that he was," Nicki said, her gaze staying on Alex's face.

"Why do you think he was murdered?" Alex asked quietly.

"Let me tell you what I saw."

She went over everything, occasionally consulting a spiral notebook she'd scribbled reminders in to be sure she left nothing out. When she'd finished, she let her gaze roam first to Alex, then to Jenna, and finally to Maxie.

"Several things could have caused him to fall and hit his head. A heart attack, a stroke, a sudden bursting of a vein in his head," Alex said. "And yes, a quick-acting poison."

"All right, doctor," Jenna spoke in her typical, matter-of-fact tone. "What made him upchuck? Besides any poison, of course."

"And before he fell," Nicki added. She shrugged when all eyes focused on her. "His body was lying on top of it."

Alex sighed. "My guess is a heart attack or poison. But it would have to be a very toxic poison. One that's easily absorbed into the blood stream, and fast acting."

"Like dissolved in a liquid, maybe?" Maxie asked. "Such as a glass of wine?"

Nicki nodded vigorously, her hair bouncing off her shoulders. "Yes. Which is why I believe he was murdered."

"O... Kay..." Alex drew out the sound. "Can you be more specific?"

"There was only one glass of wine poured. Why did he do that? He knew he was going to serve four glasses of the wine. He should have poured all the glasses on the tray and then tasted one if he wanted to. But he poured one, took a drink and died." Nicki paused, trying to judge how her logic was going over with her friends.

"So you're suggesting he poured the first glass, thought something was off, took a taste and died before he could pour the other glasses?" Alex asked.

"Yes. That's exactly what I'm saying," Nicki replied with a firm nod.

"Pretty weak, Connors," Jenna said. "A point to be sure, but still pretty weak."

"He could have poured one glass, had a heart attack before he poured the others, and never have taken a drink at all," Alex said.

"Maybe," Nicki conceded. She cleared her throat and took a firmer grip on her notebook. "Okay. What about the overwhelming odor of cherries and tobacco, along with the smell of old fish? Everyone who came near him had to cover their noses the stench was so strong. What did he do? Eat a crate of cherries while he was smoking a carton of cigarettes, before he got around to pouring the wine? And wouldn't there be smoke? There was no smoke in that room."

"But the door was open, wasn't it? You said the door was open when you and Geri got there. Perhaps the smoke escaped?" Maxie asked.

"Then what made the horrible stench?" Nicki demanded. "It was much stronger than a smell simply coming off his clothes. If the smoke in the air was gone, the smell would go with it. It couldn't have clung to those stone walls. And what about the cherry scent?"

"Yes. Very unusual. What caused that?" Maxie wondered.

A long moment of silence passed before Alex blew out a breath and shook her head.

"We need more information. We won't know until the coroner finishes the autopsy, which could be days or weeks, depending on the caseload."

"But the police might know something more," Nicki said with a hopeful glance in Maxie's direction.

Her landlady nodded. "I'll be sure to ask my Mason to find out when he gets back. He's gone fishing with his brother until Wednesday."

"That's five days from now," all three younger women chimed in together.

"I have to be back at the hospital in three days," Alex said.

Nicki's spirits sank. She'd forgotten about myMason's planned fishing trip. Five days was an eternity.

"Let's put that aside. For the sake of argument, we should assume George Lancer was murdered. Are there any obvious suspects?" Jenna looked at Nicki. "Got any ideas?"

"A whole list of them," Nicki confirmed, once again consulting her spiral notebook. "He didn't have a single friend at the event. At least no one had a nice thing to say about him. And quite a few of the attendees had a legitimate grudge. The man was that mean and nasty. Especially to the people he worked with, and I spoke to four of them at the tasting- Jim Holland, Bill Stacy, Jeremy Brennan and Geri Gant. Then there's one of the servers at the event. George humiliated him in front of a crowd that included his boss."

"Let's start with the winery owners, since I know them best," Maxie said. "Who were they again, dear? I don't remember all the names you rattled off."

Once again Nicki consulted her notes and repeated the names before her gaze shifted back to her friends. "Those three appeared to know George the best, from what I could tell at the wine tasting. At least they're the only owners he spoke to while I was there."

"They would be excellent suspects," Maxie nodded. "Especially Bill. George almost ruined him eight years ago with a very disastrous blend."

"George almost ruined Bill, yet he's still the head winemaker for Todos?" Nicki's gut feeling leaped into a wild dance in her stomach. "Why would Bill Stacy keep him on?"

"It was a business decision, I'd imagine. Anyway, George made the blends for the winery Bill owned before he bought Todos. It was named The White Crown, and Bill did decently well. Many of the winemakers work for several wineries, and George created blends at The White Crown as well as at Holland Winery."

"Was that when he went by Lancer instead of Lanciere?" Nicki asked.

Maxie laughed. "It certainly was. And he was still cozy with Stella."

"Um... who's Stella?" Alex asked, reaching for another zucchini fry.

Nicki took a quick look around the little group. Both Jenna and Alex were listening intently to every word Maxie said. It seemed she'd hooked her friends into going along with her investigation. Smiling at the warm tingle traveling up her spine, she turned her attention back to Maxie.

"His girlfriend." Maxie nodded at Alex. "She was the assistant winemaker at Holland's for a while. I recall a rumor that she had a great deal to do with the spectacular blend he brought out at Holland Winery. But she left her position there right around the time of the grand debut, and George publicly said it was because she was jealous of him coming out with a signature wine when he'd only been at Holland Winery a few years, and she'd been there much longer. She never denied it, and they broke up shortly after that."

"What's Stella's last name?" Nicki asked, diligently jotting abbreviated notes into her little book.

Maxie's eyebrows drew together. "Let me see. Kranston or Kramer? Something along those lines. But it's been almost a decade since they were an item."

"Is she still living in town?"

"I have no idea." Maxie shrugged. "I know she doesn't work in the wine industry any more. At least not that I've heard."

"Enough of the long-gone girlfriend," Jenna declared. "I'm dying to hear about The White Crown blend. What happened?"

"Nothing." Maxie smiled at Jenna's frown. "That was the problem. It was nothing of note. The local critics said it should be sold at a discount in gallon jugs to a frat house. It was a horrible embarrassment for Bill and The White Crown. Especially when George blamed it on the grapes his employer purchased to blend with the ones grown at the winery. It made the entire production from The White Crown that year come into question. George quit his job in a huff and Bill's business dropped into the ground after that."

"Is that why he changed the name to Todos?" Nicki asked.

"No, no. He bought a small winery and a sizeable number of additional acres around it and renamed *that* one Todos. It's taken a few years, but he built his business up again around the new winery. And he rehired George as his head winemaker."

"Huh. That's just weird." Jenna cocked her head to one side and gave Maxie a long stare. "What happened to The White Crown?"

"Oh, heavens. Bill had to sell it to finance his new venture. I believe there's a nice tract of houses on the old property now."

Nicki let out a soft groan. She hated to hear that a wonderful vineyard had been plowed under for boxy-looking houses set side-by-side in long rows. She exchanged a sorrowful look with

Alex before bending her head and writing "failed winery due to George" next to Bill Stacy's name.

"Well, progress marches on and all that. What about Holland Winery? I've been there a couple of times. I like their wine," Jenna said.

"George has worked there for a dozen years or so," Maxie said.

Tapping the eraser of her pencil against her lower lip, Nicki's eyes narrowed as she recalled Jim Holland's remarks at the wine tasting. "The owner told Bill Stacy that George wasn't so bad. Bill didn't agree with him. After the fiasco at The White Crown, who could blame him?"

"Given Bill's history with the man, I'm not surprised," Maxie agreed with a firm nod. "Jim didn't have as difficult a time with George. It was the signature blend George brought out at Holland ten years ago that put Jim's winery on the map. And he's managed to do very well since then."

"But George wasn't going to do the primary bottling and selling of his new signature blend at Holland Winery. He only arranged a private tasting there for the local owners, other wine-makers and a few critics. Most of the distribution was going to be through Trax. George was talking with Jeremy Brennan about being Trax's head winemaker. At least that's what Jeremy said. He claimed they were in the final negotiations."

"So it wasn't a sure thing yet?" Alex asked.

Nicki shook her head. "Didn't sound like it."

"What if it had already fallen through despite what Jeremy said at the tasting, and he was out for revenge?" Jenna gave her eyebrows a dramatic wiggle.

"It certainly needs to be checked out." Nicki scribbled madly in her notebook. Both wine owners also had reason to dislike George Lancer. Jim because he was cut out of the sales and the biggest part of the publicity for the new blend, and Jeremy Brennan, the owner of Trax, if George pulled a last-minute cancellation of their agreement.

Jenna grinned at Alex before popping the final scrap of her burger into her mouth. "Who else is on your list?" Consulting her notes, Nicki frowned. "The server at the tasting. George yelled at him for not bringing the right water to the table. The young man looked humiliated. Geri said she had to send him home."

"Waiters get yelled at all the time by unreasonable people. Not much of a motive," Jenna observed.

"Agreed," Nicki said. "But it's worth having a chat with him. And then there's Geri. She didn't like the man, and even acted afraid of him."

Alex propped her elbows on the kitchen counter and folded her hands under her chin. "Poison *is* the preferred method of female killers. But was she afraid enough to murder him?"

"And since she was afraid of him, did she have the nerve to kill him? Geri is Jim's right hand in juggling all the daily administrative details of the business. I doubt if George could get her fired, so she had nothing to be worried about on that front. I think being afraid of a bully is simply part of her personality," Maxie said.

"We'll leave her on the list but move her to the bottom," Nicki said, making a note of it. "I think the first thing to do is pay Chief Turnlow a visit and find out what he knows. Alex and I can do that tomorrow."

"Alex is sitting right here, and I'm not so crazy about paying the police a visit," Alex said.

"But I bet she would for eggs Benedict with fresh dill." Jenna looked over at Nicki and winked. "By the way, is the candy for Maxie? As in burger for me, zucchini fries for Alex and candy for our landlady?"

The older woman's eyes instantly lit up. "Candy? You bought me candy?"

"You wouldn't happen to be partial to chocolates with creamy centers by any chance?" Alex smiled.

"My favorite," Maxie declared.

When her two friends turned to stare at her with raised eyebrows, Nicki cleared her throat. "Well, I just happen to have some."

Jenna laughed and looked over at Alex who joined in.

Maxie blinked once, and then twice, before chuckling. "I know Jenna has a weakness for hamburgers, and by the way you're popping them into your mouth, I assume those fries are a favorite of yours, Alex?" At Alex's nod, Maxie's smile grew wider. "Then the candy is *my* bribe. Very clever, dear. And most appreciated. Now then. We've worked up an impressive list of suspects and have our first 'to-do' for tomorrow. All we have left to accomplish today is to go shopping."

Now it was the three younger women who blinked.

"Why shopping?" Jenna demanded.

"To buy a murder board, of course. All modern-day detectives have them. It will help us visualize and get organized. It's fortunate my Mercedes is in the shop for some maintenance, so I had to bring my Mason's van instead. Everything we need should fit nicely into it."

"That's a great idea. We can set it up in my office," Nicki said, very happy with the outcome of her little luncheon scheme and eager to get started.

A big, white board to keep track of everything they might uncover sounded perfect. Hopefully the entire investigation would go well, and they could fill the board up in no time. The murder would be solved, and she could get back to her novel.

The women put the lunch leftovers away amid chatter and laughter before trailing after Maxie down the hall and out the door. As they walked across the lawn toward the van, Jenna threw an arm around Nicki's shoulders and gave them a friendly squeeze.

"It seems we've all signed up as members of the 'Nicki Knows Murder' club. Maybe we should start our own magazine. Give Matt a run for his money."

"Well, if Nicki's in charge, it might be better named the "Food and Wine" murder club," Alex observed.

All four women were laughing as they piled into the van.

**8**

---

The following morning Nicki spent a good hour preparing an elegant breakfast of eggs Benedict, sliced tomatoes and freshly squeezed juice. In exchange, Alex reluctantly agreed to go along on what Nicki insisted was a "research" trip to the police station.

It was barely mid-morning when they climbed into the not-always-trustworthy Toyota and took the ten-minute drive into Soldoff. As they chugged down the road, Nicki cast a sideways glance at her friend. While Alex wasn't smiling, she wasn't frowning either, which was a good sign.

*Guess the breakfast did the trick*, Nicki mused as they rolled up to the stop sign on the edge of the town square.

The founders of Soldoff hadn't bothered to come up with a town layout of their own, instead borrowing ideas from their nearby neighbor, Sonoma. So like its bigger neighbor, Soldoff boasted a square in the middle of several blocks of houses. Except for a couple of fast-food stops, two gas stations and a laundromat, every business in Soldoff was located around the square. But unlike Sonoma, which stuck to adobe walls and red-tiled roofs for its buildings, Soldoff's town council never met long enough to pass any building codes to enforce a uniform look for their main tourist attraction—the town square. Anyone who bought a building and started a business was free to indulge in their own, personal style.

The fanciest restaurant in town resembled a French chateau and was flanked on one side by a square, cement-block of a building holding several tasting rooms, and on its other side by a gift shop sporting a more Southern-colonial facade. The whole square was such a mishmash of styles and colors, it drew a sizable number of tourists who came just to gawk at it.

Nicki thought it had a charm of its own. The always practical Jenna declared it a rural disaster that should qualify for federal cleanup funds, while Alex had only shaken her head the first time she'd seen it, and hadn't noticed or mentioned it since.

The center of the square boasted a walkway wandering through a lush, neatly trimmed green lawn, thanks to Maxie's husband. Mason Edwards donated his time to keep it looking that way, including planting rows of daisies around the center-piece of the square. On a tall round pedestal of marble stood a ten-foot-high statue of a cluster of grapes. Maxie had explained that since the only acknowledged founding father of Soldoff had tried to sell the entire town in pieces to the highest bidders, no one wanted a statue erected in his honor. Unless, as myMason suggested once at a council meeting, it was set up in the middle of the town dump. Instead, the residents had unanimously decided to immortalize wine grapes in bronze since it was the fruit that kept most of their businesses afloat in tourist money

One corner of the square hosted the tiny police department, its boxy building painted a discreet dark-brown. The area of street in front of it was marked off into three parking spaces, all painted in bright orange with a black "APD Parking Only" outlined on top. Nicki maneuvered around the square and took the empty spot right next to the orange asphalt. She didn't want the entire town to think she was under arrest because her car was in the "orange zone", which was reserved for the two squad cars and anyone the police wanted to talk to.

Nicki glanced over at the three empty parking spaces. "I guess everyone's out fighting crime."

"Do you want to come back later?" Alex asked.

Nicki shook her head and opened the car door. "No. I'm sure Fran is here."

"Fran?"

"She answers the incoming calls and does the office chores, keeps the paperwork in order, that sort of thing." Nicki picked up her purse and a paper bag she'd set on the console between the front seats. After a hard shove, she got the car door open and stepped out onto the street.

Alex exited the passenger side, then stood looking over the car roof at Nicki. A grin tugged at the sides of her mouth. "Paperwork? Maybe she'll have the lab reports and anything else concerning Mr. Lancer's death right there at her desk."

Nicki grinned back at her. "Do you think so? Gosh, I never thought of that."

"Uh huh." Alex followed Nicki down the short walkway into the station.

The compact front room had a long counter barely five feet from the doorway and stretching across the entire space. Behind it were crammed three desks, two filing cabinets, and a nearly empty water cooler. A woman with short, kinky gray hair and enough wrinkles on her face and neck to proclaim her well past the traditional retirement age, looked up as they came through the doorway. She squinted at them from behind wire-rimmed glasses.

"That you, Nicki Connors?" Her voice was scratchy, but a smile lit up her face as she pushed her glasses higher up on her nose. "I can surely see it is. What brings you downtown this morning?"

Nicki thought referring to the square as a "downtown" was a

bit of a stretch, but would never insult Fran by voicing that out loud. Instead she offered up a wide smile of her own. "How are you, Fran? I was wondering if I could see the chief?"

"Oh honey, I'm sorry. He isn't here. He had official business to attend to this morning."

Nicki's forehead wrinkled as she did her best to look disappointed. "Oh. Well, maybe Danny then?"

"Wouldn't you know it, it's his day off. He'll be sorry he missed you too." Fran leaned forward and lowered her voice along with a conspiratorial wink. "I'm positive that boy has a crush on you."

"He does? Well, I might have to ask him why he's never mentioned it."

Fran laughed. "Because he knows about that good-looking boyfriend of yours. Mopes around every time he sees the two of you together. Rod, isn't it?"

"Rob," Nicki supplied.

"I imagine he spends all the time he can with you." Fran nodded. "He'd be a fool not to."

At the sudden fit of coughing from Alex, Nicki gave her friend a slight, sideways kick while keeping her gaze on Fran and a smile on her face. She even managed not to wince when Alex kicked her back.

"Do you need a glass of water?" Fran asked, her attention now on Alex.

"No, no," Alex said, clearing her throat. "I'm fine, thank you."

"Fran, I don't believe you've met my friend, Alex Kolman?" Nicki said. "Did I ever mention I had two roommates in New York? You know Jenna, of course, and Alex was my other roommate."

Fran got up from her desk and walked briskly over to the counter. She took Alex's outstretched hand in her own and gave it a firm shake. "Nice to meet you. Are you out here visiting our lovely state?"

"No. I live in Santa Rosa and work..." Alex's words were cut off at another, stronger kick from Nicki.

"She's in the middle of relocating. Finding a place, looking for work. You know how time consuming that can be." Nicki sent a warning glance to Alex who raised one eyebrow.

"Why how wonderful." Fran beamed at Alex. "Always glad to have new residents in Soldoff. I heard Sandy's is looking for help on their breakfast shift."

"Sandy's?" Alex echoed.

"A local diner." Nicki gave her friend an innocent look before pushing her latest bribe across the counter toward Fran. "I guess since Chief Turnlow and Danny aren't here, you'll have to eat these without their help."

The office deputy eagerly reached for the bag and peeked inside. "Are those cranberry muffins?"

"With a pinch of orange, just the way you like them," Nicki assured her.

"Imagine that," Alex said under her breath, but loud enough to earn herself a tap on the toe from Nicki.

Fran glanced from one woman to the other. "I have a couple of granddaughters who are an awful lot like the two of you, even if they are still in their teens. Always up to something those two." She reached into the bag and pulled out one of the sugar-coated muffins. "This looks wonderful. I may have to take them all home."

"I think you should," Nicki said.

Smiling, Fran looked over at her and nodded. "I might. Now then. What can I do for you? I know you didn't come into town just to bring me my favorite muffins."

Laughing because Fran had obviously seen right through her, Nicki rested her arms on the counter and leaned forward.

"I was wondering if the chief needed to do a more in-depth interview with me, since I found the body. Along with Geri, of course."

"He hasn't mentioned it," Fran said. "But I can give him the message. And that doesn't seem like it's worth a whole bag of muffins."

Thinking she wasn't going to be very good at this investigation thing if she was so ridiculously transparent, Nicki sighed and gave up trying to be clever and sneaky about getting information. Apparently it wasn't the best approach for her to take.

"I was hoping we could trade information. What I know for what he knows?"

Fran gave her a sharp look. "Do you have information you haven't shared with him yet?"

Nicki immediately shook her head. "No. Not yet, at least."

"Are you planning on doing some detective work of your own?"

"I do have contacts in the journalism and news world," Nicki felt as if she should cross her fingers behind her back. She might be overstating that a bit, but it was true. To a certain extent, anyway. Besides, Matt *did* have a lot of contacts, and he had offered to help, so it wasn't an outright lie.

"What information are you looking for, honey? George Lancer probably died from a heart attack. No mystery there."

Nicki wasted no time in pouncing on what Fran had said. "Is that what the coroner said? That it was a heart attack?"

When Fran nodded, Nicki's face fell along with her spirits. She'd been so sure he was murdered.

"Is that the medical examiner's final ruling?" Alex asked.

"From what Doctor Tom said, he hasn't decided yet. I'm to tell the chief he won't be issuing the death certificate until he checks out a few things."

Nicki looked at Alex and then back over at Fran. "What things?"

The clerk's mouth pursed into a thin line. She gave a quick peek over Nicki's shoulder toward the front door before dropping her voice to a stage whisper. "Doctor Tom wasn't sure why George had a heart attack. Despite everyone saying the man had a severe smoking habit and being on the heavy side, he didn't show any signs of heart disease and his lungs were clear. He thought it was odd enough he needed to study it a bit further. And he said something about the blood test results."

"The blood test results?" Nicki echoed.

Fran nodded and stepped over to her desk, pulling a piece of paper out from a folder lying on top of her inbox. "Just got it in yesterday afternoon. Chief asked me to put it with the rest of the case file."

Nicki concentrated on keeping her hands still, so she wouldn't snatch it away from Fran. Taking a deep breath, she forced her voice to stay calm and even. "Does it say anything unusual?"

"Wouldn't know," Fran said. "Never could make heads or tails out of those things. Here, you can take a look."

She handed the single sheet over to Nicki, who carefully took the time to study the various bars and numbers before placing it flat on the counter between herself and Alex.

"I certainly have no idea what it says either. Maybe the chief will know since he came from a big city department. I'm sure he saw quite a few unexplained deaths in Los Angeles."

"He didn't act like he saw anything unusual, but he can keep things pretty close to the vest, if you know what I mean," Fran said.

"I do. Sometimes he's... ow!" Nicki turned a wide-eyed look at Alex who'd stomped hard on her foot. Her friend jerked her eyes toward the piece of paper lying between them.

"I just remembered I'm expected by, um, by..." Alex sent Nicki the same silent message with her eyes that she'd used back in New York when she'd needed to be rescued from an overly zealous young man in their favorite bar.

"The movers?" Nicki hastily supplied. Absolutely sure her friend had seen something significant in those test results, Nicki's nerves jittered down her spine. She grabbed Alex's arm and threw a last smile at Fran who was now frowning at them. "I forgot all about those movers. We really do need to hurry. Thanks so much, Fran. Please tell the chief I'll be calling him soon about that interview."

With one last tug, Nicki got them out the door. She did a quick-step to the car and once inside turned the key, wasting no time in setting the car into motion. She didn't say a word until they were away from the square and headed back to the townhouse.

"Okay, spill it, *Doctor* Kolman. What did you see?"

Alex turned and stared at her with huge eyes. "Raised levels of all the things which indicate a heart attack, plus one more."

"Which was?" Nicki prompted.

"Nicotine. He had very high levels of nicotine."

Confused, Nicki frowned. "He was a heavy smoker."

Her friend, the doctor, gave a dramatic sigh. "A heavy smoker with clear lungs, according to what the coroner told Fran. Which is a mystery all in itself. And anyway, those weren't levels he'd get from smoking. But they were high enough to bring on a sudden heart attack, even without any evidence of heart disease. If I had to guess, I'd say he drank it. Nicotine is used in pesticides and can make a very effective poison."

"Poison?" Nicki's blood suddenly felt heavier and her head lighter. She carefully slowed her little car until she could pull over to the side of the road. Once they'd rolled to a halt, Nicki turned in her seat and stared wide-eyed at Alex.

"Are you sure?"

"No. That's up to the medical examiner. But your victim could not have smoked that much nicotine. And from what you said happened, it certainly appears he ingested a sudden and large intake, which caused the heart attack."

"A sudden and large intake," Nicki repeated. She looked off into the distance, turning it over in her mind before glancing back at her friend.

"The wine. It was in the wine."

Alex's forehead scrunched up and her eyes narrowed. "It wouldn't take much of a sip for a heavy dose of pure nicotine to bring on a heart attack. But it might taste horrible unless it was disguised with some sort of flavoring."

"Like cherries," Nicki whispered.

The two women exchanged a long, shocked look.

"We need to go to Holland's right now," Nicki declared.

"Wait. The winery where this guy died? Why?" Alex demanded.

But Nicki ignored her. She grabbed her purse and rooted around in its depths frantically searching for her cell phone. Finally managing to get her hands on it, she punched in a number and waited impatiently for Jenna to pick up.

"So, what did Sherlock and Watson find out?"

Momentarily startled, Nicki's mind went blank. "That's what Matt called me."

"Sherlock and Watson?" Jenna asked.

"No, just Sherlock." Shaking off the distraction, Nicki clutched her phone even tighter. "I need you to get Maxie and meet us at Holland Winery."

"It just so happens that Maxie is right here getting a lesson on how not to mess up her website. What's going on?"

"We need to preserve a crime scene."

9

T he little Toyota spun into the winery parking lot. Nicki shoved open her door and leaped out of the driver's seat just as Jenna came running up, with Maxie right on her heels.

"What's going on?" Jenna's long arms windmilled as she fought to catch her balance when her feet slid on the gravel.

"The wine," Nicki said. "It *was* in the wine."

Maxie halted next to Jenna, steadying herself with a quick grab onto the tall brunette's arm. The older woman sent a stern look in Alex's direction before turning the same look on Nicki. "Now everyone calm down. Let's compare notes so we can see where we are."

Jenna frowned. "Compare notes? We don't have any notes."

The older woman patted Jenna's arm but kept her gaze on Nicki. "It's just a figure of speech detectives are fond of using, dear. I'm sure you'll become used to the lingo once the murder board is set up."

"Where did *you* learn this lingo?" Jenna demanded with a roll of her eyes before facing Nicki. "What was in the wine?"

"Nicki thinks George was poisoned with a large dose of nicotine in his wine," Alex held up her hand when Jenna's jaw dropped to her chest. "The lab report showed an elevated level of nicotine in his blood."

"The man always had a cigarette in his hand," Maxie pointed out. "Why even at the annual Wine Valley Ball he was constantly disappearing to have a smoke. He reeked of smoke the whole night." She pursed her lips and shook her head. "Such a shame to ruin that nice tuxedo too."

Praying for patience at the ridiculous direction of the conversation, Nicki clapped her hands together. When three sets of eyes turned toward her, she put her hands on her hips and gave a hard stare to each of them. "Alex read the lab report at the police station. She says the nicotine levels were way too high to be just from smoking. I think the nicotine was in the wine. We have to make sure the crime scene isn't touched until we can find the chief and let him know George was murdered."

"What makes you think he doesn't already know, dear?" Maxie asked.

Nicki took a swift glance around. "Because if he did, he'd be here, and I don't see a police car anywhere."

Her three companions craned their necks as they each did a complete turn to look around the entire parking lot.

"We look like a bunch of spinning tops," Jenna complained.

"I don't see a police car," Maxie said.

"I think we should just call Chief Turnlow, tell him what we think and let him deal with this. After all, it's his job to do that sort of thing," Alex pointed out.

"Nonsense," Maxie declared. "We absolutely should be sure the crime scene is intact and stand guard, if necessary, to make sure it stays that way until the chief gets here."

Despite Maxie's dramatic flair, Nicki sent her a grateful smile. It grew even wider when Jenna shrugged and then nodded.

"I suppose it can't hurt to call the chief after we're sure nothing has been disturbed," Alex finally said.

Before anyone had second thoughts, Nicki set off for the wine tasting room at a brisk pace. Her plan was to slip through the same door she and Geri had used the day they found George dead in his private aging room.

The others trailed behind her. Feeling a sense of déjà vu, Nicki led the small group across the parking lot and into the spacious tasting room with its large wooden beams and long bar stretching along the back. Slipping through the door behind it would have been a piece of cake if it weren't for the familiar young man tending the bar. Abruptly changing course, Nicki headed to one of the tall tables in the far corner.

"Where to now?" Jenna demanded. "Which way is the scene of the crime, so to speak?"

Nicki smiled brightly at the barman. He was the same waiter George had humiliated in front of an audience the day the wine-maker died. But right now, that young man was blocking the door leading to the private aging room.

"We need to distract the bartender, so he won't stop us going through the backdoor."

"Why would he care if we did?" Jenna asked.

"Because he might be a suspect," Nicki countered.

Jenna gave an inelegant snort. "He barely looks old enough to be serving liquor, and you think *he* might have killed George Lancer?"

"I'm sure we'll understand Nicki's reasoning once the murder board is set up," Maxie said.

Nicki bit her lip to keep from smiling. Maxie certainly was fixated on having a murder board. She wasn't even sure any of them had the foggiest idea how to set one up.

"Let's just go along with Nicki so we can get to the calling-the-police part of the plan," Alex said. She turned around, leaned back against the table, and sent a big smile along with a wave to the bartender.

"Nice flirting for an engaged woman," Jenna said, keeping her voice low, but followed Alex's lead and motioned the young man over to their table. Nicki covered her mouth and hid her grin when Kurt, at least she thought that was his name, made short work of rounding the bar. He headed in their direction with the slight swagger guys often took on when they were the center of a woman's attention, much less a whole group of them. Nicki choked back a giggle at Alex's long, drawn-out sigh.

"I think our resident blogger has made another conquest," Jenna said in a stage whisper to Alex.

Sure enough, Kurt stopped right next to Nicki. His surfer-blue eyes locked onto her even as he politely addressed all of them. "What can I get for you ladies?"

Nicki gave a polite nod before inclining her head toward her friends. "They know what I want. I need to run to the ladies' room."

"I'll go with you," Maxie turned a motherly smile on the young waiter. "We'll be back in a few minutes. Just in time for our drinks."

Alex picked up the tasting menu present on all the tables and leaned toward the unsuspecting server. "What would you recommend?"

When he started pointing out the various blends on the small menu, Nicki quietly slipped away with Maxie right beside her.

"You go check on the crime scene. I'll find Jim and ask him to call Chief Turnlow," Maxie whispered.

Nodding her agreement, Nicki split off and headed straight for the back of the bar. In less than two minutes she'd made the turn into the hallway leading to the private aging room. Even from the end of the hallway, the bright yellow police tape across the doorway stood out like a neon sign. Behind the tape, the heavy, wooden door was closed.

"Oh shoot," she said under her breath. It was probably locked. Not sure how to get a peek inside, Nicki bent over and put her eye to the keyhole. But the tiny opening only showed a patch of floor and the side of a barrel. Frustrated, she straightened up and put her hands on her hips, glaring at the offending door.

Not expecting much, she gave the handle a firm twist. To her surprise it easily turned in her hand. A light shove forward and the door opened with a soft creak of its hinges. Nicki pushed it open far enough to be able to peer into the room.

The small table holding the glasses and wine bottles was hidden behind the first row of barrels. Nicki leaned forward as far as she could, stretching her back and neck, trying to see over the barrels into the narrow aisle between the rows. Not having any luck, she took a step backwards and frowned at the triangle-shaped space on either side of the crisscross made by the police tape.

*Bet I could get through there.* Nicki gauged the size of the opening. She'd only need to slip in far enough to make sure the wine bottles and glasses were still there. Deciding it wouldn't hurt to get that closer look, Nicki gripped the doorjamb and carefully lifted one foot and then a leg through the narrow opening.

"I'm sure you aren't trying to sneak past a police barricade, Ms. Connors."

Half in and half out of the room, Nicki froze in place as her stomach sank all the way to her feet. Where had the chief come from?

While her face heated up to a full burn, Nicki slowly backed out into the hallway. She took a big step away from the door before turning to face Soldoff's police chief.

Deciding the best option was to bluff it out, Nicki took a deep breath and pasted a smile on her face. Her cheeks grew even hotter as she stared at the chief, and then at Geri standing behind him with her mouth wide open and a key held high in one hand. And behind her were Jim Holland, Maxie, Alex and Jenna. Nicki let out a soft groan and briefly closed her eyes. The only person missing was Kurt, the bartender.

"Chief..." When her voice squeaked on the single word, Nicki mashed her lips together and cleared her throat. "Chief Turnlow. You certainly got here fast after Maxie's call."

The chief raised an eyebrow. "I didn't get a call from Maxie. She walked into the office where Jim and I were having a nice friendly chat."

Nicki's gaze flicked over to Maxie who silently mouthed "sorry".

"I didn't see your cruiser in the parking lot." Nicki couldn't hold back the slight accusation in her voice.

"It's parked out back."

Nicki gave a dramatic sigh and held her wrists out in front of her. "All right. I confess. I tried to get past the police tape. Go ahead and arrest me."

"I just might do that." The chief took several steps forward. His whole audience followed right along. He stopped several feet away from Nicki and his gaze cut over to the open door. "We locked that door and Jim just told me it's stayed that way. How did you happen to get it open, Ms. Connors?"

Startled, Nicki glanced at the door and then back at the chief. "It wasn't locked."

"No?"

This time his gaze shifted to Geri, who promptly held out the key to him, dropping it into his outstretched hand as if it were a hot poker.

"I locked the door, Chief. I'm sure of it. And your deputy saw me lock it." Geri clasped her hands in front of her so hard her knuckles turned white. She flinched when Jim stepped up and placed a hand on her shoulder.

"Jim, why don't you and I and Ms. Connors go back to your office so we can talk." Chief Turnlow shook his head at Nicki. "I'll forego using the handcuffs. At least for the moment."

Jenna immediately rushed over to stand by Nicki's side. Alex did the same and wrapped an arm around her friend's shoulders.

"If Nicki said the door was already unlocked, then it was

already unlocked." Jenna staunchly defended her friend with a fierce glare squarely directed at Soldoff's police chief.

Alex nodded her head. "I can assure you, Nicki is telling the truth. And I'm a doctor."

"Which would count heavily in Nicki's favor if we were discussing her health. But at the moment, it's her snooping that's in question." The chief ran a hand over the top of his thinning, brown hair.

If he kept that up, Nicki suspected he'd be bald by the time he was through listening to her friends. Since it would be better if she simply accompanied the man, she reached up and removed the hand gripped around her shoulder while pressing an elbow into Jenna's side.

"I'll come along peacefully, Chief. You need to hear why we raced over here before you pass judgment."

Now the chief turned a narrow-eyed look on her. "This isn't the wild, wild West, Ms. Connors. I only want to have a talk in private, not hang you from the highest tree."

"Really, Paul. That is far too dramatic." Maxie frowned. She lifted her hands and gave a shooing motion to Alex and Jenna. "Come along ladies. We can enjoy a nice drink and discuss how to set up our murder board while we wait for them to finish their chat. I'm sure Nicki will be able to make the men understand how sound our reasoning is." She lifted her nose slightly when she glanced back at the chief. "Be sure you listen to her, Paul. We'd certainly welcome your help."

"Glad to be of service, Maxie." The chief's tone was as dry as dust. He slowly shook his head at the backs of the three women who marched down the hall, arm-in-arm.

"Jim, I'd appreciate it if you could lead the way."

"Should I come too?" Geri stammered, her gaze fixed on a point between Nicki and the chief. "I mean, since I was the last one to lock the door. Maybe I should come too."

Geri had kept her distance at the outer edge of their little group and was so quiet Nicki had forgotten she was there. The poor woman looked frightened as she stood in her usual, plain attire with her hands clasped in front of her. They were visibly trembling. Even though the assistant's head was bent and her eyes downcast, Nicki automatically sent her a reassuring smile.

"No need, Geri." The chief's voice dropped to a gentler level, and Nicki was surprised by the smile on his lips.

"Oh." The assistant winemaker looked from the chief to Jim Holland and back again. "Oh, well. I guess I should go back to work." She stood for a moment, still looking uncertain, before turning abruptly around and scurrying off.

With an immediate problem of her own, Nicki dismissed Geri from her thoughts and followed Jim toward his office with Chief Turnlow trailing behind.

The large office space Jim used to manage his winery was comfortably decorated and furnished. An oversized desk and a well-used chair covered in cracked leather with a patch showing here and there ate up a chunk of the space, and two overflowing bookshelves lined the far wall. The three straight-backed, wooden chairs in front of the desk comprised the only other furniture in the room. Jim headed for his usual place behind the desk and Nicki made herself as comfortable as she could in one of the rigid chairs in front of him. The chief chose to stand between them, his arms crossed over his chest.

"All right, Nicki. You start."

Feeling it was a good sign he'd dropped the formal way he'd been addressing her, Nicki nodded.

"Alex and I went by the police station in case you needed an additional statement from me. We were talking to Fran at the exact same time she had the blood test results in her hand."

"Is that right?" One of the chief's eyebrows quirked up, but he nodded at her to continue.

"She needed to do something, so she set the test results down for a moment."

"What did Fran need to do?" the chief asked.

Nicki decided he sounded pleasant enough, but the smile on his face didn't move, and his eyes certainly didn't look amused. She took a breath and plowed on with a careless wave of her hand.

"Answer the phone, or maybe she went to get a drink of water. I don't remember. But for the very brief moment the results were on the desk, we happened to glance at it and Alex... I have to apologize for not introducing you, by the way."

"I take it Alex is your friend, the doctor?"

"Yes, she is. Alex is a *doctor*," Nicki placed an emphasis on that last word. "She happened to notice the large amount of nicotine on the report."

"She noticed that from the other side of the desk?" Again the chief's eyebrow rose.

After a brief struggle, Nicki managed to keep a straight face. "Of course. She's a doctor. She's used to reading lab results at a glance."

Chief Turnlow rolled his eyes. "Now why didn't I realize that, I wonder?"

"Just a minute." Jim Holland placed his large hands flat on top of the desk and pushed himself half-way out of his chair. "Are you saying George was poisoned? With nicotine? He was a heavy smoker. Of course he'd have nicotine in his system."

Happy to have the chief's attention on something other than her, Nicki looked over at the owner and shook her head. "Not this much. It was definitely more than he'd have from smoking a pack of cigarettes."

The chief unwound his arms and turned to rest one hip on the edge of the cluttered desk. "So your friend, the *doctor,* not only read the test results from a distance, but even saw the precise amount of a drug in the victim's blood?" He sighed heavily and held up a hand when Nicki's lips formed into an "O".

"Please don't bother to explain." The chief glanced at Jim

Holland. "The ME called on my way over here. He confirmed George Lancer was probably murdered, unless he deliberately ingested the nicotine himself. The doc said it must have been fast acting, so he probably ingested it from the wine."

The chief continued to stare at the winery owner. "You told me the victim always kept that room locked. Just like it was supposed to be kept locked since we put the tape up. So the question is, how did the killer get the key to that room? The one George had on him is at the station in the evidence cabinet, and the spare was locked up in your safe until we took it out to have a look at the scene. But there was the one used during the usual work day that was kept on a hook by the door. It isn't there now." He shifted his gaze to Nicki. "And you say the door was unlocked?"

Nicki stood up. Without saying a word, she took off her jacket and set it on the desk. "I don't have any other pockets, and you can check my jacket." She picked up her purse and upended it on the desk. Her keys, checkbook, lip gloss, wallet and all the change she habitually dropped into the bottom of her purse spilled out across the broad surface.

Nicki sat and crossed her arms, her hazel eyes staring up at the chief.

Chief Turnlow looked at the scattered items on the desk but made no move to touch her jacket. "Key doesn't seem to be here." He looked over at her with a ghost of a smile. "And we didn't see you ditch it anywhere, so I guess you're in the clear."

"Why thank you, Chief." Nicki's voice dripped sweetness as she continued to stare at him.

"Now then, having settled the nagging question of whether or not you poisoned George Lancer, why don't you tell me all about this murder board of yours, and I'll just give you a stern warning about ignoring police tape over potential crime scenes."

"There's nothing much to tell, Chief." Nicki gave a small

shrug. "It's still in a box, and there isn't one word on it. I don't know what we'll do with it. Why, we might even just return it."

"Uh huh." The chief let out a big sigh. "That might be the best thing to do so you won't be tempted to get into any more hot water."

## 10

"Okay, we're set." Jenna stepped back and tapped the wooden frame with the tip of her screwdriver. She turned a grin on Nicki. "It looks great."

Nodding her agreement, Nicki walked around to the front of the large, dry-erase board stretching across the longest wall of her home office. All four women stared at the big blank, white space hanging in front of them.

"We might have gone a tad overboard on the size." Alex frowned.

"Nonsense. It's perfect," Maxie magically producing a box of felt-tipped markers and pulled out the black one. "Let's get started."

In large dramatic letters, she neatly printed across the top *George Lancer Murder,* then divided the board into quarters and put a heading over each column: Facts, Suspects, Motives and To-Do. Stepping back, she handed the marker to Alex before rubbing her hands together. "That should do it." She turned and walked over to the desk, settling herself into Nicki's ergonomically correct chair. She folded her hands in her lap and gave an exaggerated wink to the others.

Alex took a step forward and poised her hand over the board's surface. "Okay. What facts do we know?" She scrawled out *George was poisoned.* She'd barely finished the last word before Jenna came up behind her and snatched the marker away. "Good grief. The board won't do us any good if we can't read what's on it."

Alex turned around and glared at her friend. "I can read it just fine."

"Well no one else can," Jenna declared. "You write like a doctor. Only nurses and cryptologists can read it."

"Quite a few people read my handwriting every day," Alex snorted.

"Doctors' handwriting is the number one reason computers were invented," Jenna said. "So the rest of us can actually read what you've written."

"It's not that bad," Alex muttered, but gave up the argument and took a place next to Nicki. She leaned over and whispered to her friend, "Is my handwriting so horrible?"

Nicki chuckled and raised a hand to her mouth to shield her words from Jenna. "I'm going with the computer nerd on this one. Sorry."

"Traitor," Alex whispered back as she glared at Jenna. "Go ahead. What else do we know as a fact, Sherlock?"

Jenna raised her hand, ready to write as she looked at Nicki. "I'll defer to the real Sherlock in our little group. So, Nicki, what else do we know?"

"If he was poisoned, the most likely substance was nicotine." Nicki glanced at Alex, who nodded her agreement.

"Pure nicotine is odorless and colorless, but might have a nasty taste to it. The body would reject it fairly quickly, which is the likely reason for the tobacco smell. But even then, it absorbs so easily into the system it wouldn't take much to cause the heart attack." Alex paused for a moment, her gaze fixed on an unknown point outside the office window. "It would fit what else we were told. While the actual cause of death would be the heart attack, it definitely had help if he somehow ingested pure nicotine."

Nicki pursed her lips as Jenna wrote a short-hand version of Alex's explanation on the board. "We know I saw four bottles of wine in the room when we discovered George, three unused wine glasses and one broken one. Everyone who works there said that the room was always kept locked unless George was inside, and his personal key is now in the police evidence file cabinet. And the one kept hanging on a hook in Jim Holland's office is missing."

"File cabinet?" Jenna's mouth quirked upwards at the corners. "Not an evidence room? Just a file cabinet?"

"I'm sure that Paul meant it's in a file locked up in his desk," Maxie chimed in. "There isn't enough crime in Soldoff to have a room, or even a file cabinet for that matter."

"Except when someone sold the entire town off when he didn't actually own it," Jenna said before continuing with her task of listing the facts on the board. "And he was about to introduce a special blend." Jenna added that as well.

"I noticed the only way back to those rooms is through the public area, the same way Geri and I went, or through the back hallway to a door leading to the outside, across from the production building..." Nicki trailed off, her forehead wrinkled in thought. Holland's was closed to the public that morning, and George told Jim, who told Chief Turnlow, that he'd only drawn the wine the night before. Which means the killer must have either been at the event, or was one of the staff at the winery.

"What is it, dear?" Maxie prompted.

"The winery was only open to event invitees, and George probably only bottled his blend the night before the event," Nicki said.

"Which means it was most likely someone on the invitation list?" Alex asked.

Nicki tilted her head to one side and pursed her lips. "Yes. Or one of the winery employees. A stranger walking around definitely would have been noticed."

"Okay," Jenna said. "Who do we have as a suspect among the invited guests?"

"Aside from me?" Recalling the crush of humanity at the event, Nicki tapped one finger against her mouth. "There had to be at least seventy-five people there. I'm sure Geri has the invited guest list, but who actually came? I don't think they kept track, except for maybe the overall number."

"*You* have no motive," Maxie pointed out. "You didn't even know the man. Because of the salary he demanded, George only worked at a few of the wineries, so perhaps we should concentrate on those first?"

"As far as I know he only worked at two, and was about to start at a third."

Jenna stood ready at the board. "Which ones are they?"

"Jim Holland of Holland Winery, Bill Stacy of Todos, and Jeremy Brennan. He owns Trax."

"What kind of tracks?" Alex's eyebrows drew together. "And what does that have to do with wine?"

Nicki chuckled and shook her head. "T-R-A-X. It's the name of his winery. He said a marketing company came up with it."

Alex rolled her eyes in response while Jenna added the name to the board, then stepped back and examined her work.

"That should give us a good start with the winery owners."

Maxie squinted at the board. "I can't believe Jim Holland murdered George, unless the man threatened to leave entirely and take Holland's business secrets and major customers with him. Jim hates any kind of disloyalty."

"One of the keys was locked up in the safe in his office, and Jim's the only one with the combination. But he keeps a duplicate key on a hook on his office wall to use during the day. Anyone could have grabbed it if they knew it was there," Nicki pointed out, trying to ease the suddenly distressed look on Maxie's face.

The fact was, Nicki also had a very hard time imagining the winery owner getting rid of his head winemaker, especially at his own winery. And certainly not at a high-profile event. It would be much smarter to just make the man disappear and bury him in a remote part of the property. With George's nasty reputation, she doubted anyone would have spent a lot of time looking for him. Nicki bit her lip and pondered that for a moment.

"What about employees?" Jenna asked. "From what you said, George didn't treat them well at all."

"The waiter, Kurt, should certainly be on the list. He disappeared right after George yelled at him. But then George didn't treat Geri very well either, or, I would imagine, most of the employees at Holland's or at Todos."

"But the Todos employees weren't at the event, were they? So they aren't suspects," Alex pointed out.

Jenna nodded as she added Kurt and Geri's names to the board. Picking up the cap for her marker, she snapped the top back on and turned to face the group behind her.

"So, Sherlock. What are the possible motives? I can see Jim Holland not being happy about George selling his new blend over at Trax. It might cost Jim some business."

"Perhaps." Maxie clasped her hands even harder in her lap and frowned. "But he's built a strong brand with a large following, which I'm sure could stand on its own without George's new special blend. I simply can't see that as a motive for Jim. He isn't the type. Now if one of his employees didn't choose to do what's best for the winery, he might treat them the way he did Stella."

"Who's Stella?" Alex asked.

The older woman smiled. "She was the assistant winemaker before Geri, and as I told Nicki and Jenna, she and George were also an item for a while."

Nicki still had no idea where this Stella was, but at the moment anyone could be a suspect. Especially an old girlfriend. "Are they still an item?"

"Heavens, no. They broke up quite a while ago. I haven't heard about Stella for many years, since she's no longer a part of the wine community," Maxie said.

"So Geri took her place at Holland Winery?" Nicki asked.

"That's right. But not with George, I can assure you. I understand he didn't treat Geri nicely at all."

Nicki nodded her agreement and went back to studying the board. "Unless this Stella pops up somewhere, she's probably not a suspect."

"But Geri's motive might be the way George treated her," Jenna declared, scribbling away once more.

"And the waiter because of the same poor treatment. George thoroughly humiliated the guy during the event," Nicki said. "And Jeremy hadn't finalized the deal with George and was definitely on edge about that. Maybe because he thought George intended to back out of their agreement."

"Got it," Jenna called out.

"What about the last winery owner, Bill Stacy?" Alex stood on her tiptoes to peer over Jenna's shoulder at the list of names. "What's his motive?"

"I'm not sure," Nicki admitted. "But there was the old business of George contributing to the failure of Bill's first winery, and he did say something about what he called a 'bad turn' George had done to him. Bill was also the only one who wasn't at the table when I got there. He came up behind me, and claimed he'd just arrived. But now that I think about it, I didn't see him in the parking lot when I was walking in with Geri."

"Okay. I'll split that between the motive column and the fact column," Jenna said. "Which leaves the to-do list as the only one that's completely bare." She swiped a stray lock of tightly curled, dark hair off her face and looked at Nicki. "Got any ideas?"

"Time to go talk to some winery owners," The cell phone in Nicki's burst out with Carole King's voice singing *So Far Away*. She glanced at her watch. It wasn't Rob's usual time to call, which meant he was probably cancelling their weekend plans. Again. "But right now I need to answer the phone."

"Tell lover-boy we said 'hi'," Alex winked at her.

Nicki smiled. Alex wasn't all that fond of Rob. She considered Nicki's constantly traveling boyfriend not really a boyfriend at all. But as long as Nicki liked him, Alex made an effort to keep an open mind and be polite. Jenna, on the other hand...

"Yeah, tell Mr. It's-all-about-me I said hello." Jenna added a loud sniff before giving Maxie a big wink.

"He does sound a bit challenging," Maxie added as she got to her feet. "We should give Nicki a little privacy."

"I could use something to drink." Alex grabbed Jenna by the arm and hauled her out of the room as Nicki pressed the answer button on her phone.

"Hi, Rob," she said into the phone, turning her back so she wouldn't break out into laughter over the comical face Jenna was making. She didn't feel like coming up with an explanation for why she was giggling. "How's your trip going?"

Rob worked for Catalan House, a well-known restaurant with at least one location in every state. Rob liked to mention he was the national wine buyer for the chain, when technically he was the assistant to Antonio Rossi, his boss, who really was the head wine buyer for Catalan House. But Nicki never bothered to correct him.

Despite being the assistant, Rob took great pains to look the part of the head guy, with his classic features and perfectly cut blond hair shot that had been carefully shot through with even lighter streaks. He made sure they looked natural by investing in regular stops at a high-end salon in New York. Determined to claim the title of the six-foot, handsome, up-and-comer with a great body thrown in, Rob made a point of working out at every hotel stop and augmenting his 5-foot-11-inch height by always wearing one-inch lifts in his shoes.

Nicki had to admit he made very good eye candy, and she

didn't mind the envious looks they always drew on the very rare occasions they managed to go out on a date. And she'd have to disagree with Maxie. He wasn't a challenge at all. She put very little time into their relationship. She didn't have to. His conversation ran to topics that interested him, which mostly meant himself, and although San Francisco was his home base and he was supposed to spend every other weekend there, he usually chose to make a side trip or extend his stay somewhere else.

Which is why she fully expected him to cancel their plans.

And that was just as well. She had her hands full at the moment, and wasn't in the mood to go out to see and be seen by whoever it was Rob felt a need to impress. She also had an article to finish for Matt.

"Hi, babe. It's good to hear your voice," Rob said into her ear. "How's your week going?"

"Fine." Nicki thought the single word answer would suffice to cover the subject for Rob. "How's the trip to..." She hesitated, searching for the name of the city Rob had told her he'd be traveling to this week.

"Seattle, honey. I'm in Seattle."

Since he sounded hurt, Nicki was quick to give an apology. "I'm sorry. I knew that, I've just been distracted the last few days."

"With what?" Rob asked. "I thought you said everything is fine."

"It is. But I was at a wine tasting event for George Lancer when he ended up dead, and I happened to be one of the people who discovered his body."

"Who? Did you say Lancer?"

"Lanciere," Nicki corrected since Rob would only recognize the French version George had used.

"Lanciere is dead?" Rob's astonishment sounded clearly through the phone.

"Yes, he is. And I'm pretty sure he was murdered."

"Wasn't he about to announce a new blend?"

Nicki closed her eyes and sent up a small prayer for patience. "Yes, he was, but he never got a chance because someone *killed* him."

"Who will have the rights to his new blend? It would be a great coup for Catalan House if we could snag the whole pressing."

*For you too*, Nicki thought, but she kept it to herself. No use starting an argument with a voice on the phone.

"I'm not sure who his closest relative is," was all she said. "Really, Rob. The man just died and all you can say is 'who gets his wine'?"

*Looks like I'm going to start that fight after all.* Nicki closed her eyes and took a deep, calming breath. It didn't help much.

"Sorry, babe. Didn't mean to sound so insensitive, but it isn't as if he has any more use for that blend."

Nicki was sure her snort of disbelief gave him a warning to change the subject.

"I'm sure the police there in Sandstone will handle it just fine."

"Soldoff, Rob. I live in Soldoff."

"I'm only teasing, babe. I knew that. The news about Lanciere's death rattled me." On the other end of the line Rob took a deep breath. "I really wanted to talk to you about a couple of things."

She stopped pacing the room and headed for her desk chair, intending to get comfortable while she listened to all the usual excuses he was about to offer for not keeping their date this weekend, then blinked twice when she barely caught the word "company dinner".

"Dinner?" she repeated as she settled for sitting on the edge of her desk simply because it was a step closer. "What dinner?"

"The one I told you about a couple of weeks ago. It's at the Fairmont hotel in the city and being given by the chairman of the board of directors. It's pretty much a 'must attend' if you want to be taken seriously in this industry. And I need to make an appearance with my hot girlfriend on my arm."

"Rob, you know how I feel about those things, and I don't have time right now to make the drive into San Francisco." Nicki tapped her fingers on her desktop and rolled her eyes at Alex who'd made a sudden appearance in the doorway.

"It's not for another month and you need to make the time, babe. Please do this for me. And for yourself and future career prospects."

When she remained silent, he tried a different tack. "Promise me you'll come, and I promise a VIP dinner at Catalan House in the city the minute I get back. You know you like those dinners with just the two of us."

Busy trying to decipher the hand signals Alex was sending her, Nicki said an absent "fine" as she stared at Alex, who was now silently mouthing the words "lemon cake".

"But I can't take you out this weekend," the disembodied voice on the phone stated. "I can't get out of Seattle that soon. But..."

Nicki tuned out the familiar excuses and put her hand over the bottom half of her cell phone. "What?" she asked in a loud stage whisper as an oblivious Rob kept talking into her ear.

"Maxie wants to know when she should pick up the lemon cake tomorrow?" Alex whispered back.

Nicki had completely forgotten about her promise to supply her landlady, and president of the Ladies in Writing Society, with dessert for her next meeting. Nicki did a quick calculation in her head. "Late afternoon. Sometime after four."

"Okay," Alex said. "And you might be interested to know that Jenna is making dinner."

As Alex disappeared back down the hallway, Nicki's eyes widened at the thought of Jenna Lindstrom cooking any food in her shiny new kitchen. With visions of gigantic hamburgers sizzling in a pan and throwing out waves of grease to coat her walls, she quickly removed her hand from covering the receiver. "I understand, Rob. No problem. I'm very busy too. I have to go now, but I'll call later and you can fill me in on the details of this company dinner."

Without waiting for a reply, Nicki tapped the hang-up button and took off for the kitchen.

## 11

For the third time in less than a week, Nicki pulled into the parking lot of Holland Winery. After the usual wrestling match with her car door, she stepped out and looked around, half expecting to see Geri plodding up the ramp from the production building. But aside from a scattering of cars, the lot was empty.

Nicki made her way toward a low structure behind the public tasting room, bypassing the visiting areas in favor of going directly to Jim Holland's office. Since she'd called earlier and made an appointment, she didn't feel it necessary to make a stop in the area built for all the tourists. And thanks to her complete fiasco of a visit to preserve a crime scene that Chief Turnlow had already taken care of, she knew right where the winery owner's office was located. It was only a few minutes before she was peeking in through the open doorway where Jim Holland was sitting at his desk, intently studying his computer screen.

She politely knocked against the doorframe to announce her presence, smiling and waiting to be invited in when the winery owner looked up from his work.

"Nicki, don't stand on ceremony. Come in and have a seat."

Jim stood and gestured to the group of rickety-looking chairs facing his desk.

She picked the one appearing to have the least number of splinters and sat down.

"Thank you for seeing me this morning. I'm sorry it's such short notice."

The big man smiled and leaned back in his creaky, leather chair. "I'm happy to help in any way I can. You said you needed background information for the article you're writing for Matt Dillon's magazine?"

Nodding, Nicki dutifully reached into her bag and pulled out a small notebook and pen. "With all the confusion I didn't get a lot for the article. And since the tasting never happened, he's looking for a different slant."

"Understandable," Jim said. "What did you have in mind?"

"Oh, maybe a piece on George Lanciere's career, his daily life, that kind of thing." Nicki casually waved her pen in the air. "With background information on the winery, of course, to keep it interesting."

Jim frowned. "Except for his work here, I don't know much about George's career. Geri worked more closely with him on a day-to-day basis. You should talk with her."

Nicki jotted down a few words in her notebook. "That's an excellent idea. I'll be sure to get in contact with her and arrange to meet."

"She's been out ever since she found George's body. I guess the shock was too much. She needed time to recover."

"Yes, it was terrible for her," Nicki said with a mental roll of her eyes. Geri had never come within ten feet of George. She'd left most of the burden of dealing with the first responders and police to Nicki. As far as she could remember, the assistant wine-maker spent the bulk of their time in George's aging room crying on Jim's shoulder.

"She's arranging for a memorial get-together at his house

tomorrow afternoon. If you're planning on attending, you might catch her there," Jim said.

"Of course I'll be going," Nicki said, even though it was the first she'd heard about it. "But I haven't had a chance to call her and ask about the time."

"Four o'clock or so, and only for a couple of hours. He rents one of my houses on the winery property, and we can't have a lot of cars going up and down our private roads. They need to be clear to move equipment around," Jim stated, surprising Nicki with his flat, matter-of-fact tone.

Not much sympathy going on there. But still, Jim Holland had to have at least a smidgeon of remorse over his head winemaker's death. After all, he *was* putting on a memorial service.

"Well, it's nice of you to host a memorial," Nicki said.

Jim shrugged. "I'm not. It was Geri's idea and she's doing all the arranging."

"Oh." Somehow Nicki wasn't surprised. "Well, I'm sure Mr. Lanciere would appreciate it."

"Lancer," Jim snorted. "The man's dead so there's no reason to keep up the pretense he was French. And I doubt if he appreciated anything in his entire life."

Nicki tapped the end of her pen on the top of her notebook. This was interesting. Jim Holland's real feelings about his winemaker were certainly coming out in full force.

"It's very kind of you to pay for the service, whether Mr. Lancer would have appreciated it or not," she said, wondering if she was going to get another snarky response. She didn't have long to wait.

"I'm not doing that either. Geri is footing the bill. I understand she's asking the rest of the staff to bring a dish of food to help out, but she isn't getting many takers. I paid for the tasting of his private blend, not to mention his salary for all the time he was here but didn't work on Holland business. That's enough, as far as I'm concerned."

"Oh? Why do you say he wasn't working on your winery business when he was here?" Nicki asked.

"I figure he spent at least a quarter of his time out on the loading dock smoking a cigarette, not to mention the hours he spent on his personal phone, and I doubt if it was on winery business. At least not *my* winery."

Now that she had a crystal-clear picture of Jim Holland's opinion of the murdered man, Nicki switched topics.

"How long did George work for you?"

He wrinkled his forehead. "A dozen years. He started as an assistant, then came up with a personal blend that was a truly outstanding chardonnay. I not only paid for the launch, but sponsored it too."

"I understand Holland did very well sponsoring that blend," Nicki remarked, making a show of scribbling in her notebook.

"We were already building a good reputation," Jim shot back.

When Nicki tilted her head to one side and simply looked at him, he shifted in his chair before letting out a loud sigh.

"Having that blend to sell alongside our own didn't hurt us any. There wasn't a lot of it, but enough to stir a good amount of interest in our other production wines," he conceded.

Nicki mentally arranged events in her mind. "Is that when Mr. Lancer became your head winemaker?"

Jim nodded. "When that announcement went out, interest picked up even more. Bill approached Lancer about then and took him on as head winemaker as well."

"So Mr. Lancer took over at both wineries? What happened to the head winemakers you already had?" Nicki asked, not only out of natural curiosity, but also in case she had to add more suspects to their murder board.

"The one over at The White Crown, which was Bill's old winery before he started up Todos, was going to retire the following year anyway, so he only moved the date up," Jim replied.

After waiting a full ten seconds, Nicki leaned forward, her pen now tapping against her lower lip. "And how about your head winemaker at the time, Jim? Did he retire as well?"

Shaking his head, Jim plucked a piece of candy out of a bowl near his computer. "Tandry didn't like all the attention going to one of his assistants. When George took the head winemaker's job at The White Crown, Tandry wanted to fire him from my winery. But I wouldn't do it so Tandry moved on."

Nicki gave a sympathetic nod. "That must have been upsetting for you."

"It's part of the business." Jim shrugged again. "Besides, Tandry had run out his career. I would have looked for a replacement for him at the end of that year's crush anyway. It just so happens that Lancer saved me the trouble."

After writing down Tandry's name on her list, Nicki scanned the scribbled notes she'd made while Jim was talking. "You said Mr. Lancer started out as one of the assistants. Was Geri the other one?"

"No. She was only an intern back then while she was finishing up her education. There was another assistant. Another woman." Jim Holland looked away.

Despite all his signals that he wasn't comfortable with the subject, Nicki persisted.

"Someone else? What was her name? Does she still work here?"

"What does this have to do with your story about the winery and the special blend?" Jim's voice held a definite snap, but he still didn't make eye contact with Nicki.

"Oh, nothing," Nicki said. "I was just curious. Did Mr. Lancer have any family around? Parent or siblings? Maybe a girlfriend or significant other?"

"I don't get involved in my employee's lives." Jim gave his watch a pointed glance.

"Understandable. That can be messy," Nicki quickly agreed

with a smile. She'd have to find another way to track down information about this Stella person. She didn't want to alienate a potential suspect— especially on her first interview. While she was flipping through her notes, she suddenly remembered what Rob had said.

"Who gets the wine now?" she blurted out.

The winery owner frowned. "What wine?"

"George Lancer's special blend. Does he have any family?"

Jim shook his head. "No. At least he always said he didn't."

"Then who gets the wine?" Nicki asked. "Will it go to the government as part of an unclaimed estate?"

"Not according to my attorney," Jim said. "It was developed on my property, most likely during the hours I was paying Lancer, so I should have first claim on it."

"But Mr. Lancer bought the grapes to develop the wine, didn't he? Isn't that how it usually works?" Nicki asked.

"Not necessarily. He could have used Holland grapes easily enough. But if the government wants me to reimburse the estate for the cost of the grapes so I can keep the wine, then I'll do that. And I supplied the barrels, even if it was part of his employment contract, *and* paid for the party to host his tasting, whether or not the wine was unveiled." Jim stood up, signaling the interview was over.

Nicki had no choice but to get to her feet and gather up her purse and notebook.

"Thank you, Jim. I appreciate your time."

He gave her a short nod and remained standing as Nicki made her way across the room. At the doorway, she paused and turned to face him. "Did you taste it?"

"No," Jim said, not even pretending he didn't know what she was talking about.

Puzzled, Nicki frowned. "Why not?"

"On the advice of my attorney. He said I should keep the room locked in accordance with the police instructions, and no one was to touch or taste the wine so I wouldn't have an unfair advantage over any other claims on it," Jim said. "Chief Turnlow also called and told me no one was to taste any of the wine in any of the barrels."

"Who else would have a claim on it?" Nicki's brow furrowed in thought. Since the wine was on his property, she'd think the old rule about possession being nine-tenths of the law would apply.

Jim only shrugged. "It was nice talking with you, Nicki. Let me know when that article comes out."

Nicki politely smiled and left the office, turning down the hallway leading to the exit door. Once outside she glanced to her left toward the parking lot, then turned right and took the short walk to the main building. She was almost to the backdoor when a man appeared on the loading dock.

From where she stood she had a clear view of him, and since he was looking her way she assumed he also had a clear view of her. Digging into her purse for her cell phone, she took it out and dialed several random numbers, careful to keep it a couple of digits short of an actual call, and held the phone to her ear. She proceeded to engage in a purely fictitious, one-sided conversation until the man on the loading dock disappeared back inside the production building.

With no one else in sight, Nicki slipped through the backdoor and into a dimly lit hallway. She tiptoed as quietly as she could until she came to a junction. If she continued to go straight, she'd end up at the door behind the bar that led into the tasting room. Instead, she turned left into the wide hallway where George Lancer had his private aging room.

The police tape still crisscrossed the closed door. Nicki carefully tried the handle, but this time it was locked solid. She rattled the doorknob twice out of pure frustration before abandoning it and continuing down the hallway toward a wide, open archway. Curiosity had her peeking into the room that sported the same, thick stone walls as the room housing George's personal blend. She felt along the surface closest to the archway until her hand found a light switch. Flipping it on, a single dim light bulb hanging on a cord dangling from the ceiling, sort of lit up. It barely had enough wattage to show the various barrels all along the walls, lined-up in small and large groups.

"Must be the private blends for the rest of the staff members," Nicki mused out loud. "Wonder who they belong to?"

Most of the barrels were in small groups of two or three, but there were two sections, on opposite walls, that had closer to ten. Nicki did a quick count and nodded. Ten in one group, and twelve in another.

She stepped closer to the ten-barrel group and inspected them. There was nothing to identify who the blend belonged to, except for a small, almost unnoticeable "XXX" stamped on one end followed by three large dots. Another of the smaller groups had a "13", and the twelve- barrel group had one six stacked on top of another six, all very small and in places she had to get nose-to-wood to see it. She only found one, ten-barrel group that had no marking at all.

Nicki assumed it was a kind of secret identification for the owner of those barrels. She was still on her hands and knees, looking for the elusive barrel markings on a fourth group when her cell phone went off. In the echo-y chamber, it gave her quite a start. As her phone continued to blare, with the noise bouncing off the cold stone walls, Nicki couldn't get her hands on it. She frantically rummaged around the bottom of her large bag where she'd tossed the phone after she was through with her fictitious call.

Finally out of frustration, she turned her purse over and dumped everything out onto the stone floor, grabbing the cell as it slid by her. Seeing Jenna's caller ID, Nicki quickly pushed the answer button to stop the strident ring tone.

"What?" she whispered into the speaker end.

"Why are you whispering?" Jenna demanded. "Are you hiding from someone?"

"No. I'm in a room that echoes, that's all. And I'm not hiding. I just don't want to announce I'm here. I'm amazed there's cell service at all in this room," Nicki said looking around.

"Yes, it really is a wonder how strong the signals are from the cell towers anymore," Jenna snorted. "Where are you? Just in case we have to send out searchers to look for your body."

Nicki glanced across the dimly lit room at the shadows of the wine barrels creeping over the walls and wished Jenna hadn't mentioned dead bodies. "I'm at Holland Winery. In the big room next to the one George used to age his own wine. From all the wine barrels in here, it looks like other employees also make their own wine, or it could be an overflow storage for the winery."

"You can't get locked in there, can you?" Jenna asked.

"No. This room doesn't have a door. It's open to the hall through an archway."

"Okay. Did you find out anything new from Jim Holland that I should add to our murder board?" Jenna asked.

"A couple of interesting things," Nicki said. "For one, he has a lawyer to help him get legal ownership of George's wine."

"He already has the wine, why would he need a lawyer?"

"I don't know. Unless someone else has a lawyer, too," Nicki whispered. "He also made it clear he didn't like his head wine-maker at all."

"Well from what you've said, he'll have to stand in line. No one liked George."

Nicki could almost hear the shrug in Jenna's voice.

"He refused to talk about the Stella who Maxie told us about, and he was already planning on replacing George by the end of the year. He claimed his head winemaker had run the course of his career, just like the guy before him," Nicki said.

"The same is going to be said for me if I don't get back to work," Jenna replied.

"Where are you?" Nicki hoped her friend hadn't called her from the parking lot, or even the tasting room, with every intention of storming the winery to rescue her blogging-friend-turned-detective. Nicki wouldn't put it past Jenna to do something like that.

"I'm at your place. Which is why I called you," Jenna said.

"My place?" Nicki held her wristwatch up close to her face so she could read the time. "Is Alex still there? I thought she'd be headed home by now."

"She did go back to Santa Rosa, and she left you a note saying she was going to arrange for a few extra days off so she could come back and help keep you out of trouble. And no, I didn't read your personal stuff. We were both sitting at the kitchen counter when she wrote it. She also left you a map of a new route for you to try on your morning run, which she noticed you didn't take this morning, and some kind of flavored rice cakes she's gone bonkers over. Of course I'll be glad to toss those in the trash for you, being the good friend that I am."

Nicki smiled when she heard Jenna yawn through the phone. "You leave my rice cakes alone, and I plan to run this afternoon when I get back."

"Fine. I'll put your health-nut food in the pantry before I leave. And Maxie came by to remind you about the lemon cake for the Ladies in Writing Society meeting, which I gather is tomorrow morning."

With a mental groan, Nicki added one more thing to her task list in the afternoon.

"I didn't call you about lemon or rice cakes though. I thought you'd like to know that lover-boy Rob called. Your Skype kept ringing until we couldn't stand it anymore. I'll bet he's left a million voice mails on your phone," Jenna complained. "Anyway, Alex and I did rock-paper-scissors to decide who had to talk to him, and tell him to stop calling. I lost. Which is fine since I didn't want to listen to that constant ringing through the walls while I was working, and didn't mind telling him that."

Jenna gave a loud sniff. "Geez. If you aren't home, you aren't home. He should take the hint."

Having waited patiently through her former roommate's usual rant about Rob, Nicki sighed when the computer geek paused. "Well, what did he want?"

"To let you know he's coming home tonight after all, and he wants to see you. It's important," Jenna said. "Which I take to mean whatever it is, it must involve him."

"I can't drive into the city tonight." Nicki frowned. She still had to finish the article for Matt, and wanted to get a fresh start on more interviews tomorrow. And there was also the matter of the lemon cake.

"I told him you were extremely busy. Too busy to come into the city on no notice at all. So he said he'd be driving up here to see you tomorrow. About six," Jenna said. When Nicki let out a gasp, she quickly added, "I'm sorry to deliver the bad news. Well, I have to go if I want to get any work done."

The phone went dead and Nicki glared at it. "Thanks a bunch."

Realizing she was sitting on the cold stone floor with the contents of her purse scattered out in front of her, Nicki sighed and gathered everything up, dumping it all back into her bag before pushing herself up to a standing position. She was patting the dust off her pants when she froze. The distinct sound of footsteps echoed down the hallway, followed moments later by a voice from the arched entrance to the room.

"What are you doing in here?"

## 12

Nicki smiled at the older gentleman with the long droopy moustache. Dressed in jeans and a collared shirt, he didn't look at all menacing, even with the frown on his face.

"Hi. I'm Nicki Connors. I came to see Jim Holland, and thought it would be all right if I looked around."

"Nicki Connors, did you say? The woman who was with Geri when she found the body?"

That wasn't the way Nicki remembered it, but she was okay with that if it kept her from being thrown off the property.

"Yes, I am."

"Well, you come on out of there now. I'm sure it was a horrible experience, but coming back here isn't going to change anything." He made a gesture for Nicki to precede him through the archway, which she promptly did. At least the hallway had more light from its overhead bulbs. It helped lessen the feeling of being trapped in a dark room with a potential serial killer, even though the man with the big mustache didn't act like one.

"I'm Pete. I handle the security here at the winery, although that doesn't amount to much. I usually work the night shift but got switched around this week because the day guy is on vacation." Pete nodded and walked with her down the hallway, back toward the junction point.

"You said you were here to see Mr. Holland? I can take you over to his office," Pete offered.

"Oh, no. That won't be necessary," Nicki said with a smile. "I've already seen him. I just thought I'd drop in at the tasting room through the backdoor. The next thing I knew I was standing in front of the police tape. I stepped into the room next to it to get away and calm myself a bit." Nicki thought her story sounded weak, even to her own ears, and wondered if you had to be an expert liar to be an investigator. Because from her limited experience, it seemed it sure would help.

"Why don't you come into the tasting room and sit down for a few minutes? No one's in there but Victor and Kurt."

Since she wanted to talk to Kurt, the waiter George had humiliated the night of the murder, Nicki wasn't going to turn away from the unexpected opportunity, so she fell into step beside Pete. "I don't believe I've met Victor?"

"He's the warehouse foreman. We were exchanging stories about George. But we can talk about something else if you'd like," Pete said.

"No, stories about George would be fine. It will help me to..." Nicki trailed off, not quite sure what it would help her with, other than a possible clue to his murder. But she was hardly going to tell that to Pete.

"Find closure?" Pete supplied helpfully.

"Yes. Closure," Nicki repeated.

"My wife's always saying how important it is to have closure after any traumatic event in your life. Not sure I understand it all, but Phyllis is sure it's important." Pete scratched his head and shrugged at the same time. Nicki thought it was a typical male reaction to something he didn't understand, or care much about even if he did.

When they reached the door leading into the tasting room, Pete opened it and stepped aside to let Nicki go through first. She quickly walked into the public area, skirting around the bar. Pete was right. There were only two other people in the room, sitting on stools around one of the high tables. Nicki recognized Kurt, which meant the other occupant had to be Victor, the warehouse foreman.

The friendly security guard led her over to the two men and pulled out a stool for her.

"Hi, Nicki," Kurt grinned at her, pushing a lock of blond hair off his forehead. "Didn't expect to see you back here for a long time."

She smiled at the twenty-something-surfer-dude. "I had an appointment with Jim Holland."

"Found her wandering near George's barrel room, looking for closure."

"Did you find it?" the third man asked. Short, with dark hair and a dark complexion, Victor's brown eyes sparkled at the question.

Nicki took an instant liking to him. He was all smiles and open friendliness, the kind that went with people who were naturally good-natured. It would take someone like that, or a doormat like Geri, to work with George Lancer.

"I'm Nicki Connors." Nicki held out her hand which Victor took in a firm handshake.

"Nice to meet you, Ms. Connors. Kind of enjoy using that 'Ms.' for all the ladies. Saves me from having to sneak a peek at their left hand before knowing how to address them," Victor laughed. "I'm Victor. I'd go with a last name too, but everyone calls me Victor so don't see the point."

Now Nicki laughed. "I'm Nicki. I always forget to answer when someone says 'Ms. Connors'."

"I already introduced myself, and I guess you know Kurt," Pete said.

"So what can we do to help you find that closure, Nicki?" Victor asked.

"Pete said you were exchanging stories about George. I just heard a few from Mr. Holland and wouldn't mind hearing some of yours, too."

"We were mostly talking over the memorial service Geri is putting together," Victor said. "She's asking everyone to bring a dish of something and, being bachelors, Kurt and I were trying to figure out what take-out to call to pick up something."

"Phyllis is making a casserole," Pete said.

"I'm sure Geri would appreciate that. You could also offer to bring paper plates, plastic silverware, napkins—that sort of thing," Nicki suggested. "Or something already prepared at the market, like a cheese platter, or chips and dip."

Kurt's blue eyes lit up and he clapped Victor on the back. "Yeah, man. I can stop and get a package of paper plates. Shouldn't take more than a minute or two to do that."

"Well, I'm sure George wouldn't want you to put yourself out," Nicki said with a hint of dryness in her tone. "I could make a big lasagna and let Geri know it's from all three of us. Trust me, there will be plenty to go around."

"That would be great," Kurt said with more enthusiasm than the simple suggestion called for.

"I'll check with Geri later to be sure if that's okay, or if she'd rather I made something else." Nicki all but batted her eyes at Kurt. "I forgot to get her phone number. Do you have it?"

"Sure." Kurt tapped away on his phone before turning it around to face Nicki. "Here it is."

"Thanks." Nicki keyed the name and number into the contact list on her phone. "I'll get in touch with her later this afternoon."

"I'm sure Geri will be grateful, even if George wouldn't be. I worked with that man for a dozen years, Nicki. Believe me when I tell you George wouldn't have spent even two minutes going out of his way for any of us," Victor said, along with nods of agreement from the other two men. "It's nice of Geri to do this, but most of the staff are going because she asked us to and everyone likes Geri. There won't be any tears shed for George Lanciere, or Lancer, or whatever he was calling himself."

"And I don't know why Geri is bothering, either. It's not like he treated her very well," Kurt said.

Pete snorted. "The man didn't treat anyone very well." He looked at Nicki. "Never even talked to me the nights he worked late and we were the only two people here."

"Worked late?" Nicki asked. Now that was interesting. Jim Holland thought George barely worked at all, much less stayed late. Then she frowned. "I thought you usually worked the night shift?"

"I do," the guard nodded. "He'd come in around midnight, stay an hour or so, and then leave."

"Was he catching up on paperwork?" Nicki wondered, her question answered when both Pete and Victor shook their heads.

"Nope. Spent the time mostly running around on a forklift back in his aging room," Pete said.

"A forklift?"

The night guard nodded at her. "No idea what he was doing with it. I wandered back there once. He screamed at me to stay away from that whole hallway whenever he was working there, or he'd get me fired. Didn't make any difference to me what he was doing, and I like this job well enough, so I just stayed away."

"I know he was doing a lot of tasting, probably to make sure his chardonnay was barreled the proper amount of time. Too much or too little time in the barrel can ruin a good wine," Victor said. "My men complained he'd always leave the testing and tasting equipment around for them to clean up, even when he was doing his regular work at the winery. But they'd also find it waiting for them at the beginning of their shift. That's how they knew George was here the night before."

"But that wouldn't need a forklift," Nicki pointed out. "I'm surprised he even knew how to use one."

Victor casually waved that away. "Practically everyone's been here so long they've learned how to run a forklift. Even Geri and the kid here can." Victor pointed at Kurt. "The only one I know of that can't is Pete. His eyesight is too bad to let him handle a forklift. He'd be knocking the barrel racks over."

"That's true," Pete chuckled. "Got some permanent nerve damage in an accident a few years back. Can't run the forklift and don't have a driver's license either. Wife brings me here and picks me up after my shift is over."

"Doesn't that make your job a little harder?" Nicki asked.

"Not on the night shift. You use your ears more than your eyes, and my hearing is just fine."

Nicki was positive Pete's hearing was fine since he'd heard her talking to Jenna, even though she was whispering. But she sure hoped he wasn't expected to carry a gun.

"Well I'm not going to miss George's fake smoking," Kurt declared. "There was no point in stinking up the place when he didn't even smoke. But he always smelled like a full ashtray if you got within ten feet of him."

Nicki knew the autopsy had shown no physical signs of George being a heavy smoker. But how did Kurt know that? As far as everyone else was concerned, the man smoked like a chimney.

"What makes you think he wasn't a real smoker?" Nicki asked. Leaning her elbows on the table, she gave Kurt a bright smile.

The server's chest puffed out and he grinned back at her. "Because we liked to take our breaks in the same place, out behind the loading docks. And whenever he was there I'd stand off to the side, where he wouldn't notice me. He always had a cigarette lit in his hand, but I never once saw him take a puff."

Nicki blinked, surprised at the picture Kurt painted. "George just stood behind the loading docks, with a cigarette in his hand that he never smoked?"

"Well, I never saw him blow any smoke out. He spent most of his time on the phone, talking to his bookie as far as I could hear, but when one cigarette went out, he'd light another one. Never could figure out why he did that."

Nicki doubted if she'd ever figure it out either. Unless... he used the cigarette smoke to keep other people away. So they couldn't hear what he was talking about, or whom he was talking to.

"His bookie? George was a gambler?"

"I overheard him a couple of times, too," Victor said. "I don't know if it was a bookie, but he was going over the betting lines on some ball games."

"That's what I heard too," Kurt admitted. "Except for that one time he was having an argument. A loud, nasty one too. And it wasn't about sports."

"What was it about?" Nicki asked.

"Some kind of partnership," Kurt said. "Not sure exactly what, but he was talking to one of the winery owners. I heard him say the name loud and clear.

---

NICKI ARRIVED HOME LATE in the afternoon. She'd stopped at the local market to pick up fresh lemons, tomatoes and a block of mozzarella cheese. A quick glance at the driveway next to her own verified that Jenna's car was gone, so Nicki assumed she was out visiting one of her customers.

Hauling her full, reusable grocery bag into the townhouse, she set it on the kitchen counter. For a moment she toyed with making a dash down the hallway and updating the murder board, then thought better of it. First things first. She needed to get the lemon cake going, and then make the slightly spicy sauce for the pan of lasagna she intended to take to George's memorial service. Plus a dessert she hadn't decided on yet. Hopefully her food would be enough of a distraction for Geri that she and her friends could do a little undetected sleuthing. She went to the fridge and took out what remained of the hamburger mixture. She'd also need a bribe for Jenna. She was fresh out of zucchini so it was a good thing Alex was back home with Tyler.

With a quick glance into her pantry, she snagged the flour and sugar bins, setting them on the counter just as her phone erupted with *So Far Away*. With a sigh of resignation, she retrieved it from her purse and pressed the answer button.

"Hi, Rob. I can't wait to see you tomorrow."

"Nicki? Why didn't you return my calls? I must have left you at least ten messages."

Nicki got a mixing bowl out from a bottom cupboard. "I just now walked in and haven't had a chance to do anything but put my purse down."

"Then you haven't talked to Jenna?"

"I did have a chance to speak to Jenna," Nicki said, wincing at the sudden silence.

"So you can take her phone calls but not mine?"

Nicki instantly felt guilty.

"No. I had interviews all morning and Jenna happened to call when I was on a short break." Nicki drew in a breath and smiled so that it would come out in her voice. "I couldn't talk long, but she did manage to let me know that you said you were flying home after all?"

"Yes, I am. She also said you'd be too busy to drive into the city tonight. Why is that?"

"I do have a life, Rob," Nicki said, getting annoyed at his expectation that she drop everything and make the hour drive into San Francisco. "And a living to make. Those interviews need to be written up and sent in to the magazine. Finding a dead body has put me a little behind."

"Now, babe, no need to get in a huff. When your girlfriend says she doesn't have the time to see you, what's a guy supposed to think?"

"That your girlfriend might need more notice before she has to drive into the city?" Nicki accompanied that statement with an eye roll.

"Well, let's move on to something more pleasant. I should be there about six-thirty tomorrow night. I thought we could go out for dinner, unless you feel like cooking me one of those gourmet delights of yours?" Rob asked.

"I do not," Nicki said. "I have more interviews tomorrow and won't get home in time."

"Fine. Then we can go out. Pick your favorite place in Sandstone and we'll make a night of it. I have a surprise for you." Rob's voice went into teasing and flirting mode.

"Soldoff, Rob. And that's great. I can't wait." Nicki slapped her hand over the phone's speaker when the front door shut with a loud bang.

"What was that?"

"Nothing," Nicki said. "Just Jenna making her usual entrance." Nicki motioned Jenna into the kitchen and pointed at the hamburger mix. "We were about to have dinner before I have to get back to work on that article." Nicki bobbed her head up and down until Jenna, catching on, did the same.

"Is dinner ready yet? I have a customer stopping by a little later," Jenna said loudly enough to be heard by the person on the other end of the line.

"All right. I'll let you go then," Rob said. "I have a dinner engagement as well. I'll see you tomorrow."

He clicked off and so did Nicki. She glanced over at Jenna and grinned.

"Thank you. He was getting all snotty because I didn't return his calls."

"He's always snotty," Jenna observed. "Does my little white lie really get me another one of your world-class hamburgers?"

"I don't know if that was worth one." Nicki pursed her lips and pretended to think it over. "You may have to throw in something else."

"Such as?"

Nicki laughed at the wariness in her friend's voice. "Such as an hour or so of your computer skills?"

Jenna threw her head back and closed her eyes. "Tell me you did not screw up your website."

"Okay. I did not screw up my website," Nicki dutifully repeated. "I want you to search someone's computer."

"And will anyone care if I search this computer? Like, someone who can issue an arrest warrant?" Jenna asked.

"The owner is dead, so I don't believe so."

Jenna's eyes went wide. "Not George Lancer's computer? You want me to hack into George Lancer's computer?"

Grabbing her measuring cups from a peg on the wall, Nicki scooped out flour into the mixing bowl. "Not hack. Just take a look if it happens to be easy to get into."

"Looking over files stored on a computer without the owner's permission is hacking, Nicki," Jenna stated. She sat on one of the kitchen stools and put her forehead in her hands.

"Well, the owner is dead and can't give permission, so it'll be fine." Nicki went on measuring and stirring ingredients together in the bowl.

"And are we going to do some B&E too? I mean, what's a little breaking and entering in order to hack a computer between friends?"

Nicki put down her spoon and shook her head. "We aren't going to be breaking into George's house. It so happens we'll have an invitation to be there."

"We will?"

Nicki grinned and picked up her cell phone. "Of course. Just as soon as I make this call." She consulted her contacts list and selected a number. It was answered after the first ring.

"Hi, Geri. It's Nicki Connors. I was wondering if I could bring a big pan of lasagna to the memorial service tomorrow?"

## 13

"I can't tell you how much I enjoyed the lemon cake you made. Maybe you should offer baking lessons as a silent auction item at our Literacy for Kids fund-raising dinner? And that wonderful wine you brought! I could have a glass every day." Mrs. Johnson smiled, adjusting her purple hat with the fancy quill pen attached to the outer band. Each woman in the Ladies in Writing Society proudly wore her hat to every meeting. Nicki had hers on as well, although she hadn't carefully positioned it on her head until she'd arrived at Maxie's very large, impressive home.

Nicki handed Mrs. Johnson the last unopened bottle of wine. "There you go, Chloe. Please enjoy."

"If I had three small children running around my house the way you do, Chloe Johnson, I'd have a drink of something every day. That wine could hold you for a spell, but you'll want to switch to whiskey when they get to be teenagers." Frances Wilder chuckled at her own humor. She held her back straight as she leaned against her cane and shook her head at the younger women around her. "When you reach my age, it's not wine and lemon cake that make your day, but wine and beefcake."

Nicki smiled. Frances was ninety-five, at least that's what she admitted to, and as outspoken as every one of those years earned her the right to be.

"The wine is good, but that Tyrone Blackstone of yours is better. He's so much fun to read about. Wish I'd met someone like him when I was young enough to appreciate it," Frances declared.

"I wish they'd *make* someone like him," Chloe said, holding the wine close as she gathered up her light jacket and matching purse. "Not that I'm complaining about Chuck. He's a wonderful man. I'd hate for him to think I'm dreaming about someone else."

Frances reached over and patted the forty-something Chloe's hand. "Don't you worry about it. Men are blind when they look into mirrors. They all believe they're Tyrone Blackstone." She looked around the group gathering near the front door. "And women are blind too. All we see in a mirror are our faults. It's a wonder the two sexes ever get together."

Laughter flowed through the group as last goodbyes were said. Maxie appeared in the entryway to formally open the door and wish everyone well and "good writing" until they met again. Which, according to Nicki's mental calculations, would be at the end of June.

The bi-monthly meeting of the society had been occurring for two decades, ever since Maxie had finally settled down with "myMason" and shifted to doing much of her genealogy research on the Internet. The women took turns bringing dessert and wine, but the location was always Maxie's large, Spanish-style house with its generous living areas built around a huge center-patio space. Nicki loved the Maxie's place, and especially the gourmet kitchen that was at least twice the size of the one she had in her town house.

*Someday,* Nicki thought. *Someday I'm going to have a kitchen like that and a wine closet.* But for now she was content with her own space, and simply being able to admire Maxie's beautiful home.

She mingled in with the rest of the ladies moving toward the door. When she came up alongside her hostess, Maxie's hand shot out and latched onto Nicki's arm.

"Oh, Nicki. Would you be a dear and help me straighten up?"

"Um. Sure. Of course," Nicki said. Maxie had a housekeeper every day of the week except Sundays, so Nicki knew the request had nothing to do with picking up glasses and plates.

It took another ten minutes, but Maxie finally managed to herd everyone out the door, with Frances being the last one.

"You don't need anyone to help you clean up." The white-haired, ram-rod-straight woman pointed her ornately carved, wooden cane at Maxie. "I've known you for thirty-five years, Maxie Edwards, and you're up to something."

"So what if I am? It's not as if I'm breaking the law." Maxie jerked her head toward the open door. "Go on, Frances, before I call my Mason, and have him toss you out."

"He'd do nothing of the sort. Besides, he's not even home," Frances retorted, but she moved out the door, turning to look back at Maxie before continuing down the walkway. "You'll call me tomorrow with all the details of your shenanigans?"

"Of course," Maxie yelled at her back. "Don't I always?"

With a last crackle of laughter, Frances went on her way, waving a greeting to her grandson who'd been reading in his grandmother's white, Lincoln Town Car until she was ready to go home.

Maxie closed the door and ushered Nicki into a book-lined study off the main entryway. "We'll be more comfortable in here, dear. Would you like another glass of wine?"

"No, thank you. I'm fine," Nicki said, settling into a wide, over-stuffed leather chair.

Maxie sat too and folded her hands in front of her. "Well, is it?"

Puzzled, Nicki cocked her head to one side. "Is it what?"

"Illegal. Whatever we'll be doing. Is it illegal?" Maxie asked.

Nicki's mouth opened before she had a chance to come up with something to say. She didn't want to blurt out that she'd asked Jenna to hack into George's computer, but then again, she didn't want to lie to Maxie either.

"What makes you think I'm doing anything at all?" Nicki hedged.

"Well we have to do something, otherwise the case will go cold," Maxie said. "I know you spoke to Jim Holland today. That was on the 'to do' list. What do you plan to do next?"

"I thought I'd drop in on George's memorial service this afternoon. My boyfriend will be here this evening to take me out to dinner. Do you have any suggestions where we should go? Some place romantic?"

"I'm sure you've been there several times, but Mario's is your best choice. Nice Italian food, good wine, low lighting. It's perfect for a romantic night out. Are you going to the memorial by yourself, dear?"

Realizing Maxie was not going to be distracted, Nicki laughed. "No. Jenna is coming with me."

"Then you *are* up to something," Maxie declared. "I'm coming too. My car is much more reliable, in case we need to make a quick getaway."

With no ready excuse coming to mind, Nicki smiled and nodded. "I'd love to have you come with us."

---

NICKI SET the oversized lasagna pan on the back seat of Maxie's Mercedes and slid in next to it, while Jenna got into the front passenger seat.

"That's a very nice-looking dish you've made," Maxie remarked as she carefully backed out of the driveway and headed down the main road. "Lasagna, judging by the delicious smell."

Opening her car window, Nicki tried to let some air circulate into the vehicle. "I don't want your beautiful car smelling like pasta sauce for the next week. We should have taken mine."

"And break down while we're there so we'd be forced to spend the night at the winery of death?" Jenna faked a huge shudder. "No thank you."

"Winery of death." Nicki rolled her eyes. "That's kind of dramatic, don't you think?"

"Oh, a little drama makes the world go round, dear," Maxie said, smiling at Nicki in the rearview mirror. "So does an occasional bit of bribery."

"What are you implying? That our Nicki would stoop so low as to bribe someone with her magnificent culinary skills? Why I'm shocked, truly shocked," Jenna said with a grin.

Nicki leaned forward and poked her friend with her index finger. "I haven't ever heard you complain. And a few times you've even demanded that I bribe you."

"Well I'm still enjoying my candy," Maxie declared. "Who are we bribing at the memorial?"

"It isn't a bribe so much as an entrance fee. And to help Geri out," Nicki said.

"How in the world does a lasagna help Geri?" Maxie asked.

"Jim wouldn't pay for a memorial service so Geri is putting out her own funds to hold one. She asked the winery employees to each bring something to help out," Nicki explained.

Maxie nodded her understanding. "Very thoughtful to go to the trouble, and it's an excellent entrance fee."

"And hopefully a good distraction," Jenna chimed in. "So no one will notice me poking around in the dead man's computer."

"Really? You're going to break into his computer?" Maxie asked. "I imagine that's the illegal part of the adventure?"

"Hacking," Jenna said. "It's called hacking, and yes, it's most definitely illegal."

Nicki placed a protective hand on the lasagna pan as the car swung around a corner. "Hopefully all we'll be doing is turning it on and everything will pop right up. No hacking necessary."

Now Jenna rolled her eyes. "Even if he has absolutely no security on his machine, downloading personal files without the owner's permission is theft. And that's illegal."

"Well, dear, if it bothers you, then simply email the files. People email files all the time. I certainly do," Maxie said.

Jenna sighed and shook her head. "I'm not emailing files. The next person who comes along and looks at his computer, which will probably be the police, will find that email and know we stole those files." She reached into her pocket and pulled out a small, oblong object. "I brought a thumb drive. We'll download whatever we find onto this, and Nicki can pull it up and go over it any time she wants. And if I end up in jail, I expect a much better bribe than a pan of lasagna."

"It's big enough I could bake a real file into it," Nicki said.

"Ha, ha." Jenna slouched further in her seat, mumbling something about stripes and solitary confinement.

A few minutes later they pulled into the winery's driveway. Maxie bypassed the parking lot and continued past the production buildings, heading for a small house at the far end of the road. It was lit up and had cars parked everywhere around it. Maxie found a spot to park and the three of them walked toward the slightly sagging steps leading up to a small, front porch.

Maxie leaned over and whispered in Nicki's ear. "You two distract them with the lasagna while I search for George's computer."

Not sure if that was such a good idea, Nicki shook her head. "Maybe we should let Jenna find the computer."

"Nonsense. No one will pay any attention to an old woman wandering about."

Nicki didn't think Maxie was the type to blend into the woodwork. No, that was more Geri's style. Who just happened to be at the door to greet them.

"Hi, Geri." Nicki was spared the decision of whether or not to give the woman a hug since she was holding the big lasagna pan.

"Hello, Nicki." Geri turned to look at Maxie. "Mrs. Edwards. It's nice of you to come."

"It's the least I could do for a prominent member of our community. Why everyone knows Mr. Lanciere's wines helped put our little area on the map," Maxie said, her features set in a properly somber expression. She pulled Jenna forward. "Do you know Jenna Lindstrom?"

Geri nodded but didn't offer her hand. "Yes. We met when Nicki tried to break into George's aging room. How did you know George?"

"Through Nicki," Jenna said without missing a beat.

"I hope you don't mind that I brought a friend," Nicki said. "I'm not comfortable attending these types of things by myself." When Geri glanced over at Maxie, Nicki added, "We met Maxie outside."

When Geri remained silent, Nicki held out the lasagna pan. "This is getting a little heavy. Where would you like me to put it?"

Geri looked at the pan and smiled. "This will be a big help. The kitchen is that way." She pointed to an open doorway off the tiny dining room.

Nicki handed the pan to Jenna. "It's right through there."

"Okay," Jenna said, holding the lasagna pan in front of her and marching off.

Maxie nodded at Nicki and Geri. "I'd better help her."

Left alone with the assistant winemaker, Nicki rolled up on her toes and back down again, searching for something to start a conversation. Since anything brilliant eluded her, Nicki went for the obvious.

"It was nice of you to arrange for this memorial for George."

The woman shrugged. "It was the decent thing to do."

Grabbing the bull by the horns, Nicki tried a more direct line of approach. "I spoke with Jim Holland today. He told me that he wouldn't pay for a memorial and all of this is coming out of your pocket?"

When Nicki simply got another shrug as a response, she tried again. "He said he'd put out enough money for the tasting event. I'm surprised George didn't have to pay for that himself, since Holland wouldn't be sponsoring the wine."

"George promised him a case of the wine in exchange for putting on the event," Geri said. "So Jim would have been paid. Probably more than the event was worth."

Now that was very interesting. Jim hadn't mentioned that little piece of information, and Nicki wondered if Jeremy Brennan had any idea George's wine wasn't going to be exclusive to Trax.

"But no one knows that since we didn't get to taste the wine. Jim said he hasn't had so much as a sip."

Geri seemed to shrink in on herself. "I'm just guessing the wine is worth a great deal."

"Jim also said he's hired an attorney to secure his rights to the wine, since George has no family."

Another shrug had Nicki fighting a rising sense of frustration. She doubted she'd get much more information out of Geri Gant.

"The turnout is very nice." Nicki took a quick glance around the crowded living room. "Will you be saying a few words?"

Geri looked positively horrified. "Heavens no."

Nicki's mouth drooped at the corners and she nodded slowly. "I understand. He wasn't very nice to you, was he?"

The assistant's back stiffened and she looked at the ground when she answered. "No, he wasn't."

"Why did you put up with him treating you that way?" Nicki asked softly. "I'm sure you could have found a position at another winery."

"It's not that simple." Geri's head came up and for the first time she looked Nicki right in the eye. "I'm alone. I don't have the safety net of a husband, and my parents and one sister certainly couldn't help me out if I needed it. It's not easy being out on your own, having to pay bills and make ends meet year after year on an assistant's salary. Especially in an industry where women barely have a toehold. You need a hand up to make it in the wine business. I spent a long time looking for that hand up."

Before Nicki could think of a response, Maxie walked up with Kurt and Victor in tow. "Geri, these gentlemen wanted to speak with you, and there's someone I want Nicki to meet."

While Geri turned toward the two men, Maxie pulled Nicki away. She looped an arm through Nicki's and casually strolled across the living room into the kitchen. There was a veritable hoard crowded near the kitchen table, but Maxie skirted around the loitering bodies and went through a door on the opposite side. It led to a short hallway. She kept going, right out the back-door, onto the porch, around the corner, and finally through another door to a room where Jenna sat at a narrow desk. The space was so small the three women barely fit inside.

"Here she is. I'll go play lookout," Maxie stepped back onto the porch and closed the door behind her.

"I feel like we've just been shut into a closet," Nicki complained, leaning over Jenna's shoulder to peer at the computer screen. "How did you find this place?"

"I didn't. Maxie did. Looks like it used to be a storage room that George had wired for the Internet. This system of his is old, he doesn't even have a password on it. Maybe he thought this funky location was enough to keep anyone from snooping into his stuff."

"Well, did your snooping find anything useful to our investigation?" Nicki asked.

"I don't know," Jenna mumbled. "Bank records, which I've already copied onto the thumb drive, and these sheets."

"What are they?" Nicki asked.

"Again, I don't know," Jenna said. "But they look like they track some kind of sports betting." She pointed to a desk off to the side. "Maxie thinks you should go through those papers. I mean, if we're going to break the law, we may as well go all out."

Since it seemed logical to her, Nicki inched around until she was facing the desk. She quickly thumbed through a pile of papers on one corner. It resembled a hodge-podge of reading material, with each page ranked by a giant letter across the top. Setting those aside, she picked up the paper on top of another stack and began to read.

She looked up ten minutes later. "There's all kinds of notes here about sports games and someone or something named 'Benzo'."

Jenna turned her head and frowned. "Anything else?"

"A lot of unpaid bills, with quite a few of them badly over-due." Nicki continued to sift through the piles. "Now here's something interesting."

Jenna leaned over and removed the thumb drive and put it into her jacket pocket. "What's interesting?"

"It's a note that says, 'Get 25% stake from JB'."

"A twenty-five percent stake in what, and who's JB?" Jenna asked.

"JB could be Jeremy Brennan. I don't know what the twenty-five percent is referring to." But she'd certainly ask Jeremy when she talked to him. Nicki folded the note over and tucked it into her small purse.

"If you're ready, Sherlock, I think we have everything we're going to get from this guy." Jenna rose from her chair and wiggled her way around Nicki toward the door.

"I'm right behind you," Nicki said. She'd spent as much time as she could stand in George Lancer's very cramped, hide-y hole.

## 14

N icki smiled at her handsome date when he opened the car door for her in front of Mario's restaurant.

"Thank you."

"My pleasure." Rob took her hand and helped her step out before drawing it through the crook of his arm. "You look stunning, Nicki. But then you always take my breath away. I wish I didn't have to go back to the city tonight."

"You're pretty stunning yourself, Rob." Nicki glossed over his comment about having to drive back to San Francisco. "I hope I won't have to fight too many other women off tonight."

Rob grinned. "Don't worry, babe. As the song goes, I only have eyes for you."

Since the man loved being the center of attention, Nicki doubted that, but she made a small humming sound of agreement as they went through the glass doors into the restaurant.

"Hello, Lisa." She smiled at the young woman who was the part-time hostess at Mario's. "How are you doing tonight? Is it busy?"

"Just the usual mid-week regulars, Ms. Connors." Barely out

of high school, Lisa always treated Nicki like a member of her
mother's generation.

*One of the realities since I turned thirty last year*, Nicki thought.
She hadn't decided yet if she liked it or not. It seemed her only
choice with the generation a whole decade or two behind her was
to either be part of the high school crowd, or relegated to the
senior set. They didn't seem to recognize anything in between
those two.

"Hi!" Lisa beamed at Nicki's boyfriend.

*Unless, of course, you're Rob*, Nicki silently amended.

Lisa grabbed two menus and asked Rob to follow her,
leaving Nicki to trail behind them. Once they were seated, the
hostess dragged her feet as she left the couple, but had a bright
blush and big smile on her face when Rob gave her a grin and
a wink.

More amused than annoyed, Nicki hoped Lisa found a Rob of
her own someday soon. Danny Findley, Soldoff's young deputy,
instantly popped into her mind. Two more candidates for Maxie's
matchmaking list. She smiled at the thought.

"Happy, babe?"

"Um. Of course. Why wouldn't I be? I'm having dinner with
the best-looking man in town."

Rob glanced around the restaurant before turning his blue-
eyed gaze back to her. "Doesn't seem to be much of a contest."

"How did your trip go?" Nicki asked, pointedly changing the
subject. Of all Rob's personality traits, his obsession with his
appearance was not one of her favorites.

Rob shrugged. "Not bad. Had a deal wrapped up when
Antonio stepped in and took credit for it. Again. The guy is only
out for himself."

Having met "the guy" on several occasions, Nicki wasn't sure
she agreed with that assessment, but kept it to herself. Rob
looked frustrated as he frowned and drummed his fingers on the
table. There was nothing wrong with venting a little about your

boss, and if that's what he needed to do, Nicki was willing to listen.

But after a long moment, he shook his head and turned his mega-watt smile back on her. "I do have news for you."

"Oh?" Nicki gave him an expectant look.

"I talked to the owner of the Catalan House restaurant in Santa Rosa, and he'd be happy to donate the catering for your charity dinner."

Nicki gasped and clapped her hands together when he nodded. "The Literacy for Kids fundraiser? Rob, that's wonderful!"

She reached across the table and laid her hand over his. "Thank you. Maxie will be so pleased."

Rob laughed. "That's what I told the manager at the restaurant to get him to say 'yes'. Keeping on the good side of your landlady seems to be a requirement around here."

"She's very well-liked," Nicki agreed. "And should be. Maxie's a wonderful person."

"You're gaining some pretty good popularity yourself with that blog of yours," Rob said. "I had another idea for the fundraiser. You should give a gourmet cooking class, or even a small series of them. With all the profits donated, of course. I'm sure it would fill up in no time. Maybe get one of these restaurants to donate the use of their kitchen during the hours they aren't open? I'll bet Maxie could swing that pretty easily."

Nicki's forehead wrinkled in thought as she considered it. Chole Johnson had suggested the same thing, but without the practical idea of using the kitchen in a local restaurant. It wasn't a bad idea. She could probably wrangle a few ladies from the Ladies in Writing Society to help with the prep and cleanup. Something to run by Maxie.

"Thanks, Rob. That's a wonderful idea." Giving his hand a last squeeze, she leaned back and picked up her menu, very pleased he'd just reminded her why she enjoyed spending time with him.

Beneath that it's-all-about-me exterior of his, Rob could really be a sweet guy.

The waiter came up and rapidly repeated the evening's specials before taking their drink orders. Within two minutes he was back at the table, delivering their wine and noting their dinner choices before retreating again.

Rob lifted his glass and tipped it toward Nicki. "To continued success in your career."

She lifted her glass and tipped it slightly back at him. "To yours as well."

Taking a quick sip, Rob set his glass down and cocked an eyebrow. "I read the last article you did for Mark's magazine."

"Matt. You know his name is Matt." Nicki shook her head when Rob flashed his grin.

"Right, right. Matt. Anyway, it sounds like a nice little winery up there near Healdsburg. I may have to drop in and take a look."

Pleased he'd read her work, and that it might mean new business for Bon Vin, Nicki smiled and nodded. "It really is a wonderful boutique winery. I think you'd be very pleased with their wine."

Rob reached over and took one of her hands in both of his. "Have you recovered from discovering Lanciere's body? That must have been quite a shock."

"It was," Nicki said. "A horrible tragedy."

"Have you found out anything new since his death?"

Startled at the question, Nicki's eyes opened wider. She didn't remember telling Rob she was doing a little sleuthing of her own into the winemaker's death.

"What do you mean?"

"About his wine," Rob said. "Now that he's dead, who will get his wine?"

"Oh." Nicki quickly realigned her thoughts from murder to something more practical. "Well, no family member has come forward to make a claim, as far as I know. I guess it will be a matter for the courts to settle his estate."

Rob frowned. "That might take quite a while."

"Yes, it could," Nicki agreed. "Jim Holland has hired an attorney to secure his claim on the wine, and it wouldn't surprise me if Jeremy Brennan did the same."

"So it could take quite a while *and* become messy." Rob toyed with the stem of his wine glass.

Nicki bit her lip and considered him for a moment. "There's also some positive evidence that George Lanciere may have been murdered."

Rob sat up a little straighter and his gaze narrowed on her face. "Really? Then maybe I should check into it."

"Check into what?" He couldn't mean doing any investigating of his own. It was impossible for her to visualize Rob Emerson running around the wine country, trying to find clues about who killed George Lancer.

"The wine. With Lanciere being murdered, the price of his special blend will go sky high."

She sighed. "Not my first concern at the moment, Rob."

"Sorry, babe. Didn't mean to sound insensitive."

For the next hour they ate excellent pasta and enjoyed another glass of wine, while Rob told stories about the various places he'd been and customers who had placed large orders since the last time they'd seen each other. But by his occasional fidgeting and furtive glances, Nicki could tell there was something on his mind. After they'd both refused the offer of a dessert menu, she set her napkin aside and placed her elbows on the table, resting her chin on top of her interlaced fingers.

"There was something you wanted to talk to me about?" Nicki asked. "Your company dinner maybe?"

"Not much to talk about there. I have to make an appearance and need a date." He raised an eyebrow at her. "Which I assume will be my very hot girlfriend. We'll be the talk of the party."

Nicki bit her lip to keep from making a comment about his smug tone. It wasn't as if she hadn't shown him off on occasion at an event or two, but that was at the beginning of their relationship. She'd hoped that after more than a year together that kind of behavior would have worn off a bit. But knowing she should be flattered, Nicki put a smile on her face.

"Be sure to send me the date so I can put it on my calendar. Anything else on your mind?"

"Oh. Yeah. There is something else. Glad you reminded me." Rob also put a smile on his face, but looked slightly past her to a point over her left shoulder.

It was a telling sign that she probably wasn't going to like whatever he was about to say.

"I know you've been getting more and more into the wine scene here." He paused, waiting until Nicki gave him a wary nod. "So it would be a good idea, every bit as good as the one about that cooking class, if you learned more about the history of wine and the winemaking process in general."

*Uh oh*, Nicki thought.

"Do you have a good book on the subject you would recommend?" She accompanied the question with a sweet smile and small tilt of her head.

"Not a book. Something better. A class." Rob put a lot of enthusiasm into that statement, which instantly made Nicki suspicious.

"A class?"

"It would be perfect! I found one near here, at the local college in Santa Rosa. If you like it enough, you might even mention it in your blog. Or maybe in one of your magazine articles."

Learning more about the history of winemaking was a good idea, and would help give a tad more color to her writing. But taking a class for something she could just as easily read in a book? Hmm...

"What's the class called? And do you know who's teaching it?" Nicki asked.

"Well, that's the best part," Rob said. "I'm not sure of the exact name of the class, *Wine through the Ages* or something like that. And it's being taught by an expert in the industry."

"What expert, Rob?"

"Antonio Rossi."

Nicki leaned back in her chair. "THE Antonio Rossi? As in the same one who's your boss at Catalan House?"

Rob nodded vigorously. "The very same one. Isn't it great he's going to be in the area for a few months, and has agreed to teach this class at the exact time you really need it?"

"Gee, thanks. And it is amazing how you happened to stumble across it," Nicki said. "Did you also happen to tell him I'd give him a mention in an article for *Food & Wine Online*?"

"Don't get huffy, babe. I only told him that you wrote for the magazine." Rob shrugged and lifted his wine glass. "Which you do."

"And have you already told him I'd be taking his class?" Nicki crossed her arms and stared at him over the low, flickering candle.

"I didn't think you'd mind, and it would be helping me out in a small way. Learning that stuff is a great idea, isn't it?" Rob raised his glass to his lips and stared at her over its rim.

"It's a good idea," Nicki conceded. "But my time is a little short right now, Rob, so..."

He cut her off, sounding relieved. "I'd knew you'd be okay with this, babe. Antonio offered to enroll you, so all you have to do is show up." Rob reached into his coat pocket and pulled out several flyers. "Here's the details. The first class is early next week."

With a sigh, Nicki reluctantly took the flyers. "Great."

## 15

"Well, isn't this interesting," Nicki said to herself.

She was alone in her townhouse and looking forward to Alex's imminent arrival. Her friend was true to her word and had managed to finagle a few extra days off, much to Nicki's delighted surprise. She'd picked up Alex's voice mail message about two minutes after Rob had dropped her off the night before. While she was waiting, Nicki decided to go through the information Jenna had collected on her little thumb drive. Most of them were bank statements.

She'd never found bank statements so fascinating.

"He didn't have any money." She frowned as she scrolled through the screen and found images of several checks made out to Holland Winery with the notation of "barrels" on them. Now why would George be paying for barrels when it was in his contract that the winery had to supply them to the head winemaker for free? She walked over to the murder board and added the barrel payments under the fact column. The payments started about a month ago and continued every week until his death.

She searched further back but couldn't find any more

payments to Holland or any other winery. But she did see a check every month for a sizeable amount that she would have attributed to a small mortgage, except George lived in a house on Holland property. And the amount seemed too high for his rent. As far as Nicki knew, he didn't have a mortgage. But the same amount popped up every month as far back as she could go, which was a good two years. Right up until three months ago when they'd stopped. The electronic statements Jenna had copied off from George's computer didn't have an image of the actual check, so she couldn't see what, or who, the payments went to. All she had was a check number and the amount.

She pondered it for a moment, then decided against adding the payments to the murder board. They may have been a fact, but she had no idea if it was in any way related to George's death.

Her computer rang with a Skype call. Nicki groaned when Matt's picture appeared on the screen. She'd forgotten to call him last night. By the time she made it home, she'd been too tired and too annoyed about Rob enrolling her in a wine class, to do more than listen to Alex's voice mail and fall into bed.

Hoping her editor had something else on his mind and hadn't even noticed her failure to call him, Nicki clicked on the answer button and smiled as Matt came on screen.

"Hi, Matt. How are you this morning?"

"Tired. I was up late last night waiting for your phone call." With his eyes drooping behind his glasses, Matt not only looked tired, but grumpy too.

"I'm sorry," Nicki said, instantly contrite. "I should have called, but by the time I got home I only had the energy to fall flat on the bed and didn't move until this morning."

"Did you at least take your shoes off?" A smile tugged at the corners of his mouth.

Nicki laughed. "I did manage that much."

He grinned. "What were you doing to keep you out so late? A girls' night out with Alex and Jenna?"

"No. I had dinner with Rob."

Matt's smile faded into a flat line. "So. How is lover-boy?"

She deliberately rolled her eyes at him. "He's fine. What do you have against Rob?"

"Nothing." Matt rubbed the back of his neck. "Is he the reason you're so tired this morning?"

"Matt! Are you kidding me?" Nicki leaned away from the screen and narrowed her eyes at him. In the three years she'd known him, Matt had never asked her anything like that.

"Sorry," he mumbled before clearing his throat. "I'm sorry. It's none of my business."

"No, it isn't," Nicki said. "But since you apologized so nicely — no, Rob isn't the reason I was up late last night. I mean, he was the reason I got in late. We had dinner before he drove back to San Francisco. I'm tired because I got up very early to look at these bank records."

"Are you having money problems?" Matt frowned. "Do you need more work? I can advance you money against future work."

Nicki held her hand up and waved it in front of the screen. "Stop, stop. That's a very nice offer but these aren't *my* bank records."

"Okay. Whose are they?" Matt pursed his lips for a moment before looking up at the ceiling. "They aren't George Lancer's by any chance, are they?"

"Now that you mention it," Nicki grinned.

"The police gave you his bank records?"

Her smile faded and she squirmed in her chair. "No."

"Did a member of his family give them to you?"

"I don't believe he has any family."

Matt's mouth flattened into a thin line. "So the answer is 'no'. How about Jim Holland, or someone else from the winery?"

She shook her head.

"Okay. How long have you had them?" Matt asked.

"Since the memorial service yesterday. I took a big pan of lasagna, and it was a huge hit."

"Who were you bribing this time?"

Nicki gave up her attempt to distract him and leaned forward to glare at him instead. "I cook all the time, Matt Dillon. And it's rarely to bribe someone."

He nodded. "Yes, you do cook all the time. But for your friends. Why go to all the trouble to feed a bunch of people you hardly know?"

She could have argued more with him but didn't see the point. He was just going to get it out of her anyway.

"Out of human decency. It was a memorial service."

When Matt stayed silent and continued to stare at her, Nicki threw up her hands. "All right. Jenna, Maxie and I went to the memorial so we could sneak a peek at George's computer."

"Jenna hacked into Lancer's computer?" Matt closed his eyes. Nicki could almost hear him praying for patience.

"No hacking involved. He didn't have a password."

Matt's eyes flew open and he pinned her with a hard stare. "And then you, or rather Jenna, sent his personal information to your email?"

"Of course not," Nicki said with a wave of her hand. "Jenna downloaded it to a thumb something or other."

"Drive," Matt supplied. "It's a thumb drive. I'm surprised Maxie didn't manage to talk you out of this."

Nicki shrugged. "She was the lookout."

Matt groaned and put a hand to his forehead. "You are aware that what you were doing is illegal."

"Strictly speaking, maybe." She concentrated on not squirming under his sudden glare.

"In any 'speak' you want, Nicki Connors. What did you find? And I want to know all of it," Matt insisted.

"Wouldn't that make you some kind of accessory to our crime?"

Matt didn't even blink at that. "All of it, Nicki."

"Well, he seemed to have a gambling habit," Nicki said slowly. "We found all kinds of sports betting spreadsheets to track games. Apparently he dealt with a man named Benzo."

"Benzo," Matt repeated, his voice sounding grim. "What else?"

"He didn't seem to have much money, and a lot of his bills weren't paid," Nicki said, warming up to the subject. "I also found a note that stated, 'get 25% stake from JB'. I think he was talking about Jeremy Brennan, the owner of Trax."

"Hello? Is anyone here?"

"Who's that?" Matt asked.

"Alex. She left a message saying she'd be here this morning and intended to stay a few days." Nicki swiveled her chair around to face the office door. "We're in here, Alex."

Her friend appeared in the doorway. "Who's 'we'? Is Jenna here? How was your date with..." Alex immediately trailed off when she rounded the corner and saw Matt's face on the computer screen. "Oh. Hi, Matt.

"Hi, Alex," Matt said. "How's everything going in the doctoring world?"

"Fine. People getting cured, lots of happy endings." Alex looked over at Nicki. "He looks annoyed. What's going on?"

"He *is* annoyed," Nicki replied. "He's not happy with me right at the moment."

"*He* can hear you both." Matt's raised voice came clearly over the speakers. "Alex, I need to yell at Nicki. Would you mind giving us a little privacy? She can tell you all about it later."

"You know I'm just going to go around the corner and listen to every word, don't you?" Alex smiled at him.

"Are you female?" Matt asked. He sighed and ran a hand through his hair. "Fine. As long as I can't see you,"

"Okey-dokey then." Alex disappeared around the corner.

"If you two are through," Nicki said as Alex slipped away. "I'm not sure I want to sit here and listen to a pre-planned yelling."

Matt snorted. "Lancer was dealing with a bookie, Nicki. Generally speaking, bookies are not nice people. You need to take this to the police, and you need to do that today."

"You want me to go to the police and tell them we hacked into George's computer?" Her eyes grew wide.

"You're the one who said it wasn't hacking. And I don't care what you tell them about how you got the information. Just tell them what you found out." He leaned over and looked past her. "What's that behind you?"

Nicki knew exactly what he was looking at. Next time he called, the first thing she'd do was cover it up. "It was Maxie's idea. It's a murder board."

Matt groaned and dropped his head into his hands. "You know you're all getting carried away?" He raised his head and looked at her. "Go to the police, Sherlock. And if you don't, I'm getting on a plane and we'll go together."

"Okay, okay. I'll go as soon as I finish the article I'm writing for the magazine. It's due today," Nicki hedged. She wasn't too sure about telling Chief Turnlow they'd snooped into George's computer.

"I'll take care of that deadline. I know the owner." Matt grinned before he switched back to his serious expression. "Today, Nicki. Give me your word."

"Fine. Today," Nicki said. It was obvious he wasn't going to let this go until she agreed.

"Then I'll talk to you tonight." Matt's voice became quieter. "Don't forget to call. I did uncover a couple of things that might be of interest. I made a promise to let you know about anything I found and I'm going to keep that promise. But don't make me regret it. Maybe I should spend the rest of the day getting a bail fund together. Talk to you later."

He clicked off, leaving Nicki to look at a blank space where his face had been a moment before.

"He's getting very bossy," she groused, standing up and stretching her back.

"He's also very right," Alex said from the doorway. She had a coffee cup in one hand and her car keys in the other. "Grab your purse and let's go."

---

"Are you going to tell me *how* you know George Lancer was up to his eyeballs in gambling?" Chief Turnlow crossed his arms over his wide chest and raised one eyebrow. "We didn't find anything to indicate that, and we did a search of his house. And we opened all the cupboards and drawers. We didn't see anything having to do with him gambling."

"Kurt said George was always talking on his cell phone whenever he went out on break. That he'd light a cigarette but never smoke it, and spent the whole time on the phone. And George didn't have much money in his bank account."

"And Kurt works in the tasting room at Holland Winery?"

Nicki nodded. "Yes, he does. He also said he overheard an argument George had with someone he called 'Jeremy'."

"An argument with Jeremy. Huh." The chief uncrossed his arms and laid them on his desk. "Did Kurt happen to overhear what the argument was about?"

Sitting across from him in a hard, straight-backed chair, Nicki smiled. "He didn't say."

"Neither did Jeremy Brennan."

Nicki jerked back slightly and frowned. "You've already talked with Jeremy?"

"He was in here this morning. Fact is, you just missed him." Chief Turnlow shook his head. "He was a bit vague on what the argument was about, but he admitted to having it."

"Oh." Nicki felt a little deflated. The chief's next comment didn't help, either.

"We've already seen Lancer's bank statements, but I'm a little curious how you managed to get a look at them too. And we could see he didn't have much money in there. I didn't see any payments I would have attributed to a bookie. But then that's usually a cash-only business, so it'd be hard to find out who he had been dealing with."

"Benzo," Nicki said absently, her mind still mulling over the fact that the chief already knew everything she did. Well almost everything. He didn't know about the note she'd found.

"Benzo?" Chief Turnlow echoed. "You know the name of Lancer's bookie?"

He blew out a breath and folded his hands, his eyebrows drawn together. "All right, Nicki. I'm aware Jenna Lindstrom is a computer whiz so I'm not going to ask you how you got that information. I *am* going to ask you where, though. When Danny searched the house, he didn't find a computer anywhere." The chief leaned forward. "I heard you were at the memorial yesterday afternoon because I talked to the warehouse manager this morning before Brennan came in, and Victor mentioned it. All I'm going to ask you, more in the line of a friendly, general conversation, is if you happened to take... well, let's say a tour of Lancer's house while you were there."

She'd have to be a moron not to take the gift he was offering by overlooking their hacking. Getting her friends in trouble had been her biggest worry.

"Why yes, Chief. I did take a tour of the house." She gave him a polite smile. "Very compact, serviceable place. But I did find the location of the personal office space a bit odd."

"Why is that, Ms. Connors?"

"Because you had to go out the kitchen door onto the back porch, and then follow the porch around the corner until you came to the second door on your right. It certainly wasn't very convenient."

"I have to agree." Chief Turnlow sighed before looking past her and yelling for Danny to get his tail into the office.

When his young deputy stuck his head around the doorway, the chief scowled at him before giving him the location of George's closet-sized office. "Go out and pick up his computer, and any other papers lying around."

"Yes, Chief," Danny said before giving the other occupant of the room a shy smile. "Hi, Nicki. Are you doing okay after finding the body and all?"

"She's fine, Officer Findley. Now go get that computer," the chief barked, keeping his gaze fixed on his deputy until the young man disappeared. His running footsteps rang down the police station's short hallway.

Chief Turnlow looked over at Nicki, a frown on his face. "As for you and your band of amateur sleuths, I want you to keep clear of this investigation."

"But we really aren't..." Nicki stopped when the chief held up his hand.

"I know a bit of your history, Nicki." His voice softened. "I know about your mother and that her case has gone cold. I dealt with enough families when I was a homicide detective to understand how tough that is on everyone. But trying to find out who killed George Lancer isn't going to make up for your mom."

Nicki's mouth opened, but nothing came out. Was that what she was doing? Trying to compensate somehow for her mother's murder never being solved?

When Chief Turnlow stood up, she automatically did the same.

"You need to stay away from this, Nicki," he said. "There's a good chance that George owed money to this Benzo character and paid the price. That particular branch of humanity plays by its own rules, and I don't want you to stumble into their line of fire. Am I making myself clear?"

She nodded and gathered up her purse and sweater without saying a word. She walked out into the main room with him.

"If we find out who did this, I'll personally give you a call." The chief nodded at her and then at Alex. "Have a nice day, ladies."

Alex trailed after Nicki as she trudged toward the car. Still silent, she climbed into the passenger seat and stared straight ahead as her friend put the car into gear and drove away from the town square. Several minutes passed before Alex threw her a sideways look.

"All right. What did the man say to put that look on your face? That you'd have to do five to ten in the State penitentiary?"

"No," Nicki sighed. "He said I'm trying to solve George Lancer's murder because I couldn't solve mom's." Nicki dropped her gaze to her hands lying in her lap before looking over at Alex. "Do you think that's true?"

"In my best medical opinion? Not really," Alex carefully negotiated the turn onto the highway leading to Maxie's large property.

"So why am I doing this?" Nicki asked. "I didn't even know the man. I'd barely said a dozen words to him, and to be honest I didn't like him at all. He was rude, arrogant and whether or not he actually smoked, he smelled like an ashtray."

"Because you're naturally nosy," Alex said. "The chief's explanation is way too complicated. If he knew you better, he'd realize that you love to pry into everyone's life."

"Well that's a mean thing to say," Nicki declared.

Her friend laughed. "Not at all. It's one of the things I love most about you, and so does Jenna. You love hearing everyone's life story and how they got into the place they're at. You like it so much, you're willing to spend hours cooking just to create the perfect bribe to get someone to start talking."

"I like to cook," Nicki protested.

"And you're nosy. That's why writing a blog and doing interviews for Matt's magazine is the perfect career for you."

Nicki snorted and then chuckled, which turned into a full-blown laugh. "Only your real friends will tell you the truth."

"That's me," Alex nodded. "One of your real friends."

"I'd give you a hug if you weren't driving at seventy miles an hour down this country road," Nicki said.

"And I'd take that hug if I weren't driving at seventy miles an hour down a country road," Alex replied, but she eased off the accelerator. "So not to change the subject, but how did your date with Rob go last night?"

"It started out very well, but slid into annoying."

"All right, Connors. Explain."

"Well, he began by telling me that the local Catalan House restaurant will donate the catering for our Literacy for Kids fundraiser. Which reminds me, I still need to call and let Maxie know as soon as I get home."

"That's wonderful," Alex said.

"And he had a fantastic idea about offering a cooking class to help raise even more money," Nicki continued.

"Also wonderful. So, when does the annoying part happen?"

"Right now," Nicki said. "He thinks I should take a class on the history of wine which his boss happens to be giving at the local college."

"Can't you just read a book?"

"Why bother when he's already enrolled me in the class?"

Alex's mouth dropped open. "He *what*? Okay, start from the beginning, and don't leave a word out."

## 16

"I simply love your coffee, dear." Maxie took another sip and made an appreciative noise in the back of her throat. "Such a lovely start for an early morning meeting."

"It's almost ten, Maxie," Alex pointed out from her perch on one of the tall stools pulled up to the kitchen counter.

"Which may be the middle of the day in your profession, dear, but for the rest of the civilized world it's definitely early in the morning. I was up a bit late last night doing research for a client. An absolutely fascinating family in Sweden. Their genealogy is positively intriguing. And I love the Nordic countries in the fall. I might deliver my results personally."

"That sounds like a great idea. I wish I could join you," Nicki stiffled a yawn.

"Were you up late too?" Maxie smiled, her brown eyes crinkling at the corners when Nicki nodded. "What kept you up late? Working on an article, or taking a romp with that dashing hero, Tyrone Blackstone?"

"Nothing that exciting. I was on a business call."

"Sounded a little more personal than business to me." Alex laughed when Nicki stuck her tongue out at her.

"Oh?" Maxie tapped a finger against her lips. "That occasional boyfriend of yours? Bob, isn't it?"

"Rob," Nicki corrected. "Which reminds me. He told me that the Catalan House restaurant in Santa Rosa will be donating their catering for the dinner at the Literature for Kids fundraiser."

"Rob, of course. How generous of him." Maxie clapped her hands together. "Such a thoughtful boyfriend. Did he call you last night?"

"Not that boyfriend," Alex said. "Her other, wanna-be boyfriend, Matt."

Nicki let out a snort of exasperation. "Matt does not want to be my boyfriend."

"I wouldn't say that, dear. In my opinion, he very much would like to be your boyfriend." Maxie took another sip of coffee and winked at her hostess. "Dr. Alex and I agree on that point."

"You're both crazy. Right now he doesn't even like me much. He really didn't want to tell me the information he found out that might have a link to George's murder, even though he promised he would. But it was worse than pulling teeth to get it out of him last night."

Alex leaned toward the end of the counter where Maxie was standing.

"He doesn't like her getting so involved in this murder investigation now that she's doing illegal stuff," Alex said in a loud stage whisper.

"It wasn't illegal," Nicki countered. "Or at least it was barely illegal, and he's having a fit over the whole thing. I told Chief Turnlow what we found out. He knows we looked in George's computer, and yet I'm not parading around in jail stripes."

"Probably more due to the chief being afraid of Maxie than believing you were innocent," Alex pointed out.

"Very glad to be of service, dear." Maxie smiled at Nicki. "Is that all Matt is upset about? A little snooping around in a dead man's house when there was no family we could ask for permission?"

"He wasn't very happy about a bookie being tossed into this mix either," Alex supplied.

Nicki rolled her eyes. Honestly. She would have thought at least one of her friends would know how to keep a confidence.

"Nonsense." Maxie airily waved the comment away. "It was simply a name. There isn't a shred of evidence the gentleman was involved in George's murder."

"That's right," Nicki declared, squaring her shoulders and giving Maxie a 'thumbs-up'. "It was just a name. There's a lot more reason to suspect one of the winery owners killed George."

"Such as...?" Alex asked.

"Jeremy for one. Especially after what Matt finally did tell me last night."

"Let's go to the murder board, ladies." Maxie picked up her coffee cup, a huge smile on her face.

Nicki and Alex exchanged grins. Maxie Edwards really loved the murder board.

Less than a minute later they were all standing in front of the large, white erase board, staring at their trove of information.

"Since Jenna has declared my handwriting is unreadable, someone else will need to fill in the latest information from Matt," Alex said.

Maxie grabbed a marker and stood at the ready, her hand poised over the board as she looked at her hostess, one eyebrow raised in an unspoken question.

"Right." Nicki walked over to her desk and consulted the pad she'd taken notes on the night before while Matt was talking. "He said there's been a buzz for the last month and a half that both Jim Holland and Bill Stacy had feelers out for a head winemaker."

"Do you think George Lancer might have heard those rumors?" Alex frowned.

"Maybe. It's a pretty small industry when it comes to gossip, so he probably did, which would explain why he was so rude to them the day of the tasting event."

"Unfortunately, he was always a rude man, so it could be just George being himself and he wasn't aware of the rumors at all," Maxie said as she wrote the latest information under the *motives* column.

Nicki thought that was also a likely possibility. "True. It's interesting, though, that Matt said only Jim Holland has been inquiring about a head winemaker for the past few weeks. Not a word has come out of Bill Stacy."

"So do you think Bill decided to keep George after all?" Maxie asked. "Which leaves Jim as the only owner with a motive?"

"Or he found another winemaker, and killing George was much cheaper than having to buy out his contract," Nicki said. "It was Bill who mentioned George would get a large sum of money if he was let go for any reason."

"It's a great motive." Alex nodded. "George might have been entitled to full pay for a year or more. It could be very hard, if not impossible, for a winery to pay two head winemakers."

"Oh my. We may have found the answer," Maxie said.

"George was probably nervous, so he was negotiating for a stake in Trax. Matt told me there was a rumor going around that Trax was selling a twenty percent stake in the business to someone. I think it was George." Nicki nodded at her audience and held up a small, scrap of paper. "And I'll bet he wanted more, so was going to demand twenty-five percent. That's what this note means."

"Let me add it all to the board, then we can decide what to do next," Maxie said.

As she was scribbling away, Alex gave her good friend a long intense look. "I guess we'll be visiting the owner of Trax to find out if the rumors are true?"

"And if that's the reason he had the argument with George," Nicki said.

———————

"IT WAS nice of you to take the time to show us around the winery." Nicki's lips curved up into a slow smile. "Maxie's been telling me for a while now that I had to pay Trax a visit."

"Indeed, I have," Maxie said to a beaming Jeremy Brennan. "I've heard wonderful things about how you're bringing this property back to life."

"Thank you." Jeremy's gaze fell to the sparkling ring on Alex's third finger. "And I gather congratulations are in order, Dr. Kolman?"

Alex smiled. "Yes, they are. Thank you. And please, call me Alex."

"Who's the lucky fellow?" Jeremy's blue eyes warmed up as he led the three women to a table near a large picture window in Trax's newly renovated tasting room.

"Tyler Newman," Alex said. "He's a fireman with Santa Rosa County."

Jeremy shook his head. "I should have known. Those firemen get all the beautiful girls."

Nicki sat back and kept quiet. She was more than happy to let the winery owner fall all over Alex. It gave her a chance to look around and note all the new furnishings and equipment at Trax.

"You've done a wonderful job with this public room, Jeremy," Nicki said after Alex gave her a hard nudge under the table with her foot. "There's a lot of new equipment in the warehouse and production rooms too."

"The place needed a major overhaul when I bought it." Jeremy signaled to the tasting room server, who quickly came to the table bearing a tray with a bottle of wine and four glasses already poured.

"That would take a good sum of money. Do you have investors?" Maxie put the question in such a matter-of-fact tone that it sounded like a simple business discussion.

Nicki sent her an approving look and a grin.

Jeremy shook his head. "Just an inheritance and a desire to produce excellent wine."

"It must have been quite an inheritance. I mean, to put so much into updating the winery, and purchasing the land and vines as well." Nicki picked up her wine and swirled the amber liquid almost to the rim of the glass.

"What are you getting at, Nicki?" Jeremy asked.

She did a slow look around the room before returning her gaze to him. "There's a rumor that a twenty percent stake in Trax is for sale." She paused for a moment. "To George Lanciere."

She watched carefully as most of the color drained out of Jeremy's face.

"That doesn't mean I killed him."

His blunt statement had Maxie gasping and eyes widening all around the table.

"I hear rumors too. And one of them is that you and your friends are doing some investigating of your own into Lancer's murder. And yeah. I knew he wasn't French." Jeremy lifted his glass and drained half the contents in one gulp.

Nicki straightened her back and stood her ground. "Really? Well I also heard George had wanted a bigger stake in Trax. Say, twenty-five percent?"

"Where did you hear that?" Jeremy demanded.

"I work in the media, Jeremy. We have all kinds of sources." Nicki tried to sound as if it was an everyday occurrence for her to access inside information.

"Oh, come on. You write a blog. How many connections can you have with a blog?"

She shrugged. "In a community this size, how many do you need?"

After a long moment of silence, the winery owner sighed. He turned his head to look out the big window to the rows of vines beyond. "Good point. Not many, especially depending on who your friends are." He glanced over at Maxie who gave him a polite-looking smile.

"It *was* quite an inheritance," he said, looking at Alex. "But still not enough to cover everything. After all the expenses to fix the place up and get it going again, I couldn't afford a top-flight winemaker."

"Like George?" Nicki prompted.

"Like George," Jeremy confirmed. "Or I thought he was. I found out both Holland and Todos were in the market to replace him. George said it was because he'd decided to use Trax as the sponsor for his new personal blend. It sounded reasonable to me. I mean, his last blend put Holland on the wine map as a major player, and his criticism destroyed The White Crown."

"But twenty percent is a pretty hefty chunk of your business," Nicki said.

"It was in place of the salary I couldn't afford to pay him. And he promised to put up all ten barrels of his wine. That's over three thousand bottles." Jeremy downed the rest of his wine, reached over for the still-full bottle the server had left on the table, and refilled his glass. "I was willing to give it to him, and then he demanded twenty-five percent or he'd take his precious wine elsewhere. He gave me until the tasting to agree, or he'd make the announcement right there at the event that he'd changed his mind."

Nicki wasn't about to tell him that he never was going to get all of George's wine. At least one barrel had been promised to Jim Holland to pay for the tasting event.

"Is that why you were in such a bad mood that day? Because you'd had an argument and told him 'no'?" Nicki asked.

He shook his head. "We had the argument because we'd already made the deal, and now he wanted to change it. He agreed to give me the first taste at the event, and would act according to my final answer right then before the others were served their sample."

Nicki felt more than a small twinge of sympathy for him. George Lancer had given him a terrible choice. Either turn over a quarter of his ownership in the winery, or face the winemaker's public criticism and the possible ruin of his business.

"You need to tell Chief Turnlow what the argument was about before he finds out on his own." Nicki nodded when Jeremy frowned at her.

"If I do that, he'll assume I killed the little snake," Jeremy said. "Him getting murdered got me out of a bind."

"Except you still don't have a winemaker," Alex pointed out.

"I'll find someone who's young, talented and looking for a break," Jeremy declared. "And will work for something a great deal less than a king's ransom."

Nicki considered that for a moment. "Speaking of being worth a king's ransom, are you planning on taking any action to claim ownership of George's wine?"

"You mean hire a lawyer like Jim has?" Jeremy shook his head. "George never signed a formal contract so I don't have a claim to it. And a piece of my winery won't be going into his estate. Jim can keep the wine. It seems to be bad luck anyway."

"Did George mention anything that would make you suspect he had a gambling problem?" Nicki asked.

Jeremy blinked at the sudden change in topic. "Not that I recall. Why? Did he have a gambling problem?"

"Could be," Nicki hedged. "Is there anything else you remember about the time he spent here? Was he on his cell phone a lot?"

"No more than I considered normal. And he only had one visitor, although she came a couple of times."

"She?" Her ears perked up. From the corner of her eye Nicki saw Alex and Maxie sit up a little straighter.

"He never introduced her. But the last time she was here they had one big, blow-up fight. I heard him call her Stella."

The three women exchanged a look.

"Stella?" Nicki shrugged. "I've never met a Stella." Which was true—she hadn't met Stella.

Alex leaned over the table to get Jeremy's attention. "I suppose you'll need to start looking for that young and ambitious winemaker right away?"

Nicki said a silent *thank you* to Alex for distracting the winery owner.

"I've already put out inquiries," Jeremy said.

"In the meantime, you need to talk to Chief Turnlow," Nicki insisted.

"Or you will?" Jeremy glared at her, his palms slapping down on the table.

Maxie put an arm around his shoulders. "It's best if you do, dear. These things always come out. It would weigh a great deal in your favor if you offered the explanation first."

Jeremy hung his head. "I guess."

"I'm sure the chief will let us know that you came to him on your own to tell him why you were arguing with George." Maxie gave him a pointed look.

"Then I'd better rearrange my schedule today to take care of that." Jeremy picked up the bottle of wine and bent at the waist in a slight bow. "If you'll excuse me, ladies."

A few minutes later Maxie backed her car out of the parking lot and onto the street heading back to Soldoff. The silence dragged on, with each woman looking out a different window.

"Well, that was intense," Alex finally said. "Do you think he'll really go to Chief Turnlow?"

"If he doesn't, we certainly should," Maxie declared. "Jeremy Brennan has an excellent motive to murder George, and he was at the tasting event so he had the opportunity as well."

"I don't know if he does or not," Nicki said. "He did have a good reason for wanting George dead, and an equally good reason for wanting him alive."

"Now dear, I thought you wanted to solve this case," Maxie said.

"I do," Nicki frowned. "But I want the real killer caught, and I'm not convinced that's Jeremy Brennan."

"Then who, dear? Because I'm certain it isn't Jim Holland. He simply isn't the type."

"It could be that bookie after all," Alex chimed in. "That's what Chief Turnlow thinks, and he was a homicide cop. They have instincts about these things." She leaned forward from the back seat and tapped Maxie on the shoulder. "But he also believes Nicki got involved in all of this because her mom's case was never solved."

"Of course that's ridiculous," Maxie declared. "Men have the strangest notions sometimes. Even former homicide cops, it seems."

Curious, Nicki looked at her landlady. "Why do you think that's a ridiculous idea?"

"Because, dear, it's obvious why you're investigating George's murder."

"And that is...?"

"The same reason I'm helping you, and why we're researchers and writers." Maxie reached over and patted Nicki's knee. "We're nosy."

Alex plopped back against her seat and laughed. "And there you have it, folks."

---

## 17

The following morning Nicki made an emergency ingredient run to the local market. French toast simply could not be made without whipping cream and fresh berries. Having purchased those, plus a few other essential items that happened to catch her eye, she pulled into the circular drive in front of the townhouse, only to see the police cruiser outside her door. Chief Turnlow was standing next to it, talking to Jenna and Alex. All three looked over when her little Toyota sputtered to a stop behind the chief's car.

*Uh oh*, Nicki thought. *This can't be good.* But at least the chief wasn't dangling a pair of handcuffs from his fingertips. A sudden picture of her having to call Matt to ask for that bail fund flashed through her mind. She could deal with anything short of that.

"Nicki," Chief Turnlow said, holding out his arms. "Let me take that for you."

While she handed him the grocery bag, Nicki sent a questioning look to Jenna who held her arms out to the side and shrugged. A quick glance at Alex got her the same response. It seemed the chief hadn't told either of them why he was paying her a visit first thing in the morning.

"Mind if I come in so we can talk for a minute?"

Nicki couldn't help but smile at the big man standing on the tiny patch of lawn, holding a bag of food and looking like a papa bear trying to understand his cub.

"Well, Chief, you can either come inside or hand over my groceries. I planned on using them for breakfast."

Behind his back Jenna rolled her eyes. Alex gave the computer geek an elbow in the side to get her to behave. The chief barely raised an eyebrow when they followed him into the townhouse.

Nicki led the group to the kitchen, pointing at the counter when the chief asked where she wanted him to put the grocery bag. She watched him do a quick, cop-like scan of the room.

"I'm not hiding anything, Chief Turnlow. You're free to search the premises if you want to."

"Nice place," he said, making himself at home on one of the tall stools.

Alex and Jenna moved around the island to stand on either side of Nicki.

Soldoff's Chief of Police chuckled. "I guess you three come as a set?"

The women linked their arms through Nicki's and stared back at him.

"Yes, we do," Alex said.

"Absolutely," Jenna stated at the same time.

Nicki sighed. "Stop this. He isn't going to haul me off to jail."

"I rarely do that to anyone who has so many powerful friends. It's not considered a politically correct move." The chief smiled at the two women intent on protecting Nicki, whether she needed it or not. "I'm referring to her other powerful friend, besides you two."

"You mean Maxie?" Nicki smiled.

"Her, too," Chief Turnlow said. "But I'm talking about your boyfriend."

"Rob?" All three women said at once.

"Wait, wait." Nicki held up her hand. "You spoke to Rob? When?"

The chief shook his head. "Who's Rob?"

"Rob Emerson. My boyfriend?"

He rubbed his hand across the back of his neck. "Ah. Then I talked with your other boyfriend. The one who owns that magazine you write for."

"Matt?" Nicki's jaw dropped to her chest. Why in the world did the Soldoff police chief talk to Matt?

"Is he in some kind of trouble?" she asked.

"It's more likely that Matt thinks *you're* in some kind of trouble," Jenna said while Alex nodded her agreement.

The chief smiled at Nicki. "She's right. I didn't call him. He called me. First thing when I walked into the department this morning the phone was ringing, and your boyfriend was on the line."

"He's not my boyfriend," Nicki protested.

"Funny you didn't say that right off," the chief said.

At Nicki's glare, he blew out a quick breath. "I don't have any kids, so I have no experience in dealing with guys hanging around a daughter. But I'd say from my conversation with Matt this morning, if he isn't your boyfriend, he sure wants to be."

"We know," Jenna and Alex said in unison.

"The only one who doesn't know is her." Jenna tilted her head in Nicki's direction.

"All right, all right." Nicki could feel her face lighting on fire. "Enough about my personal life. Why did Matt call you this morning?"

"Because he wanted to know if I had any idea who killed George Lancer, and how dangerous was it for you to be poking around in my investigation."

"She can't help it," Jenna said.

"She's naturally nosy," Alex added.

"Yeah. I got that," the chief replied before turning his attention back to Nicki.

Nicki stepped away and shook off her friends. "You two, go sit." She pointed at the other side of the counter. "I'm putting on fresh coffee, Chief Turnlow. Would you like a cup?"

"I would," the chief said. "It was too early in the morning to be dealing with an irate boyfriend."

"He's not my…"

The chief held his hands out. "Okay. He's not your boyfriend. Just an overly concerned friend who happens to be male. And told me he's considering giving you an assignment to review a restaurant he's particularly fond of… in Alaska."

"Fine," Nicki grumbled, dumping the last of her freshly ground coffee into the filter before plucking a bottle of water from underneath the counter.

"You use that expensive bottled water for your coffee?"

"Because I enjoy good coffee. Ninety-eight percent of a cup of coffee is water." Nicki finished pouring it into the tea kettle and lit the burner to heat it up before turning back to the group on the other side of the counter. "Now. Why did Matt call you?"

"Because last night you told him about your talk with Jeremy Brennan."

Nicki's eyebrows drew together. "So? I agreed to call him every night about our case."

"*My* case, Nicki," the chief corrected. "Well, apparently he thinks Brennan is an excellent candidate for being the murderer, and there you were, his girl, sorry, I meant his employee, talking with a killer like you were at a tea party."

Nicki raised her hands, palms up and glanced over at Alex and Jenna. "What has gotten into him? Why would Matt call the chief at all, especially over something like that?"

"Because he wants to be your boyfriend," Jenna repeated.

"Ty would do the same thing if he thought I was talking to a murderer," Alex said.

"Ladies, you can argue about it later. Boyfriend, only a friend, or whatever he is, this Matt guy has a good point." Chief Turnlow looked at Nicki. "I was coming out to talk to you anyway to let you know Jeremy Brennan came by the station yesterday afternoon to explain the argument he had with George Lancer. Brennan's out the money he spent in preparing for the launch, but he'd stopped most of those expenses when he and Lancer got into their beef over the percentage stake in Trax. He might have a motive for wanting Lancer dead, so he wouldn't need to deal with the man bad-mouthing his business. But I'm not seeing the opportunity."

Nicki's mouth opened into a wide "O".

"You mean how could he have poisoned the wine?" Alex asked.

Chief Turnlow nodded. "The owner of a rival winery would have been very noticeable wandering around in the back area of the building where he had no business being. Unless he was there with an escort. And all his time was accounted for at the event."

"What about Bill Stacy? Is all his time accounted for too?" Nicki asked.

"Stay out of this, Nicki. A homicide investigation is no place for amateurs. Especially when the best suspect is a bookie." The chief stood up just as the kettle on the stove started to sing. "Wish I had time to taste that coffee."

"I always keep to-go cups, Chief." Nicki opened a cupboard and grabbed one. "It will only take a minute for this to finish dripping."

"Then I'll take that minute to warn you again. Murder is no place for amateurs. And when you call that editor friend of yours tonight, like you promised you would, be sure to mention I stopped by. I have better things to do than to try and calm down worried boyfriends."

Nicki poured coffee into the cup and placed it on the counter. "Do you need cream or sugar?"

"No, thank you. I drink it black."

She handed him the coffee accompanied with a stiff smile. "And Chief, he's not my boyfriend."

Chief Turnlow picked up the cup and lifted it in a short salute. "Thanks for this, Nicki. And remember what I said. Now I'm going to pay a visit to Maxie to tell her the same thing, and to let Mason know what his wife's been up to. I really don't care whether or not that's politically correct."

Silence reigned over the kitchen for several moments after the front door closed behind the chief.

Nicki stirred her coffee and looked over at Jenna and Alex.

Jenna grinned back at her. "Want to update the murder board?"

"Of course she does," Alex picked up her cup and slid off the stool.

"Of course I do," Nicki echoed with a broad smile. "Just as soon as I call Maxie to warn her that the chief is headed her way, and then put together a cheese plate for us to munch on. I'll make the French toast for lunch."

"Perfect," Alex rolled eyes. "Nothing like having a last meal before we're dragged off to jail. Because if the chief catches us playing amateur detectives again, he probably *will* toss us in the clink and throw away the key."

"After he tastes Nicki's coffee, I'm betting she can bribe our way out," Jenna said with a shrug.

Nicki hung up the phone, laughing. "Maxie found an urgent errand that myMason has to do right now. She'll be over as soon as she gets rid of the chief. Her words, not mine."

"Gotta love her," Jenna said. "Not sure why at times, but still gotta love her."

"I'll get the cheese, you two go uncover the murder board," Nicki directed.

Alex frowned. "Why is it covered up?"

"So Matt wouldn't see it," Nicki admitted. "He got all wonky about it, even after I told him it was Maxie's idea."

"Matt's always wonky around you, period," Jenna said before hurrying out the kitchen door when Nicki glared at her.

Five minutes later the three women were staring at the white board and nibbling on an excellent Brie and crackers.

"Who's the best suspect?" Alex wondered, looking over the names. "And shouldn't we add the bookie? What was his name?"

"Benzo," Nicki said. She picked up the pen and wrote the name at the bottom of the list.

"Yoo-hoo?"

Maxie's voice was followed by the sound of her heels clicking down the hallway. She stepped into the office and put her hands on her hips.

"Paul came by to give me that lecture. Imagine talking to his elders that way. What is this world coming to?" Maxie shook her head. "What are we doing?"

"Looking over our list of suspects," Jenna said. "And eating cheese."

"An excellent combination." Maxie walked over and joined them in front of the murder board. "Now, who is that at the bottom?"

"The bookie," Alex volunteered. "Chief Turnlow's favorite suspect."

Nicki wrinkled her nose. "I don't think so. Remember the three questions? Means, motive and opportunity? Mr. Benzo, or any of his cohorts, might have a motive if George owed them a lot of money, but how would they get into the room to poison the wine without anyone seeing them? And whoever heard of a hit man using poison? Why wouldn't he simply shoot George when he was at home alone at night? I think the chief already knows all that and he's using the bookie slant to scare us off."

"It's certainly working on Matt," Alex pointed out.

Jenna winked at Maxie. "Nicki's mad because Matt called

Chief Turnlow wanting to know how dangerous this investigation is, and mentioned sending her on an assignment to Alaska."

"Oh, that's not surprising, dear." Maxie smiled at Nicki. "It's obvious the poor man wants to be your boyfriend."

"We know," Alex and Jenna sang out.

Tired of hearing about Matt and the status of a relationship that didn't even exist, Nicki picked up the snack plate and held it away from the group. "We either drop the whole Matt thing and get back to our suspects, or you've had your last bite of cheese and crackers."

"You play dirty, Nicki," Jenna complained. "But all right. Back to the suspect list, and not another word about Matt. At least not today. Unless, of course, *you* bring up his name."

Nicki set the plate down and turned to the board.

"We have the three winery owners," she began, looking over the list. "Jeremy who George threatened to dump and then ruin his winery's reputation the same way he did to Bill a decade ago."

"But George's death means he's lost out on all the revenue and publicity from being the sponsor of George's special blend," Alex pointed out.

"But now he can keep his winery all to himself." Nicki tapped one finger against her lower lip. "Jeremy could have poisoned the wine, but he'd run a big risk of being seen in an area of Holland he shouldn't be in. And all his time is accounted for at the event, according to the chief."

"Then there's Jim Holland." Jenna squinted at the board from behind her oversized lenses. "He wanted to replace George. But now that his winemaker's dead, Jim will probably get to keep the special blend *and* not have to pay out the termination clause in George's contract."

"Which Bill Stacy said was a big sum of money," Nicki pointed out. "Jim could have easily poisoned the wine, since it's his winery."

"But it doesn't seem smart to do that at your own place and your own event," Alex said. "And what about Bill Stacy?"

"Bet he had a grudge with George, big time," Jenna said.

"Over The White Crown going under because of George's gossip?" Nicki pursed her lips and considered Bill's name on the board. "I don't know if all his time at the event is accounted for, but he'd have the same problem poisoning the wine as Jeremy would. How to sneak into George's private aging room without being noticed? But he is definitely on my list to visit next."

"Then there's Geri and Kurt, both of whom were treated badly by George, and either could be anywhere in the winery and no one would pay any attention since they work there," Nicki said.

"Are hurt feelings really enough motive to commit a murder?" Alex asked.

"Well, George never did anything to help Geri's career along," Nicki said. "But neither has Jim Holland, at least as far as I can tell, and he's still alive."

"And let's not forget Stella," Maxie put in. "The former girl-friend George had a fight with, according to Jeremy Brennan."

"We'll need to track her down," Nicki agreed.

"I already have, dear. She recently took a position on the morning shift at Sandy's diner."

Alex laughed. "Isn't that the job the clerk at the police station, thought I should try to land?"

"Sounds like you're out of luck. Stella beat you to it." Nicki grinned at her friend.

"Too bad, Dr. Kolman soon-to-be Dr. Newman. It would've been a nice back-up for you if this whole medical thing doesn't work out," Jenna chuckled.

"Such a shame," Maxie agreed amid the laughter. "Well, it appears we have our to-do list. First we should to talk to Bill Stacy, and then to Stella."

"Which I'll get started on tomorrow," Nicki said. "Today I

need to finish that article for M..." She stopped herself when Jenna sent her a wicked smile.

"For my editor," Nicki finished. She'd already decided to send the article tonight along, with an email telling Matt she was going to bed and wouldn't be calling him.

---

## 18

"You didn't talk to Matt last night?" Alex frowned. "I thought you two had a deal that you would call him every night?"

Nicki grimaced but kept her eyes on the road. Thanks to Alex being used to working all hours, they'd managed an early start and were only a few minutes away from Todos Winery, where they were hoping to catch Bill Stacy by surprise.

"I wimped out and sent him an email telling him I was going to bed and wouldn't be calling."

"He probably thinks you're mad at him for talking to Chief Turnlow," Alex said.

"Then he'd be very perceptive, because I *am* mad at him for calling the chief. *And* for saying he can order me to go to Alaska on an assignment," Nicki sniffed. It really was arrogant of Matt to believe she'd just up and leave in the middle of something obviously important to her. Otherwise she wouldn't be spending so much of her time on it when she should be working on her newest Tyrone Blackstone novel.

"Is that the only reason? Because you're mad at him?"

Biting her lip, Nicki gripped the wheel of her little Toyota a little harder. "No. All that talk about him wanting to be my boyfriend weirded me out."

Alex laughed and gave her a light tap on the arm. "Half the men you meet want to be your boyfriend, and we all ignore what the other half wants. Matt's a very responsible, caring kind of guy. He'd have the same concern for any of his employees."

"Well, that's true." Nicki's mood picked up at the thought. So her editor might have had a fantasy or two on occasion. It's not like she didn't either. After all, he's good-looking, in a nerdy way. And she liked nerds. It was natural and perfectly harmless if you looked at it as a temporary-imaginary-only thing.

"It is true," Alex nodded. "Of course, he wouldn't care at the same intensity he shows for you, but..."

"Quiet shall now reign in the car," Nicki declared, glancing over at her friend. "And I don't want to talk about it anymore."

They passed another vehicle coming out of the Todos driveway as they were pulling in.

"Well someone sure gets an early start on their winery tours," Alex commented as they slid by the small compact with faded blue paint.

Nicki frowned and pulled into the nearest parking spot in the empty lot. Quickly opening the door and stepping onto the gravel, she watched the other car disappear around a bend in the road.

"What?" Alex climbed out of the passenger seat and turned her head to peer in the same direction as Nicki. "What are you looking at?"

"Geri Gant, unless I'm mistaken. And I don't think I am." Nicki's brows lowered. What was the assistant winemaker from Holland's doing here at this hour of the morning?

"Checking out the competition?" Alex guessed before stifling a yawn. "Let's get this over with so we can do some serious sampling at the tasting rooms around the square. I promised Tyler I'd have the wine for our wedding picked out by the time I came home. It's the excuse I gave him for coming back to your place so soon, and for so long."

"Okay. Let's go," Nicki said. She grinned at her friend as they walked along the path toward the public tasting room. "Since when have you considered four days a long time? Is that all you can stand being away from your hunky fireman?"

"Or all he can stand being away from his hot fiancée," Alex countered. "Besides, he's working extra shifts this next week since he's changed his mind about the honeymoon again. Now he wants to go snorkeling in Belize."

"When did you take up snorkeling?"

Alex laughed. "When I met a hunky fireman. Thank heavens for videos on YouTube so I could at least talk coherently on the subject. He'll spend a lot more time at it than I intend to. There will be a beach, a lounge chair and several drinks with little umbrellas in them calling my name that I simply won't be able to ignore."

"Sounds like the perfect plan to me," Nicki said. She pulled on one side of the double glass doors leading into the tasting room that, according to the hours posted on the wall, had only opened five minutes ago. Hopefully the owner was already at his desk, working away.

The two women walked into the charming stucco-and-pink space, which had the definite vibe of a cozy cantina. Nicki spotted a lone server stacking glasses behind the circular bar in the center of the room.

She walked up and leaned against the gleaming wood top and smiled at the woman who barely looked old enough to be pouring wine. "Hi."

"Can I help you?" The server's long bangs didn't quite cover the diamond-looking stud over one eyebrow.

"Yes, thank you. I'm here to see Bill Stacy."

The girl with a flat, thin fall of blond hair trickling down her back blinked at Nicki. "Okay. I think I saw his car out back. Um. Do you have an appointment?"

"Not exactly," Nicki improvised. "But we spoke at a Holland's tasting event and he asked me to stop by any time." Nicki couldn't remember if Bill Stacy had said that, but she was sure he would have if he'd had the chance.

"I write for *Food & Wine Online*," she threw in for good measure.

"Okay." The server looked over at Alex.

"I'm a doctor," Alex supplied.

"Of what?" the girl asked. "I mean, a couple of my teachers at the college are doctors. The one I have right now for Modern English Lit is one."

Alex shot Nicki a sideways glance when her friend raised her hand to hide a smile. "I'm one of those doctors you'd see if you went to a hospital."

"Oh." The server went back to looking bored, but at least she walked to the other side of the bar and picked up the phone.

Nicki could only hear one side of the conversation, which consisted of a couple of single-syllable words, but as soon as the girl hung up she turned around and smiled at Alex.

"Bill says to come right up. The stairs are through that door over there." She pointed toward the other side of the room. "His office is at the end of the hallway."

Once they were in the stairwell, Nicki poked Alex in the back. "I guess being a doctor counts more than a lowly writer."

"Well, she knew other doctors. She probably doesn't know any other writers," Alex pointed out. Then she winked at her friend. "Or she thinks doctors are smarter than writers. It's a common misconception."

"Funny," Nicki muttered.

The fact that Alex was much better at school than Nicki went without saying. But to be fair, Alex always maintained that there were a lot of other ways to be smart than just in a classroom.

Given how many times she'd had to rescue her friend, the extremely intelligent doctor, from awkward social situations, Nicki had to agree with that. Then there was the time Alex had been robbed because she'd decided walking through a shabby part of New York City at three in the morning was a good shortcut to take after her long shift at the hospital. Nicki had lectured the not-so-street-smart doctor for over an hour after that one.

"Where did she say his office was?" Alex peered down the dimly lit hallway as Nicki climbed the last stair.

"At the end of the hallway." Nicki stepped around Alex just when the door opened. Bill stood on the other side with a smile on his face.

"Welcome, ladies. Come in and make yourselves comfortable."

Nicki, with Alex half a step behind her, crossed into the sparsely furnished room with a large window on one side, and a picture of a bull rider on the opposite wall.

Bill grinned at Nicki. "That's my baby brother. He preferred the rodeo circuit over going into the family business. Did okay for himself, too. But he's retired now. Bull riding is a young man's game. He owns a feed and grain store in Colorado."

He went to stand behind his desk, waiting until Nicki and Alex took their seats before settling into his office chair.

"What *is* your family business, Bill?" Nicki asked.

"I forget you're fairly new to the area." Bill chuckled. "It's making wine. My parents owned The White Crown and did pretty well there. Everyone believed dad was the winemaker and mom kept the books, but the truth is that dad ran the business and mom had the final say on the wine production. She had a great instinct for when a good wine had aged exactly the right amount of time."

"Then you're the second generation of winery owners?" Alex asked.

"I am. And I don't believe we've met."

Nicki immediately apologized. "I'm sorry. That was certainly rude of me. This is my good friend, Dr. Alex Kolman. Alex, please meet Bill Stacy, the owner of Todos."

"It's a pleasure to meet you, Mr. Stacy." Alex smiled. "I was admiring your tasting room earlier. It's very warm and inviting."

"Thank you, and call me Bill. I'm glad to meet you too. My sister's a doctor. Has a practice up in Portland."

He leaned back in his chair and winked at Nicki. "Been expecting you. I wondered if my feelings should be hurt because I wasn't higher on your list of suspects."

"Higher?" Nicki wrinkled her nose slightly. "What do you mean?"

"Winery owners may be business rivals, but we do talk to each other. I know you've been out to grill Jim and Jeremy, so it was only a matter of time before you showed up here. But I heard a rumor the chief isn't too happy about your nosing around and asking questions."

Nicki bit her lip. Like Jenna would say, you gotta love small towns and the efficiency of their gossip mills.

"Are you going to tattle on me to the chief?" she asked, relieved when he shook his head.

"Not me. You go ahead and throw out any question you want. I'll do my best to answer it." He smiled and lifted one foot to rest it on the opposite knee. "Shoot."

"I didn't realize The White Crown belonged to your parents. Do you blame George for your family losing it?" Nicki asked. It was a bold question, and out of the corner of her eye she saw Alex's neck and arm tense up.

But Bill only shrugged. "If you know the story then you know the answer to that. Of course I do. Wouldn't you?"

"But you rehired him as head winemaker at Todos. If you blamed him for losing your parents' legacy, why did you do that?"

"Business is business, Nicki, and the wine industry is a cutthroat one. Lancer put it out that I had inferior grapes in my production and so an inferior wine. He'd just introduced one of the best chardonnays to ever come on the market, so my mediocre production couldn't logically be blamed on him, even if it should have been. Lancer was the reigning winemaker in the region when I opened Todos, so it was good for business to hire him again." He paused and rubbed a hand over his chin. "There was no love lost between us, so I'd bet he took the job out of guilt. Probably the last decent feeling the man had."

"Then the dislike you were showing at the tasting event was real?" Nicki asked.

"Absolutely. But I didn't kill him. I might have come back here and had a toast to the guy that did, but it wasn't me."

"Actually, that's a healthy reaction," Alex observed. "A scary one, too."

The winery owner laughed. "If your friend, the amateur detective, intends to interview everyone who disliked Lancer, you'll both be talking to a lot of people."

"You mentioned rumors earlier. I heard one that you were looking to replace George even before he was killed."

"You've got powerful ears, Nicki. I kept that pretty quiet."

"So it's true?"

"Yes." Bill didn't sound as friendly as he had before.

"Also heard a rumor that you stopped looking for a new head winemaker a few weeks ago," Nicki went on, keeping her gaze on him and not backing down from his intense stare.

"All right. I'll admit to that too."

Nicki raised one eyebrow. "You found someone to replace George?"

"I have," Bill said. "But that's off the record or I'll deny I ever said it. It won't be announced until next month. I've sampled this winemaker's blend, and it will beat anything Lancer could have come up with."

"Then why the delay?"

He shrugged. "Business reasons that have nothing to do with

Lancer's murder." He glanced at his watch. "Is that all your questions?"

"No. Why was Geri here?" When he looked startled, Nicki smiled. "She was driving out as we came into the parking lot."

Bill relaxed back into his seat again. "She was doing a barrel swap. Wineries trade barrels sometimes, depending on what type we need."

"You mean such as American or French oak?"

Bill nodded. "Is that it then?"

"Only one more thing," Nicki said. "Where did you disappear to during the tasting event?" She wasn't sure he had, but thought she'd try the shot-in-the-dark approach.

"Who told you that? Chief Turnlow?"

Nicki didn't confirm or deny that, but simply smiled back at him.

"Like I told the chief, I went to the men's room."

"Can anyone verify that?" Nicki was proud of how professional she sounded, even if she had heard that line a thousand times on TV.

"I have no idea." The owner of Todos rolled his eyes. "Treating a trip to the john as if it was a social occasion and looking around for someone to talk to is what women do. Men don't. I didn't notice if anyone else was in there while I was doing my business."

## 19

"Remind me why we're here instead of enjoying a nice lunch in town? Or better yet, the smell of that wonderful eggplant Parmesan that you make? The one with the buttered breadcrumb topping?" Alex asked. "Accompanied by a fabulous red wine, of course."

"Well first, to get a fabulous red, you'd have to go further inland than Sonoma or the Russian River wine countries. And second, it's just a quick stop to take Geri up on her offer of a tour, so my special eggplant Parmesan is way too much of a bribe."

"Fine. But I expect a decent lunch in town after this, and if anything strange or annoying happens on this little detour, then making eggplant Parmesan is in your immediate future," Alex followed Nicki into the tasting room at Holland Winery.

"Agreed." Nicki spotted Kurt behind the bar, and at the far end was none other than Geri, drying glasses. *Lucky break for me,* Nicki thought. *Now I won't have to go searching all over the winery for her.* She waved at the assistant, hiding her smile at the pained expression on Geri's face.

She and Alex strolled over to the bar, with Alex turning to talk with Kurt and Nicki to face Geri.

"Hi. Taking a break from your winemaking duties?"

Geri picked up a glass and started drying it, keeping her gaze firmly on her hands. "It's a quiet week after the hard work from the crush."

"Well, I wanted to stop in and see how you're doing after everything that's happened." Nicki waited patiently until Geri finally finished with the glass and looked up.

"I'm okay. Planning the memorial helped a little."

Nicki slowly nodded. "I can understand that. It helped to make that lasagna. It made me feel as if I was doing something useful in the middle of all the chaos."

"Oh. Yes. Well." Geri cut short her stammering by clamping her lips into a thin line. She took a deep breath. "I can't remember if I thanked you for bringing your lasagna to the memorial gathering. I didn't realize that you might want the aluminum pan back."

"I don't," Nicki hurried to reassure her. "That's why I used it, so you wouldn't have to bother with returning a dish."

"Oh, good. Well then, I should..." Geri froze when Nicki cheerfully cut in.

"But I would really like to take you up on your offer of a tour of the winery. It would be helpful for my blog to see as much of the production operation as I can."

"I don't remember offering to give you a tour," Geri stammered.

"You didn't?" Nicki did her best to look crushed. "Are you sure? Between going with you to find George and discovering his body instead, and the articles I've had to get finished for the magazine, and making the lasagna for the memorial, I was so certain we talked about a tour. I've really been looking forward to it too." Nicki hung her head.

"Well, I guess I could arrange it."

Even though there wasn't a drop of enthusiasm in the assistant's voice, Nicki jumped on her words anyway.

"Do you have time now?"

"Now?" Geri held her towel over the row of glasses. "I'm pretty busy today."

Nicki cast a pointed look at the drying towel in her hand. "Oh. I thought you said it was a quiet week." She looked over at Alex and Kurt who were both listening to her conversation with Geri.

"I don't know if you've ever met my good friend, Dr. Alex Kolman? We shared an apartment in New York City before we both decided to move to California. Alex, this is Geri Gant, the assistant winemaker at Holland."

Alex leaned forward and held out her hand. "We met the day Chief Turnlow came to look over the crime scene and found Nicki poking into it. But I'm pleased to see you again, Geri."

Geri briefly shook the outstretched hand before snatching hers away to continue drying the glasses while remaining stubbornly silent.

"I'd love a tour of the winery," Alex said. "Nicki's told me how difficult a time it's been for both of you."

"Oh go on, Geri," Kurt said. "You love telling people how wine is made, and Nicki's lasagna really was great. It's the least we can do. I can handle the customers alone for a while." He grinned. "The crowd isn't that big."

Nicki and Alex looked over at the lone customer in the room before returning their gazes to Geri.

Scrunching her face up into a grimace, Geri gave a short nod and tossed her towel on top of the bar. "I guess I can spare a few minutes. Why don't we start in the private tasting area? It's that way." She pointed to the opposite end of the room, over near the doors.

"That would be great," Nicki was all smiles as Geri led the way while Alex fell into step beside her.

For the next fifteen minutes, the two women listened to Geri go on about how the smaller, separate room was used for the different private parties the winery booked there, and even how

the decor was changed with the seasons. They asked polite questions until Geri relaxed enough to take them through the front
doors and around to the rear of the building. When they were
right across from the backdoor leading into the hallway and the
room where George Lancer was murdered, Nicki stopped.

"Before we see the production areas, Geri, I noticed a barrel
room next to the one that was sealed off by the police. With all
the excitement, I haven't had a chance to see it yet."

Nicki didn't give the assistant time to answer. She made a
beeline for the backdoor, yanking it open and heading straight
down the dark hallway. She heard the swift clip of shoes behind
her. Satisfied the other two had come along as well, she breezed
past George's private room and stepped through the archway into
the large space with the separated rows of barrels.

"So, what is this used for? It's a bit far away from the production area, isn't it?" Nicki asked.

Geri barely stood inside the archway. With a deep sigh she
leaned over and flipped on the light. "The winery doesn't store
any of the production in here. This is strictly for the employees
who make their own personal blends."

"Really?" Alex said. "Isn't that interesting? Do you or Kurt
have any wine in here?"

The older woman walked further into the room and started
pointing at the various stacks against the walls. "That group
belongs to Victor, and those over there are more of George's.
Mine are right here."

She gestured to the twelve-barrel group Nicki had seen
marked with one "6" on top of another. Nicki realized it wasn't a
"6" at all, but a "G", for Geri Gant.

Nicki did a slow turn, pretending to inspect each stack. "Why
didn't George put those into his private room?"

"He probably didn't feel they were good enough to be in
there," Geri said.

"Makes sense," Nicki agreed. "We waved at you this morning, but I guess you didn't see us."

"What?"

"This morning," Nicki repeated. "When you were driving out of the Todos parking lot."

"Oh," Geri got the one word out, then stood and stared at Nicki.

"Checking out the competition maybe?" Alex asked, a teasing note in her voice.

"No. That is, I wasn't spying. I mean I was there on business." Geri stopped and rubbed her hands together. "Delivering barrels. They needed a few extra and we could spare them."

She hurried over to a cabinet next to the archway and opened one of its doors revealing a row of wine glasses. "Would you like a taste?"

"A taste? Of George's wine?" Alex asked.

"No, no. I can't do that. I meant of *my* wine," Geri said, already pulling out glasses.

Nicki and Alex exchanged a look while Geri's back was turned. Nicki shrugged in answer to Alex's silent question.

"Of course. We'd love to try it," Nicki said.

Geri brought a couple of glasses and a thin pipette called a wine thief, over to her double line of barrels. She stepped around the front two barrels and put her hands on a third. She removed the bung, which was simply a large cork, from the hole all wine-makers drew samples from when tasting the wine still in a barrel. Using her wine thief, she withdrew a small amount of wine and piped it into the glasses before closing the barrel up again. With a tiny smile, she handed the glasses to Nicki and Alex.

"I've been creating a personal blend using American oak barrels for the last eight years. It takes a lot of practice."

Nicki took a tentative sip and quickly pursed her lips together. She shot a look at Alex whose eyes were practically crossed.

Peering into her glass, it dawned on Nicki why Jim Holland hadn't even considered promoting Geri to head winemaker.

Clearing her throat, Nicki managed not to wince. "It's certainly an interesting blend."

"It still needs another few weeks of aging, I think," Geri said with a nod.

"Yes, I believe so." Alex's voice was faint, but Nicki had to give her points for putting a tad of enthusiasm behind her words.

"Geri?" Victor suddenly appeared in the opening of the archway. "Kurt told me you were giving a tour to a couple of friends. I'm sorry to break it up, but Jim wants to see you right away."

"Okay." Geri turned back to Nicki. "I'm sorry. We'll have to continue this another day." She reached over and plucked the two glasses out of her audience's hands. "I'll take care of these. Victor can show you the way to the parking lot."

"Sure, sure," Victor said as Geri walked past him. He smiled at the two women she'd left behind.

"You ready to go?" He took a second, closer look at Alex. "Hey, I know you. Don't you work in the Emergency Room over at the hospital in Santa Rosa? I was there last month with my cousin, and I remember seeing you."

Alex took a deep breath and held out her hand. "I'm Dr. Kolman. It's nice to meet you."

"Victor is the warehouse foreman here at Holland," Nicki said. "Alex is a good friend of mine who wanted to see how a winery works. I wish we'd had time to see the production area."

"I'd be happy to show you," Victor offered. "If you aren't in too much of a hurry. I know doctors have pretty busy schedules."

*Unlike writers who spend their days lounging around conjuring up stories in their heads*, Nicki thought. But she kept a smile on her face and nodded.

"That would be great. Thanks."

"Well c'mon, Nicki." Victor waved them through the archway and fell into step beside Alex.

"Hey, Doc. I've been getting this pain along my lower back. It comes and goes—nothing steady. Do you think I should get it looked at?"

"Tell me a little more," Alex said. As Victor launched into a description of his back pain, Alex turned her head toward Nicki and mouthed one word--*eggplant*.

Twenty minutes later, having wandered between the huge tanks in the fermentation area, Victor took them into a room where barrels were stacked on top of each other.

"This is where we store our barrels to replace the ones that have reached the end of their lifespan for aging wine."

Alex looked around. "What do you do with the old barrels?"

"We sell them, mostly. Sometimes a few of the smaller wineries, or places just starting out, will come and buy them, but mostly we sell them to decorators or furniture stores. People like to use them in their gardens." He pointed to the one closest to them. "That's a brand-new, French oak barrel. It costs well over a thousand dollars."

"Wow!" Alex said, her eyes getting bigger. "For a barrel?"

Victor nodded while Nicki glanced over at the wall. Two clipboards hung there. She walked over and picked one up and started flipping through it while Victor kept on with his talk.

"The stock room is only open during the day, and every barrel taken out has to be entered into the inventory sheets along with what wine it was being used for, the date, and who took it. There's enough money invested in this room that it's locked up every night, and the only key is in the owner's safe. Not even the master key will open this room."

"That's very interesting," Alex said, her eyes narrowing at the signal Nicki was sending her behind Victor's back. "I'd love to learn more, but to be honest, I have one of those doctoring things I have to get to."

She looked over at Nicki when Victor frowned. "Don't we

have to go? You also have that story you need to send to your editor today, don't you?"

"Yes, I do," Nicki said. She headed for the door, grabbing onto Alex's arm on her way. "I didn't realize how late it was getting. We really have to be on our way." She glanced over at Victor and waved. "Loved the tour, thanks! Please let Kurt know this was more than enough payback for making the lasagna."

"Nice touch to keep him from asking us why the sudden rush," Alex said in a low voice as Nicki pulled her along. Once they'd reached the parking lot, she tugged her arm away. "All right. I can take it from here. Care to tell me what that was all about?"

"I'm not sure, but I'm glad we stopped by." Nicki unlocked the passenger door before heading around the car to the driver's side.

Alex got in and snapped on her seatbelt. "What did we learn besides the fact Geri is the world's worst winemaker? And I'll be tasting that concoction of hers in the back of my throat for the next week."

"It really was awful, wasn't it?" Nicki laughed. "That clipboard I was looking at? It listed all the French oak barrels that have been used at Holland Winery for the last year, either by staff for the winery, or bought by employees for their personal use."

"So?"

Nicki drummed two fingers against the steering wheel. "So, George Lancer hasn't taken one barrel out in over a year, even though it was in his contract that he could. And during the tour, I asked Victor if George fermented his wine in just the steel tank or in the tank and the barrel, and he specifically said the tank, and then the final aging in a barrel."

"And so?" Alex prompted.

"Well, after wine is fermented in a tank, it's transferred into barrels. What helps make each wine batch special is knowing not only what grapes to blend together, but how long to age the wine in the barrel," Nicki explained.

"Something Geri has never mastered," Alex said. "At least not that blending part. But what does this have to do with anything?"

"More than a year is too long for the barrel-aging process of a chardonnay," Nicki said.

Alex frowned. "Oh. Then where has George been getting his barrels for the last year? Or do you think he just had some extras lying around from last year? And by the way, I expect extra cheese on that eggplant Parmesan."

## 20

J enna and Alex were in Nicki's office, enjoying the perfectly prepared eggplant Nicki had made for dinner. It was past eight at night and none of them felt like doing dishes. Luckily, Nicki staunchly believed the taste of food was not altered in the least by the plate it was served on. So by unanimous vote, it was eggplant, on paper plates, in the office, as they enjoyed an excellent red Barbera wine from Amador County, over near the Eastern border of the State, and worked on the murder board.

"I'm not seeing anything jump out at me," Jenna said before forking up a big bite of eggplant, sauce and cheese from her plate. "Any one of the owners had enough reason to do in George— Jeremy for the possibility of being ruined, Bill for revenge and Jim for being cut out of the profits from the new blend. And they all disliked him."

"Which means we should keep Geri and Kurt on the list, because they didn't like the man either," Alex pointed out. "And they could have gained access to George's private room by simply walking into Jim's office and taking the key. Which hasn't turned up as far as we know."

"It's one of my questions for the chief." She sat at her desk and studied her computer screen as she brought up the rest of the documents Jenna had copied off George's machine. The man had certainly been obsessed with spreadsheets. He'd kept track of everything that way. Even his daily medications, which had included an extensive list of vitamins.

Jenna's fork froze midway to her mouth. "You're going to talk to the chief? After what he told you the last time he was here?"

Nicki's gaze stayed on the screen as she waved one hand in the air. "We're not doing anything illegal, and if we find something, it's our civic duty to let him know." She looked up and sighed. "Besides, Matt will make me tell him anyway. And if I don't, he'll call Chief Turnlow himself. And that'll *really* get me another visit from the local police."

"How about copying those documents you're looking at? That isn't illegal?" Alex asked.

"Probably. And if I'm sued by someone in George's family for invading his privacy, I'll be sure to apologize."

Jenna continued to eat her dinner and stare at the board. "Since George has no relatives, I guess that isn't going to be a problem."

"Back to this problem then," Alex said. "Jeremy and Bill have the strongest motives, but Jim, Geri and Kurt had the best opportunity."

"What about means?" Jenna asked. "That's the third thing, isn't it? Means, motive and opportunity? Or is it the first thing?"

Alex picked through her eggplant. "All of them. With the unfortunate rise in e-cigarettes, it isn't that hard to get hold of liquid nicotine anymore. You can even buy it already flavored. I checked on that. It can also be made fairly easily, if you're careful and don't get any of it on your skin. There's instruction videos on the Internet."

"Okay, we're back to motive and opportunity." Jenna put her empty paper plate down on the desk.

"And contradictions," Nicki said. When the other two stared at her, she walked over to the board and picked up a marker. She blocked off a space and titled it "Questions".

"Why go to the trouble of only poisoning the four bottles of wine? I mean the killer had no way of knowing which bottle George would use first, so of course all four of the bottles had to be poisoned. But why not just dump the nicotine into all the barrels and really ruin George? It's faster and there's less chance of being caught."

Alex shook her head. "It would take too much pure nicotine to contaminate an entire barrel much less ten of them. At least with enough to kill a person."

Nicki smiled. "Okay. We eliminate that. But why not ruin the other barrels anyway? If hurting George was the killer's intent, why leave most of his wine untouched? At least we're assuming they're untouched. We won't know for sure until the chief has them tested. Next question. Why hasn't anyone tasted the wine?"

"Because George was keeping it a secret?" Jenna asked.

"But these are business men. And good ones. Would Jeremy really give up twenty percent of his winery, and Jim take on the expense for the tasting event for a single case of the wine, not to mention hiring an expensive team of attorneys to get hold of the rest of it, if neither man had ever tasted it? Even Bill made sure to get a sample of a blend from the new guy he's hired. Why wouldn't the others have demanded one from George if they were going to invest a good amount of money into his blend?"

"You think they're both lying and really have tasted George's wine?" Alex made the question sound like a flat statement.

"It would be easy enough for Jim to sneak a sample, and Jeremy probably demanded one as well," Jenna said.

"I don't know," Nicki replied turning back to her screen and opening another spreadsheet with the title of "Monthly Budget" across the top. "It doesn't make any sense."

"If it's true that they've tasted the wine, then there's a couple of things we do know for sure. The blend is worth fighting a legal battle for, or giving up a chunk of your winery." Nicki glanced at her friends and reluctant co-conspirators. "And someone wanted George dead, but not ruin his new blend. I don't think George was killed because he was universally despised. If none of the barrels were touched, then I'd bet he was murdered for his wine."

Alex looked over at the board. "Who wanted George's special blend the most? Jim?"

"That won't make Maxie very happy," Jenna observed. "She thinks he's innocent."

"Maybe Stella?" Nicki stared at her computer screen.

"Who?" Jenna and Alex said at the same time.

"Stella, the ex-girlfriend. I'm looking at George's monthly budget, and he was way over his head with gambling losses. But he also paid this Stella a nice sum every month. I saw the amount on his bank statement but didn't know what it was for. Now I do. He has her name listed on this spreadsheet as one of his expenses, and for that very same amount. Except..." Nicki trailed off as she squinted and scrolled through the sheet.

Jenna put her plate down and stood up, peering at the spreadsheet over Nicki's shoulder. "Except what?"

"See here." Nicki pointed at a row. "He paid her every month going back as far as I've been able to look. But three months ago he stopped listing it as an expense, and it didn't show up anymore on his bank statements from then on either."

"It could be they had a love child and he decided to cut costs by becoming a deadbeat dad," Jenna said. "Kind of sounds like something he'd do."

"Stella left the winery around the same time George came out with his spectacular blend ten years ago." Nicki leaned back and frowned. "Maybe he was paying her off."

"Paying her off for what?" Jenna asked. "A love child makes more sense."

"Maybe. But tomorrow while Alex is out on her morning run and you're sleeping in, I'll go have a talk with Stella."

Jenna shook her head. "How do you propose to do that?"

"By enjoying a very nice breakfast at Sandy's diner." Nicki glanced at the clock display on the bottom of her computer screen. "Oh shoot. It's almost nine o'clock. I'm supposed to call Matt at nine."

"Since you're still annoyed with him, why are you calling him? Let him stew for a while," Alex advised.

"He could stew enough to refuse to give me any more assignments, or demand I take one far away from here," Nicki said. And her bank account could not afford for Matt to cut her off, even for a few weeks.

"Well, he might do that anyway. I hear Alaska is nice this time of year," Jenna said.

Nicki scooped up a handful of paper clips and threw them at the computer geek.

---

THE NEXT MORNING Nicki pulled into a parking spot right in front of Sandy's diner. The restaurant, with cute, checked curtains across its front windows, was the only business with any customers at 7:30 a.m. on a Tuesday. Except for the Starbucks on the opposite corner of the square. But most of the permanent residents in and around Soldoff preferred drinking coffee in their own kitchens, so the street in front of Sandy's had more activity than the one facing its well-known rival.

Nicki smiled at the young, gum-chewing hostess standing behind the front desk.

"Good morning."

The teenager looked up and popped her gum before offering up a bored "hi" in return. She picked up a menu and stepped around the desk. "You here by yourself?"

"Yes, I am. And I wonder if Stella is working this morning?" Nicki asked.

The girl sighed and put the menu down. "Yeah. She's on station three. But she can't come over and talk to you while she's working. Sandy doesn't allow that. You'll have to wait until she goes on break."

"I'm an old friend of hers. Do you think I could sit at one of her tables?"

The hostess gave her a suspicious look. "Are you going to eat or just order a cup of coffee?"

Not wanting to miss her opportunity to talk with Stella, Nicki figured a breakfast at Sandy's was a small price to pay. "Oh, I want breakfast. And I'd prefer to sit at one of Stella's tables."

"Okay. It's a slow morning, so there's plenty of empty ones." The girl picked up the menu again and started walking toward the back of the restaurant. Apparently being a newer employee, Stella drew the section away from the front windows and back by the kitchen and bathrooms.

"I'll tell her you're here." The hostess tossed the menu on the table and sauntered toward the front of the place.

Nicki tore off a paper towel from the roll on the table, assuming it was meant to be the napkins since there weren't any others in sight, and placed it across her lap before picking up the menu. At least the table was clean, and so was the silverware. She'd certainly eaten in worse establishments.

A woman with bright red hair and lipstick to match, wearing a yellow uniform that was too short and tennis shoes that had seen better days, approached the table, her green eyes looking Nicki over.

"Hi. Kelly says you asked for one of my tables because we're old friends. But I don't recognize you."

*So much for polite, introductory small talk*, Nicki thought.

"I needed an excuse to sit here so I threw out the first one that came to mind," Nicki said, going with the honest approach. If this whole investigation had taught her anything, it was that she wasn't any good at lying.

Stella raised a heavily lined eyebrow. "Why did you need to sit at one of my tables? I don't serve the food any different from the other waitresses."

"But I don't want to talk to them," Nicki said. "I want to talk to you."

"Fine. But you have to order something, and it has to be more than coffee."

"That's what Kelly said." Nicki smiled and pointed to a vegetarian omelet. "I'll take that with egg whites and fruit."

Taking out her notepad, Stella wrote the order down, commenting without looking up. "The egg whites are extra."

"That's fine."

"Toast or English muffin?"

Nicki folded her hands and patiently walked through the various choices until Stella finally looked up.

"Anything else?"

The waitress was making it very clear she wasn't going to engage in a social conversation, so Nicki decided to take a bold chance.

"Only a few words."

"Okay," Stella laughed. "You can have ten or so, and I'll expect a decent tip."

"I know about George's wine and the money."

Stella's jaw dropped open and she took a quick look around. "Keep your voice down."

"I will if you agree to talk to me. Otherwise the police chief might be interested in hearing about it. The station is right across the square, so I wouldn't have to walk very far." Nicki didn't actually say she wouldn't tell Chief Turnlow anything because she certainly *was* going to tell him. But she didn't want Stella to know that. At least not yet.

"Fine," the waitress said. "My break is in thirty minutes. We can talk then. In the meantime, I'm going to put your order in."

When Nicki's food came, she picked her way through it. The omelet wasn't bad. The vegetables still had a crispness to them, so the line cook hadn't turned them into mush. But she didn't touch the canned fruit swimming in a small bowl. Luckily she didn't have to wait long before Stella caught her attention and jerked her head toward the front door.

Nodding, Nicki stood up and left a generous tip on the table before hurrying to pay the rest of her bill at the front cashier's desk. Stella passed close to her halfway there.

"Meet me around the corner," she whispered.

Now completely curious about the big mystery surrounding George's wine, Nicki made her way to the designated spot and stood waiting, feeling she stuck out like a sore thumb loitering on the nearly empty sidewalk. Fortunately, Stella showed up within five minutes and led her further down the street until they came to a bus bench. The older woman sat and indicated Nicki should do the same.

"Who told you about the wine?"

"George did, in a way," Nicki said. "Stella, he's dead, so there's not any reason to keep it secret anymore."

She pulled out a cigarette. "Do you mind if I smoke? We're outside and all, so it shouldn't bother you."

"Go ahead." Nicki didn't like anything about cigarettes, but she didn't want Stella to be uncomfortable and clam up.

The waitress lit one end and took a long drag. "I wish I could say I picked up the habit from George."

"George didn't smoke," Nicki said.

The waitress laughed. "You *did* know him. No, he never got in the habit. He only used it as an excuse to spend time on the phone with his bookie. And he only lit up outside so he could keep the smoke blowing away from him. Told me he was allergic to it, but I think he was scared of getting cancer. He was always talking about the diseases he didn't want to get."

Nicki smiled. "He took a lot of vitamins."

"Yeah, he did."

"Tell me about the wine," Nicki said.

Stella pursed her very red lips and eyed Nicki for a long moment. "Not much to tell. It was ten years ago. He and I were both assistant winemakers at the time and he desperately wanted the top job. More pay, more prestige, more of just about every-thing. But he needed something to set him apart. We all made our own blends, even back then, and George was no different. He was a good winemaker, but not a great one. Didn't possess the nose or the palette. But I did."

Nicki's mind raced, putting the pieces together. "The wine he introduced ten years ago was actually yours?"

"Sure was," Stella said, her eyes staring straight ahead. "But there was no way Jim Holland was going to let a woman be his head winemaker. I doubt if he would have bothered to even give me credit for the blend. So, I made a deal with my boyfriend." She looked over at Nicki and smiled. "George and I were an item in those days."

"I did hear that." Nicki smiled back at her. "The deal was for George to bring your blend out under his name?"

"For a price. I sold him the wine. And when it became a spec-tacular hit, he had to pay me every month to keep my mouth shut."

"You were blackmailing him?" Nicki gasped. That certainly explained the regular payments.

"And enjoyed my life, not having to work and being able to take a nice trip every once in a while."

"Until three months ago, when he stopped paying you."

"He told you that?" Stella's voice rose a notch. She snorted when Nicki's shoulders lifted into a shrug. "Did he tell you why? He said he didn't *need* to pay me anymore. That if I told anyone now, no one would believe me, especially because he had a new blend coming out that was even better than mine." She smoothed out the too-short skirt of her uniform and lifted one leg straight out from the bench. "When the money was cut off I had to find a job, and now I stand on my aching feet all day."

"Were the payments being cut off the reason you had that argument with him at Trax?"

"I wanted him to face me and tell me he didn't care about our deal anymore. I couldn't show up at Holland Winery. Even after all this time, Jim would have tossed me off the place. He was furious when I left. He considered it being disloyal to him. When I told him I was leaving, he threatened to make sure I'd never work in the wine industry again. And I didn't want to go to Todos because Bill Stacy might recognize me, and he's good friends with Jim Holland. That left Trax. I didn't know that owner, and he didn't know me."

"Who else knows about your wine switch?" Nicki asked.

"You're the first one I've ever heard of who George told," Stella said, taking a drag on her cigarette.

Nicki waved a hand in front of her face to keep the smoke away. She didn't correct Stella's assumption that George had confided the secret to her. "What about you? Did you ever tell anyone?"

"A couple of people," Stella admitted. "But none that would blab. One of the interns I stayed friendly with, and Victor knew, of course. We were all tight back then."

"Victor? The warehouse foreman?"

"That's his title now, but back then he drove a forklift and did mostly manual labor. He helped move my wine to George's personal spot in our shared barrel room. It was about that time we all came up with the idea to mark our barrels." Stella grinned. "A little secret we kept from George."

Nicki had already seen the marks, so that wasn't news. "Anyone else?"

"My mom, but she passed away a few years ago," Stella said. She dropped her cigarette and ground it out with the toe of her shoe. "I wonder if you could do me a favor?"

"What's that?" Nicki asked.

"Take my cell number. If you find out who killed George, can you let me know? He meant something to me once, and in a strange way he always has. And not just because of the money."

"Sure." Nicki tapped Stella's phone number into her contact list. "Is there anything else you can think of that might help find his killer?"

Stella shook her head. "No. I don't know who hated him enough to want him dead. But there's one thing I *do* know. If George really had a spectacular new blend like he claimed, there's as much chance that he came up with it as there is that he was French. Like I said. The man didn't have the nose or the palette. You can't change that, even after all these years."

## 21

"I was stunned. It's a wonder I didn't fall off that bus bench when she told me their big secret." Nicki finished pouring a class of the lovely chardonnay she'd picked up from her last trip to the Russian River wine region near the coast.

"I still can't believe it," Maxie declared. "George passing off someone else's blend as his own? Why, it's the biggest scandal to ever hit our Sonoma wines. And it could ruin Jim Holland!"

"It certainly would be a huge scandal if it became public knowledge," Nicki said. "But Stella wants it kept confidential, and we should honor her wishes. It was ten years ago. That wine is long gone, and now George Lancer is too. There's no point in dragging Holland Winery and Stella through the mud."

"The one who gains the most from keeping the secret safe is Jim Holland." Maxie didn't look happy about that conclusion at all.

The four women were gathered around Nicki's kitchen counter, enjoying an afternoon glass of wine while they pondered murder.

"I agree. Jim Holland has the most to lose if it got out, but why worry about it ten years later?" Alex wondered out loud. "Besides,

George was right when he told Stella no one would believe her now. Why should anyone believe her? And what does it have to do with his murder? It can't be over him revealing he didn't blend the wine that made him famous. Why kill him to keep him quiet over something he'd never talk about anyway?"

"It's scary that I actually followed that," Jenna said. "Maybe Stella is right, and he didn't create this new one either. Would someone kill him to keep that a secret? Because then the winery sponsoring the new blend has the most to lose. And that would be Trax."

"But to make it a real threat, it would need to be after Trax was officially announced as the sponsor. George was killed before that," Nicki pointed out.

"What are we missing?" Alex glanced around the group.

"Besides another bottle of this excellent wine?" Jenna poured the last of it into her glass. "I don't have a clue."

They all looked at Nicki, who held her hands up and laughed. "I don't either."

"What do we do next?" Maxie asked.

Alex hopped off her stool. "Jenna and I are going to do a little shopping before the crowds roll in for the art and wine festival tomorrow. You're welcome to come with us." She glanced over at Nicki and winked. "Our writer-blogger friend will very likely be forced to call on Chief Turnlow in the morning after she makes her nightly call to Matt."

"Well you'll certainly have an earful to give him tonight." Maxie smiled at Nicki before switching her attention to Alex. "I'd love to go shopping. I have my eye on a lovely pair of sandals at one of the shops on the square. They're very expensive, but I'm sure my Mason won't mind since he's in the dog house for that lecture he gave me after he found out about Chief Turnlow's visit."

"He is?" Alex looked fascinated by the idea. "I didn't realize men could still be relegated to the dog house. Tyler always claims that's old-fashioned, and just a way for women to get make-up gifts."

"Of course it is," Maxie said. "What's wrong with that? Doesn't your fiancé enjoy buying you a trinket or two and spoiling you a bit?"

Jenna laughed. "Ah. So it's really for his own good? To let him do something he enjoys?"

"Of course, dear. There's a lot of things couples enjoy when it comes to making up."

"Thank you for that mental picture," Jenna groused just as Nicki's phone rang.

Rob's picture popped up on the caller ID. Nicki sighed. Naturally she loved seeing him, but she hoped this wasn't one of the very few times he managed to get home early from his business trip.

"Hi, Rob." Nicki rolled her eyes as three sets of feet hit the floor. Within seconds she was all alone in the kitchen.

"Nicki? Are you there?"

"I'm here." Nicki sat on a now vacant stool and took a deep breath. "It's nice to hear your voice. How's the trip going?"

"It was fine until last night. I talked to Antonio, and he said you missed the first class. Where were you?"

Nicki threw her head back and closed her eyes. The first class was last night?

"He covered the beginning of winemaking from ancient times to the middle ages. He said it was very well received by his students."

"I'm sure it was," Nicki replied. "It sounds fascinating."

"Okay. It sounds deadly dull. But the next class will be all about barrel making, selling and storage. That should give you plenty of color for your magazine articles and blog."

Nicki wasn't so sure. What was so interesting about how to store barrels?

"So, why didn't you go to the class?" There was a distinct note of impatience in Rob's voice.

Nicki decided to stick with being honest. "I forgot, Rob. That's all. I've been very busy here with a project and the time simply got away from me." She didn't mention the project was murder, and refused to count that as being dishonest. It fell more into the category of avoiding an argument. She might even use that same rationale later tonight when she called Matt.

"I'm sure everything you're doing now is important to your career today, but you should also invest a little in your future," Rob said.

She laughed. "I don't have any plans to go into barrel making or storing, Rob. I'm not very good at making or fixing things. That's more Jenna's forte. I usually call someone."

"Funny." Rob's impatient tone scaled up a notch. "What I mean is that you shouldn't ignore the opportunity to meet the movers and shakers of the future. Who knows? One of the people in this class might be the next greatest winemaker in California. Maybe even the world. It could happen. *Someone* will be the best winemaker one day in the future. Why not someone from the class? And that guy would then be in your network. It's a terrific chance to meet an up-and-coming genius."

"Geez, Rob. You're in the wrong end of retailing. Instead of buying, you should be selling," Nicki said. She carried the phone down the hall and into the bathroom. While Rob continued to point out the enormous opportunities she was missing by not going to Antonio's lectures, she reached into the medicine cabinet and grabbed the bottle of aspirin.

Telling herself it wasn't her boyfriend's conversation but the shock of hearing Stella's story that had given her a headache, she headed back to the kitchen for a glass of water.

"That's why the established people in the industry give these classes, you know. It's a good way to find the emerging talent in the field."

"Uh huh," Nicki responded automatically then suddenly stopped and frowned. "Wait a minute. What did you say?"

"I said that there's usually someone in these classes with the talent to be an important force, and..."

"No. I mean about people in the industry teaching these classes." A sudden picture of a stack of papers with red letters across the top flashed through Nicki's mind. Not simply letters, but grades. Of course!

"Rob, I need to go. But I promise, promise, promise I will be at Antonio's next class. Okay?" She only waited long enough to hear his grumbling agreement before adding, "I have to go. We'll talk later."

She tapped the disconnect button, slipped the phone into her back pocket and headed for her office. Within five minutes she had the local college's current class catalog up on the screen. She put the cursor into the search box and typed: *Winemaking.*

---

"AND THEN SHE said that the wine was hers, and she'd made a bargain for George to bring it out under his name."

Matt whistled. "Whoa. That is huge, Nicki."

"I know. But I'm not going to print it anywhere, Matt. Stella told me it was off the record."

"Did she?" Matt's eyes narrowed behind his glasses. "Was that before or after she admitted it wasn't George's wine?"

"After. And that might make her statement fair game. But it's not ethical and I won't do it," Nicki said quietly.

He frowned at her. "Stop giving me that half-accusatory, half-kicked-puppy look. I'm not going to publish it either."

Nicki let out a sigh of relief. She'd debated with herself on whether to tell Matt what Stella had said, and in the end decided he was not the kind of editor who'd go after a sensational headline just to make a profit. And she'd been right.

"Thank you," Nicki said softly, a happy smile blooming on her lips. It was nice to be so sure she could count on Matt to do the right thing.

"The fact we're not going to blast it all over the magazine doesn't mean it won't get out. I'm amazed it's stayed a secret this long." Matt rubbed his chin. "Who else have you told?"

"Only my group," Nicki said.

"So that means Jenna and Alex. Which in turn means Tyler too."

"And Maxie," Nicki added.

"So Mason will also know." Matt gave her a crooked smile. "You remember Mason? The former police chief who still talks regularly with the current police chief?"

Nicki groaned. "He does, doesn't he? But I mean, what's the point? How does something that happened ten years ago affect George's death now? If someone wanted to kill him so he'd keep silent, they would have done it a long time ago."

"Jim Holland has a reason," Matt said. "If you just found out the secret, he could have just discovered the secret too. With George dead, his winery's reputation stays intact, and he'll likely get his hands on the new wine. Brennan over at Trax had a good reason too. He's already in debt, and George breaking their agreement would make a bad situation worse. Or Stella, because he stopped paying her and cut off her life style."

"Or a young rising talent who George promised the moon to, and then realized that the famous winemaker couldn't deliver. Or rather, George didn't intend to deliver," Nicki said.

"And that was a definite sidetrack." Matt leaned closer to the screen. "Care to let me in on why you went there."

"Okay, but hear me out. George must have known that Holland and Todos were looking to replace him. The wine industry is like a small town when it comes to rumors and gossip. I'm sure he'd heard something."

"Go on," Matt said.

"The fame from his last personal blend had faded away."

Matt snorted. "That's an understatement. It died a good five years ago."

"Are you going to listen or not?" Nicki demanded.

"Sorry," Matt mumbled. "I'm listening."

"George simply couldn't make a blend to match his last one. Stella said he didn't possess the nose or the palette. Which means he could have been searching for another Stella. Someone with the talent but not the means to get the wine to market."

"And he'd go looking for that where? You said Geri was definitely not on that list. Maybe Victor?" Matt asked.

"Or someone outside their little circle. Like a college student studying winemaking. Someone young who works at a winery and brought George one of his blends to get the expert opinion of his professor." Nicki nodded at Matt.

"Professor? You think George Lancer was moonlighting as a college professor?"

"I know he was. I found his name in the class catalog at the local junior college. He was teaching *Beginning Winemaking*." Nicki ended on a triumphant note.

Matt was silent for a full minute. She could almost see the wheels turning in his head. "That's not something George would do out of the goodness of his heart. But why would he look there?"

"Simple," Nicki said. "Between paying Stella and his growing gambling debts, George was broke. How was he going to make another deal like he had with Stella when he had no money?"

Matt took up the narrative. "So he starts looking for an unknown talent. Someone who'd be willing to work for peanuts, or even for the promise of a big payoff in the future?"

"But the part I haven't figured out yet is why would this unknown talent kill George? That's cutting off your nose to spite your face, isn't it?" Nicki curled her lips inward as she tried to reason it out.

"We don't need to figure it out. Chief Turnlow does. That's his job. You have to talk to him tomorrow." Matt crossed his arms over his chest and waited.

"Why? It's only my little theory. There are all kinds of reasons George might have had for teaching at the college," Nicki said.

"Uh huh." Matt's arms didn't budge. "What you're saying is that someone may very well have killed George to keep whoever the real winemaker is a secret. Which means *anyone* who knows would be a threat. And you know the secret. So do your friends. To keep out of trouble, go tell the chief and let him deal with it. Despite your murder board and persuasive bribes with delicious goodies, the police can still tap into more resources than you can."

Nicki thought it over. She didn't like taking orders but Matt had a point. Everything she knew, her friends knew as well. If there was even a sliver of a chance that the knowledge could put them in danger, she wasn't going to take it.

"All right. I'll go see the chief in the morning."

## 22

"This is very cozy," Maxie said, causing a burst of laughter to erupt behind her.

All four women were piled into Nicki's car for the short trip into Soldoff. Jenna and Alex had sandwiched themselves into the back seat, leaving Maxie the marginally roomier passenger space in front.

Nicki grinned at her landlady. "When I become as well-known in my field as you are in genealogy research, I'll be happy to buy a Mercedes, so we can ride around in comfort and style. But until then, this is what you get."

Jenna leaned forward. "It's good to see how the other half lives, Maxie."

"I've already lived this way. When I was your age, as a matter of fact. I didn't have one qualm at leaving it behind." She cast a look over at Nicki. "Are you sure we'll make it there and back? The engine doesn't sound happy."

"The car's fine," Nicki assured her. "I'm more worried about finding a parking spot. It's sure to be a madhouse in town today with the festival in full swing."

Her prediction proved to be true. The latest art and wine festival had kicked off the day before and was getting an early start today. The square was already jammed, with cars and pedestrians occupying every available inch of ground. Nicki slowly maneuvered her car toward the tiny Soldoff Police Department on the opposite side of the square.

"Since you'll be stopping in to see Chief Turnlow before joining us for a bit of wine tasting, I'm sure we're entitled to one of the spots in front of the station," Maxie declared.

"It's a little early for wine tasting," Alex said. "I've heard you say that alcohol is an afternoon drink."

"It is, dear. Except on festival days, of course. The rule doesn't apply then." Maxie craned her neck as the compact car rounded the far corner of the square.

"And there's Danny, keeping a spot open for us." Maxie pointed to the young deputy standing on the sidewalk in front of the police department, watching the crowds of people stream by.

Since they were right there, and the space was indeed empty, Nicki pulled in. She gave Danny a friendly wave as the engine did its shuddering act before turning off.

"Hello Danny," she called out once she'd exited the car.

"Hi, Nicki." The brown-haired, brown-eyed deputy who had kept his linebacker form from his high school football days, flashed an ear-to-ear grin as he walked over and held the door for Maxie.

"Thank you, Danny. That's very gentlemanly of you." Maxie accepted his helping hand.

"Happy to help, Mrs. Edwards. But I'm not sure I can let you park here. The chief says we need to keep it open."

"Whatever for?" Maxie raised an inquiring eyebrow as she carefully draped her scarf back over her shoulder.

Danny looked from her to Nicki. "In case someone needs to come talk to us on police business."

"Well then, we don't have a problem. Nicki is here to see Chief Turnlow. On police business," Maxie assured him.

"You are?" Danny was back to smiling at Nicki.

"I am," she said. "Is he here?"

Danny nodded. "Yes, he is. I'll take you right in."

After a last nod to the other three women, Danny latched onto Nicki's arm and walked her into the police station. Nicki was sure if any of the town's residents had seen them together, they would have leaped to the conclusion that she was under arrest.

Fran looked up when they came through the door. "Hi, Nicki. If you've come into town to do alittle shopping, you picked a dreadful day for it. The place is bursting at the seams. And it isn't even lunchtime yet."

"Nicki's here to see the chief," Danny announced.

"Oh? Is that why you're dragging her around like a sack of potatoes?" Fran shook her head at the young deputy, who immediately turned a dark shade of crimson all the way up to his hairline. "You go on and walk through the square like the chief told you to. I'll tell him Nicki's here."

"No need." The chief filled the entire space of the narrow doorway leading into his office. He motioned for Nicki to follow him before he disappeared back inside.

"Thank you for the escort, Danny," Nicki said. The young deputy snatched off his hat and ducked his head in response.

Once he was out the front door, Fran laughed and winked at Nicki. "He sure has it bad for you. Now you go on in, the chief's waiting."

Nicki skirted around the counter and walked into the chief's office. He was sitting behind his desk with his hands folded in front of him. She took the same straight-backed chair she'd sat in the last time she'd been there.

"I hope you're here about something other than George Lancer's murder."

"Why is that, Chief?" Nicki asked.

"Because I remember asking you to stay away from it. Now please don't tell me you've been disobeying a direct request from your police department."

Nicki shrugged. "Fine, I won't tell you what we found out. I guess I can always write out an anonymous note and drop it in the mail."

When she made a move to rise the chief held out his hands and motioned for her to sit back down. "All right. I'll save the lecture for later, after I hear what you've come to tell me."

Nicki smiled. She'd been sure he'd want to know. "Have you had a chance to go over the information in George's computer yet?"

Chief Turnlow shook his head. "We've had our hands full preparing for this festival. But we'll get to it. I have a request into the State Police for more computer help."

"Well, one of the many spreadsheets George kept, had his monthly budget on it, and up until three months ago he was making regular payments to Stella, his former girlfriend."

"I'm guessing it wasn't for child support," the chief said.

"No. It was blackmail." Nicki kept any expression off her face when the chief sat up straighter in his chair.

"Blackmail? What was she blackmailing him for?"

"George didn't produce the blend that made him famous ten years ago. Stella did."

The chief lowered his brows and scowled at Nicki. "Did this Stella also make the wine George was going to serve at that special tasting event the day he died?"

Nicki shook her head. "No. But she doesn't believe George did either. She said he didn't have the talent."

He let out a breath and reached for a pad of paper and a pencil. "Go ahead and start at the beginning."

She did just that, telling the chief everything she'd learned since they'd last talked. Fifteen minutes later she sat back in her chair and looked at him expectantly. "Well, that's all of it. What do you think?"

"If you're expecting me to have some kind of Charlie Chan moment and name the killer, I'm going to have to disappoint you."

"Charlie Chan?" Nicki laughed at the reference to the 1920's detective.

"I'm a major fan. Sherlock Holmes is fine, but give me a good old Charlie Chan mystery any day. And I'm also a big fan of being listened to. Why didn't you come to me first and let us conduct the interview with Stella?"

"Because I wanted to hear her story first-hand," Nicki said.

"And because you're nosy." He smiled at Nicki's annoyed look. "Your friend, who's also a red-blooded, grown male, told me that."

"Matt. His name is Matt."

"Uh huh." He shifted in his seat and reached for a folder from the inbox on his desk. "I should be annoyed with you and probably will be later, but right now I'm going to do some sharing too." He flipped open the folder and picked up a sheet of paper. "The lab test came back on the wine. Aside from the usual readings you'd get from wine, there was also a high concentrate of pure nicotine and components that make up a cherry flavoring in all four bottles. Nothing in the eight barrels. There was no nicotine in any of them." He dropped the paper back into the folder and looked over at Nicki. "Which means the wine was definitely poisoned, and this case is now officially a homicide. That entitles the department to request more help from the State guys, and the police department in Santa Rosa."

"That sounds like a good thing," Nicki said.

"It also means you can go back to your blogging and magazine work and stop playing Sherlock Holmes."

Nicki smiled. "Not Charlie Chan?"

The chief finally relented and grinned. "Nobody is good enough to be the great Charlie Chan."

"There's a lot of possible suspects. Our board is completely full."

He sighed and leaned back in his chair again. "Yeah, there are. And now you've given me one more with this Stella person."

"But it does make you wonder if this whole thing is about the wine, and George was incidental damage."

"Collateral. The term you want is collateral damage, and I wouldn't go that far. He was the guy slapping his name on something that wasn't his, and that could have been the reason he ended up dead. Probably was. It seems to fit better than a sudden burst of anger at George." The chief made a steeple of his fingers and gazed back at Nicki. "We haven't found Benzo the bookie yet either. He could be in another state."

"He's in New York," Nicki said absently. At the chief's narrowed gaze, she shrugged. "His number is on one of the spreadsheets in George's computer. I recognized the area code."

The chief uncrossed his legs and stood up. "Okay. A New York bookie is a step too far. Go out and do some shopping, or go home and make a cake. I don't care what you do. Save the world if that's what you want, but don't do it in my town. I want you to let us do our job, and you go home and do whatever Matt has you doing for that magazine. Which reminds me..." He pinned her with a direct stare. "Is he aware that you're still involved in this? Or do I have a repeat phone call to look forward to?"

Nicki rolled her eyes and walked out of his office. She waved at Fran on her way to the front door. As she stepped out into the sunshine, she almost collided with Danny.

"Sorry, Nicki. I was on my way in."

She smiled and skirted around him. "And I'm on my way out, but I should warn you, Danny. I'm not moving my car. You'll just have to give me a ticket."

The deputy did an about-face and walked with her. "I guess

I'll have to do that. I'm pretty busy right now, but should get to it sometime this afternoon."

Laughing, Nicki opened her car door then frowned down at her seat. There was a jar with liquid in it, sitting on top of a piece of notebook paper. Nicki picked up the jar and set it on the hood of her car before opening the note.

She gasped and took a quick step back, right into Danny. He reached out to steady her as his eyes went straight to the note in her hand and the message spelled out in large, block letters.

*STICKING YOUR NOSE WHERE IT DOESN'T BELONG MIGHT GET YOU HURT AND YOUR FRIENDS TOO*

Danny grabbed Nicki's arm and backed her away from the car as if it might explode. He turned his head and pointed at a young teenager walking by.

"Jimmy Pasten. You go in and tell Chief Turnlow he needs to come out here right now."

The boy took off like a rocket as Danny removed the note from Nicki's limp hand. "Why don't we sit on this curb and wait for the chief?"

Nicki's hands and legs began to tremble so she locked her knees to keep them from giving out on her. The message was so simple, and frightening. And she had a good idea what was in that jar. Jumping when the chief put his hand on her arm, she took a deep breath before looking up at him.

"Are you all right?" he asked, genuine concern in his voice.

When she nodded, he walked over to the car and used a large handkerchief to lift the jar and remove its lid. He took a short sniff of the contents before screwing the lid back on.

"Danny, I'll take Nicki inside to my office while you go find her friends." He looked at Nicki. "Who came into town with you today? I heard Maxie Edwards' voice through the open window. Was there anyone else?"

"I know who they are, Chief," Danny said before Nicki could answer.

"Good. Go find them." The chief helped Nicki to her feet. "Let's go inside."

She walked in front of him and went straight back to his office. Fran bustled in a minute later with a cup of coffee that she handed to Nicki without a word. Nodding her thanks, Nicki took a sip before setting it aside. Her hands were shaking too much to hold it.

The chief came in and set the jar down on the far side of his desk.

"It smelled like cherries," he said, answering her silent question.

They sat quietly for ten minutes before there was a commotion in the tiny bullpen area and three women came bursting through the door.

"What happened?" Jenna demanded. "Dudley Do-Right here wouldn't tell us anything."

"What's going on, Paul?" Maxie put her hands on Nicki's shoulders.

Alex squatted next to her friend's chair. "Are you okay?"

"I'm fine. Had a little scare is all."

"Scare? What kind of scare?" Jenna asked, her glare settling on the chief. "What did you say to scare her?"

"Not me. This." The chief slid the note across his desk so all four women could see it. He waited until their gasps subsided.

"It came accompanied by a jar with a liquid in it," he added.

Nicki stood and looked at her friends. "It smells like cherries."

"You think it's the same stuff that killed George?" Jenna's eyes were twice their normal size.

"What I think," the chief said over their rising voices. "Is that you need to go home. And stay there. And erase that murder board, forget about this case, and go back to your normal lives."

He nodded into the sudden silence in the room. "This is serious stuff. We don't know who murdered George Lancer. It could be someone familiar to you, and who could get to you easily enough. Or it could be someone sent from the bookie in New York, and I don't have to tell you what that means."

"Go home and forget this case," he repeated. "And this time it's not a request but an order. If I have to contact the governor himself to keep you all out of this investigation, then that's what I'll do."

## 23

"I'm sorry, Nicki, I have to go. Tyler got home from his shift early this morning and picked up a voice mail from Chief Turnlow. He called the chief and then turned right around and called me. I just got off the phone with him." Alex took a seat at the kitchen counter and reached for the cup of coffee Nicki slid toward her.

"How angry is he?" Jenna asked.

"If I don't show up at home within an hour, he's coming to get me. And there was no talking him out of that."

Nicki visibly winced. She had never, never meant to cause so much trouble for her friends. When they'd pulled up to the house yesterday afternoon, Mason Edwards had been standing on the lawn, waiting for them. Even with all of Maxie's assurances that she was an expert at handling her husband, Nicki's heart broke when she barely had time to wave before the former police chief ushered his wife into their car and drove off.

Nicki spent the whole evening hoping she'd call, but no such luck.

She was sure myMason probably hated her at this point, and now Tyler did too.

"I'm going to have to cut our visit short and go home to calm him down." Alex's lower lip started to quiver. "But I don't want to leave you here alone either."

"Hey." Jenna wrapped an arm around Alex's shoulder. "I live right next door. Nicki won't be alone, and neither will I. You need to deal with Tyler."

"Alex Kolman, don't even *think* about staying here instead of going home to your fiancé. He's probably worried sick after talking to the chief, and you can hardly blame him. I managed to get your life threatened, so I'm counting on you to explain to him why he shouldn't hate me for getting you into this mess." Nicki pasted a smile on her face so her friend wouldn't break down and cry. Lord knew *she* certainly felt like it, and Nicki suspected it would only take one tear from any of them for all three to burst into sobs.

Dabbing at the corner of her eye with the paper towel Jenna handed her, Alex stood up. She leaned over and gave Nicki a fierce hug.

"I'll be back as soon as I can," she whispered. After swiping a kiss along Nicki's cheek, she turned and left the kitchen.

A miunute later Nicki heard the front door open and then close behind her.

Jenna picked up her coffee cup and shook her head. "Relationships can be the very devil, can't they?"

Instead of going along with Jenna's attempt to lighten the mood, Nicki chose to stick with the invisible cloak of rejection she'd been wearing ever since the drive back from Soldoff. Why would anyone want to be her friend? She'd dragged them over half the county and had them neglecting their own work and family to go chasing after the killer of a man none of them even knew. Well, except for Maxie. But still, he was a man no one really wanted to know. And now they all had to live with the fear they might be poisoned every time they went out to eat, or had a pizza delivered. It was unnerving. And frightening.

Jenna and Alex were the only family she had left, and they had seen her through the worst times in her life. And how did she repay them? By making them a target for a killer. If the police didn't catch George Lancer's murderer soon, they might have to be on their guard for months, or even years. Maybe forever. Nicki bit her lower lip and fought to keep the tears from slipping down her cheeks.

She and Jenna both jumped when her phone rang. Shaking her head Nicki looked over at it. The caller ID flashed Matt's name. She ignored it and let it ring until voice mail kicked in.

Jenna quietly sipped her coffee. After a few minutes, she glanced over at the now-silent phone lying on the counter. "Is that the way you intend to deal with Matt?"

Nicki sank lower onto her stool. "It is for now. I simply can't listen to any more lectures on the subject of amateur detectives."

"Can't say I blame you," Jenna agreed. "I can stay here tonight. It might make us both feel better."

"Better or safer?" Nicki's voice held a trace of bitterness in her voice. "I've made a fine mess of things, haven't I?"

"If you did, you had lots of help. This wasn't your fault, Nicki. We all wanted to solve the murder."

"Only because I did, and you're the best friends in the entire known universe to go along with it," Nicki said.

When she saw the mutinous look in Jenna's eyes, Nicki gave the computer geek's hand a squeeze. "Would you mind being the best friend in the universe a bit longer and stay in your own place tonight? Unless you really are uncomfortable, then of course I want you to stay with me. But I need some thinking time."

When the computer in Nicki's office started to ring, she exchanged a long look with Jenna.

"That's probably Matt on Skype," Jenna said. "Are you going to ignore that too? Because he'll only keep calling."

"There are ways to deal with that." Nicki picked up her phone and scrolled through the settings until she could set the phone to silent.

"I'll turn the computer off later."

---

THREE DAYS CRAWLED by in relative silence. Nicki was sitting at her computer in her pajamas, even though the clock showed it was only an hour away from noon. She'd told herself, and Jenna who'd dropped by earlier that morning, that she was simply being comfortable while she worked on her latest spy novel. But thirty minutes into her writing session she'd switched over from the Word program on her laptop to her favorite, online game. The biggest issue on her mind at the moment was whether or not to make a run to the market later to refill her potato chip and chocolate-covered peanut stash.

Since she still had her phone on silence, and was using her laptop which did not have Skype, she'd managed to avoid talking to Matt. Or anyone else for that matter. But Alex and Maxie knew if they needed to get hold of her, they only had to call Jenna. Nicki was sure her very good friend and next-door neighbor had explained the whole avoiding-Matt-for-the-foreseeable-future thing to the other two women.

A loud knock on the door rang through the townhouse. Nicki listened for Jenna's signature door bang, or Maxie's familiar *yoo-hoo*. When neither occurred, she shrugged and ignored it. It was probably somebody who pretended not to see the "No Trespassing" signs posted all over the property's fence and was selling something.

When the knock sounded a second time, a little louder and a little more insistently, Nicki uncurled herself from the sofa and padded over to the door. She looked through the peephole before stepping back with a frown.

It was Chief Turnlow.

The way her life was going, he was probably here to arrest her for obstructing justice, or maybe for jaywalking. As tempting as it was to ignore the man and go back to her game, Nicki decided to do the adult thing and find out what he wanted.

She opened the door just far enough to stick her head out. "What can I do for you, Chief?"

"I've had a complaint I have to respond to, Ms. Connors, so I have to ask you to step out here."

Nicki frowned. "I'm still in my pajamas and I don't feel like stepping out there. What was the complaint?"

The big man gave her a polite smile. "Then I need to come in, if that's agreeable with you."

"It isn't, Chief Turnlow," Nicki said, not opening the door even one more inch.

"Stop pouting, Nicki. I need to talk to you."

She pulled the door open. "Fine. Come in. Do you want a cup of coffee?"

"That would be nice, thank you."

Nicki marched back to the kitchen and pulled a bottled water out from the cupboard as the chief settled himself on one of the stools at the counter.

"So, what's the complaint?" Nicki asked, pouring the water into the tea kettle and turning on the burner.

"I'll get to that in a minute. I also want to talk to you about the Lancer case."

Nicki looked over her shoulder, her eyes wide with surprise. "You do? Why?"

"Because you should know that I've been in touch with the State boys, and a resource or two at the Santa Rosa PD, but I don't think it's going to do much good."

She continued to measure out the coffee. "Okay."

"I'm not meaning to make a bad pun, but we've hit a dead end. All we know for sure is that someone got into that room and poisoned the wine that killed George. We didn't find any fingerprints in that private aging room besides the victim's, and while a lot of people didn't like the man, no one has a strong motive to kill him. And everyone has an alibi for the time of death, including Stella and that bookie we tracked down in New York."

When he paused, Nicki turned around to face him.

"What does that mean? That the case will go cold?"

The chief ran a beefy hand through his thinning hair. "I'm afraid so, Nicki. I'll keep picking at it when I can, but with nothing else to go on and no family to push for it, I don't think we can solve this one." He looked down at his hands. "I'm sorry."

"It's not your fault. It's just one of those things, Chief."

She sighed. If the police backed off and she and her friends stayed away, maybe the killer would disappear too, and they could all return to their normal lives. Accepting a cold case involving a man no one liked was a small price to gain back peace for her friends. And for herself, too.

"Now, about that second thing," the chief said.

"What second thing?" Nicki asked more from habit than any real curiosity. She was still thinking about the murder going cold. Just like her mom's case had.

"The wellness complaint."

"What? Someone complained about me being well?"

Chief Turnlow chuckled. "No. The complaint is he doesn't believe you're well at all, and demanded I come out and check on you."

She didn't have to think twice about who the "he" was.

"Matt called you? Again?" Nicki was exasperated. Why did her editor feel he had a right to interfere in her life, anyway? She was only one of a hundred contract writers he gave assignments to. He wasn't her keeper.

"Again? Your friend-who-happens-to-be-a-male is driving Fran nuts with all his calls. According to this friend of yours, no one on the entire West coast is answering their phones. Not Maxie, not Jenna, not Alex, and not you. He swears we're the only ones in this entire part of the State who's answering calls, and that's because we're the police department and we have to." The chief rolled his eyes. "He's a little upset."

Nicki put a cup of coffee in front of the chief before folding her arms with a shrug. "It sounds as if he has a problem."

"He does," the chief said. "You. And he's made it my problem. So now I'm making it *your* problem. You need to call him."

"He's just going to lecture and yell," Nicki said. She was sure of that much.

"Then let him get it out of his system so we can all have some peace." The chief picked up his coffee and took a long drink. "I'll wait while you get him on the phone."

Nicki gaped at him. "Are you serious?"

"Yes, I am."

Fuming, Nicki picked her phone up from the stand and dialed Matt's office number. As she hoped, his efficient assistant answered on the third ring.

"Hi, Jane. It's Nicki. I'm sure Matt is busy, so would you take a message and let him know the chief was here and I called?"

"Just a minute, Nicki," Jane said. "Let me grab something to write with."

Nicki sighed when Jane put her on hold, but then clicked back on almost immediately.

"Great. Do you need me to repeat the message?" Nicki asked.

"No, I don't," Matt said. "And if you hang up on me, Nicki Connors, I'm getting on the next plane to California."

"Oh." Nicki bit her lower lip. "Well. I wasn't going to hang up, I just didn't expect you to be on the line."

"Obviously, since you called my office number rather than my personal cell like I've left a million messages for you to do."

Nicki glared at the chief when he mouthed a "good luck" and left the kitchen.

"My phone's been turned off."

"And your computer too?"

"I've been using my laptop," Nicki said. "Is this what you wanted to talk about? The status of all my electronic devices?"

"No. I want to talk about your meddling in a murder investigation to the point you put your life in danger." By the time he'd reached the end of that sentence, Nicki could feel his anger even through the phone.

"Well, you don't have to worry about it anymore," Nicki said. "The chief stopped by and told me the case has hit a dead end, so to speak, and will probably go cold. Just another unsolved murder tucked away into the police files."

"Which is how you're going to leave it," Matt stated.

"I am?" Nicki only said that because she didn't like the way he was barking out orders that had nothing to do with the magazine and everything to do with her life.

There was a long, charged moment of silence while Nicki held her breath.

"You'll leave it alone, Nicki, or I won't give you one more hour of work for *Food & Wine Online*. And I'll be calling the chief to be sure you keep to your end of that bargain.

"Matt!" Nicki couldn't believe he'd just said that. He couldn't mean it. He knew how much she depended on the income from the magazine to keep herself above water financially. Now he was using that knowledge to hold it over her head so she'd fall into line. It was a low blow. And a vicious one from a guy she'd always counted on to never be that way.

"I mean it, Nicki. Don't test me on this."

The phone went dead in her ear. Nicki held it away and stared at it.

After a minute, she carefully put it back into its holder as big tears rolled down her cheeks.

## 24

N icki hit the send button on her email, then frowned at the computer screen. She was back working on her desktop since there was no need to deal with unwanted Skype calls. She hadn't received so much as an email from Matt in four days. She vaguely wondered if she'd ever hear directly from the owner of *Food & Wine Online* again.

This latest article was simply one in a string of assignments she'd received from Jane. She could usually count on a new assignment to be in her email inbox every morning, and corrective edits to the article she'd submitted the day before to show up in the afternoon. Both came like clockwork. Both came from Jane. No other communication necessary.

Nicki glumly felt this new arrangement was a good thing in the long run. All the assignments were interest pieces, the kind that only required a moderate amount of Internet research, and on occasion a phone call or two. She could crank them out right from home, which left her plenty of time to work on her own blog and very neglected spy novel. Or even sit and enjoy a cup of coffee whenever she wanted one. Yes, it was a great gig.

And she hated it.

With a sigh that was half frustration and half resignation at the fate she'd brought on herself, Nicki opened the email that had been waiting for her since morning. With a definite lack of enthusiasm she read through the details of the assignment. She blinked and sat up straighter as she read through it again, a spark of anger growing into a full-blown eruption. Really? The varieties of wildflower that naturally grow around grapevines? Who writes about that?

She was glaring at the screen when the front door slapped loudly against its frame. Something else she hadn't heard in days. It suddenly dawned on her that whenever Jenna dropped by lately, she'd quietly come into the house and just as quietly left. But today she was back to her usual door-banging habit. Nicki smiled.

"Where are you?" Jenna called out, her flip flops smacking against the boards of the hallway.

Laughing, Nicki jumped to her feet. "I'm in the office but headed for the kitchen for coffee and a cookie."

She was already ripping open a bag of Oreos when Jenna appeared in the doorway.

"Cookies? Really?" Jenna's gaze zeroed in on the bag in Nicki's hand. "And store-bought ones?"

Nicki dumped them out onto the counter. "I haven't made any cookies lately, but I just might find the time this afternoon."

Jenna rushed over the space separating them and wrapped her arms around Nicki in a breath-stealing hug. Stepping back, Jenna held her off at arm's length, a grin slowly spreading across her mouth.

"And she's baaaaack!"

"Let go of me, you nut. I didn't go anywhere," Nicki laughed. She reached down and picked up an Oreo. "Here. A cookie for my freedom."

Jenna took it out of Nicki's hand, then snatched up another one. "Make that two and a glass of milk, and you have a deal."

Plopping down on one of the stools, Jenna eyed her friend as Nicki poured out a tall glass of milk. "So, what finally snapped you out of the stupor you've been in for the last five days?"

"Matt's stupid assignments," Nicki said, setting the glass down in front of Jenna.

The computer geek paused with her cookie in mid-air. "You talked to Matt?"

"No. He's not speaking to me. I'm getting the assignments from his admin, Jane."

"Okay. So what's wrong with the assignments?"

Nicki shrugged. "Nothing. If you're a staff writer for the magazine."

Jenna's brow wrinkled. "Well, aren't you?"

"No. I. Am. Not." Nicki emphasized each word. "I'm a freelance writer who takes field assignments. Field. As in going out into the field and visiting wineries, eating establishments, food and wine festivals, that sort of thing."

"Oh. What kind of assignments has the very scary Jane been giving you?"

"Desk assignments. You know what I'm talking about. Anything I can write with a little help from research and done from the comfort of my desk. The latest one? The varieties of wildflowers that grow naturally around vineyards." Nicki snorted her disgust. "Wildflowers. Really?"

"Maybe Jane lacks imagination when it comes to thinking up interesting magazine articles," Jenna said.

"Oh no." Nicki shook her head and glared at nothing in particular. "This is all Matt. Jane would never come up with such lame ideas much less assign them to one of the mag's freelance writers."

"Ah. The man's trying to keep you keying away at your computer in your safe-and-sound townhouse." Jenna nodded and bit into a cookie. "Not very clever, but points for the considerate thought."

Nicki turned her glare on Jenna. "He doesn't get any points for that. I'm not someone he can wrap in cotton and stick wherever he wants."

"No, no. You're definitely not the cotton ball type."

"First the man crushes me and brings me to tears with his stupid ultimatums, and then he pawns off a bunch of fluff assignments that are an insult to my intelligence and lifestyle. I don't sit at home and do research. I *like* going out in the field." The more she talked, the madder Nicki got. Matt Dillon had become an impossible jerk.

"Whoa, wait. Hold up there." Jenna slapped a palm flat on top of the kitchen counter. "What do you mean he brought you to tears? You cried over something Matt said?"

"Only briefly," Nicki sniffed. "And anyone would have if they'd had over half their income threatened."

Jenna's jaw dropped. "He said he wouldn't pay you?"

"Not outright, but that's what he meant. He said if I stuck my nose into the investigation for even one more minute, he'd stop sending me any assignments for *Food & Wine Online*."

"And then he sent you fluff assignments to be sure you stayed at home and behaved?" Jenna shook her head. "Well, that was low and dirty, and astonishing."

"Yes, it was. Low and dirty, I mean," Nicki clarified. "Why was it astonishing?"

"First, because he's never acted that way before, at least not toward you. And second because you've actually been doing the fluff assignments instead of throwing them in his face."

Nicki sighed. "I have to find a way to replace that income first. I'm too old to be that irresponsible anymore."

Her friend laughed. "Well, old lady. I'm positive plenty of magazines would love to take you on as a freelance writer."

"Thanks," Nicki said with a smile.

"Yoo-hoo?"

Nicki's smile grew even wider at the sound of heels click-clacking down her hallway.

"We're in the kitchen, Maxie," she called out, laughing when Jenna groaned out loud.

The silver-haired landlady marched over and gave Nicki a kiss on the cheek, and then gave another to Jenna before settling onto a stool.

"Well, ladies. Where were we before we were so rudely inter-rupted?" Maxie beamed when Nicki and Jenna burst into laughter.

"Does your husband know you're here?" Nicki finally managed to ask.

"Of course he does, dear. I'm too old to go sneaking around. I told him I was coming to check on you and any updates to our murder board, and if he didn't like it, he should get his mind onto other things. Like pruning a bush." Maxie smoothed away an imaginary stray piece of hair. "By the way, he said to be sure to tell you 'hello'. He was very upset when I informed him that after his boorish behavior the other day, you most likely think he hates you."

"Oh, I would never think something like that," Nicki lied, her mouth still turned up into a grin.

"Of course you wouldn't." Maxie patted Nicki's hand. "But he doesn't need to know that, does he? Now, what shall we do for lunch?"

"Hold that thought for a few more minutes," Jenna said. "I'm waiting on a surprise for Nicki. Should be here any minute now."

"A surprise?" Nicki pursed her lips. "Tell me it's the name of a contact you have at a major magazine."

"Not quite." Jenna grinned when the doorbell rang. "And there it is."

Less than a minute later Alex walked into the kitchen. Nicki gave a happy yelp and ran to give her other BFF a hug. Jenna joined in while Maxie beamed at them.

"Together again," Alex laughed. "I know it's only been a few days, but it feels like forever."

"I'm sorry." Nicki leaned back and gave her two best friends a misty-eyed smile.

"For what?" Alex asked.

"For weirding out on you. I should have had a backbone and told the chief and Matt they can't order me around."

"Matt?" Alex glanced at Jenna. "What happened with Matt?"

"He made her cry," Jenna whispered back. When Alex narrowed her eyes, Jenna shook her head. "We'll talk about it later."

"Much later," Nicki agreed. "Just because you're whispering doesn't mean I can't still hear you."

The three women widened their circle to include Maxie. Alex smiled at the older woman.

"Where's your husband?"

"Pruning a bush, I would imagine. He'll be around later to walk me home." She winked at the others. "Simply as a romantic gesture. And to apologize to Nicki for his rude behavior."

"How did you get past Tyler so you could visit me again so soon?" Nicki asked. Everyone turned to look at Alex.

"I told him that he couldn't keep me from being with my friends, especially when they needed me and I needed to be with them. He'd have to figure out a way to deal with it."

"Perhaps he should take up gardening," Maxie suggested.

Jenna laughed. "So what's he doing? Lounging in a man cave somewhere and pouting? In a macho way, of course."

Alex smiled. "No. He's getting our luggage out of the car and giving us some time alone. He refused to be caught in the middle of what he was sure was going to be, and I quote, 'a girl fest with tears'. He should be here any moment."

Right on cue, a masculine "hello" called out from the front of the townhouse.

"Just drop the luggage anywhere, honey, and come to the kitchen."

A very wary-looking Tyler walked into the room, stopping a mere foot or two inside. His deep brown eyes swept over the women. Nicki thought it was comical to see the well-built fireman, sporting a close-cropped haircut, looking so unsure of himself.

Alex motioned him in. "It's all right, Ty. There aren't any tears going on."

All the women laughed at the look of sheer relief on the fireman's rugged face.

"We were about to invade Nicki's office to update our murder board," Maxie announced. "You're welcome to join us."

Just then the phone rang. Nicki glanced at the screen display and smiled. "It's Rob. Everyone stay where they are, this won't take long and then we can talk lunch and murder."

Nicki smiled when Tyler instantly perked up. She hit the answer button and lifted the phone to her ear.

"Hi, Rob." She waited a second. "That's okay, I don't have much time either." Nicki fell silent, quietly drumming her fingers against the counter top.

"Oh yes, that does sound interesting," she finally said. "Uh huh. Okay. Yes, absolutely. Right. I'll talk to you later. Bye."

"Not a very lengthy conversation for a boyfriend, dear," Maxie said.

"At least he didn't make her cry, so points for that," Jenna put in.

Tyler's brows drew together as he stared at Nicki. "Who made you cry?"

"Matt," Jenna supplied.

"The magazine guy who wants to be Nicki's boyfriend?"

"We know," the other three women said in unison as Nicki glared at Alex who only shrugged in response.

"He made Nicki cry?" Tyler looked at all the women who nodded their heads. "The guy's toast."

"Now Tyler, dear, I'm sure Nicki doesn't need you to fight her battles," Maxie said gently.

The fireman grinned at her. "I'd be happy to, but I wasn't talking about the dude having to deal with me. He made one of the friends cry. He's got a real big hole to dig himself out of."

"What did your boyfriend, of a sort, want?" Alex asked.

"To remind me Antonio's class lecture is tonight." Nicki tapped a finger against her lower lip, remembering the graded papers on the end of George Lancer's desk. With the abrupt departure of the teacher, she wondered what had happened to all the students in his class. All those potentially rising stars.

"Did you say something about lunch?" Tyler looked around the kitchen.

Nicki glanced at him and smiled. "I did. How do you feel about ordering pizza?"

## 25

"You should let Ty go with you," Alex declared for the third time.

And for the third time, Nicki shook her head. "I don't need a bodyguard, Alex."

"Well, I don't think he is one," her friend retorted.

Tyler looked up from his afternoon snack of a ham sandwich and a beer. "Hey. I could be a bodyguard."

"I'm sure you could," Nicki laughed. She glanced at Alex and raised one eyebrow. After all these years, she knew her friend very well.

"And I don't need someone to make Rob jealous."

The fireman grinned. "I'd do my best if that's the way you want to go."

"Hey," Alex protested, poking a finger into her fiancé's side.

It took another ten minutes of arguing, but Nicki finally got her way and chugged off in her Toyota without Tyler's company. She arrived at the college half-an-hour later and pulled into one of the designated student lots. Quickly paying for a parking permit, she slapped it on her dashboard and went looking for the small lecture hall where Rob's boss, Antonio Rossi, was going to enlighten the attending students on the history of wine.

The class wasn't due to start for another few minutes, but there were already several groups lingering in front of the double doors. Nicki did what she did best and started mingling with the small crowd, introducing herself and asking a subtle question or two before moving on to the next group.

She hit the jackpot when she strolled up to three, twenty-somethings, standing off to one side and huddled together.

"Hi. Are you here for the History of Wine class?"

The young men nodded in unison then stepped back to make room for her in their group. Nicki smiled. Sometimes the face she'd inherited from her mother really helped.

"I wasn't at the first class," she said, keeping her tone light. "I couldn't make up my mind between this one and the class on winemaking. That ones being taught by a local winemaker, a George Lanciere, and I've never heard of this Rossi guy. But I thought I'd give him a try." Nicki secretly crossed her fingers and said a silent apology to Antonio.

"He's the wine buyer for Catalan House restaurants," the student with the sparsely grown beard said. Nicki remembered he'd introduced himself as Brian. "And you're lucky you decided on this class instead of the other one. It was canceled last week."

"It was?" Nicki frowned. "Why?"

The short, muscular man who'd given his name as Shane, lowered his voice to a loud whisper. "I read in the paper the dude was killed. Right there in the winery he worked at."

The other two boys in the group nodded their agreement when Nicki let out the expected gasp of horror.

"Oh no! One of my friends knows him and said he was really nice to the students."

Nicki didn't have to wait long for a reaction to that statement. Shane immediately snorted and rolled his eyes.

"Couldn't prove that by any of us. The guy rarely showed up

for class on time, didn't stay after to answer questions, and wouldn't post any office hours."

"Never saw him so much as say 'hi' to one student," Brian piped in.

The third boy, whose name she couldn't remember, gave her a shy-looking smile and nodded.

"Oh. Then I guess what else I was told isn't true either. That he liked finding new talented winemakers in his class?" Nicki wasn't surprised when all three shook their heads.

"It was a beginning class," Shane stated. "What kind of talent can you see in a beginning class, especially when we hadn't made any wine yet?"

"I see your point," Nicki said. She hung out with them for a few more minutes, listening to the latest news on a local rock band she'd never heard of, before politely excusing herself.

Feeling the lead about George's winemaking class wasn't going to work out, she was about to head to her car when someone tapped her on the shoulder. She turned around and found herself looking right into the very dark eyes of Antonio Rossi.

"Nicki! I'm glad you could make it tonight." He took one of her hands in his, and as was his habit, raised it to his lips and dropped a light kiss on the back.

Knowing she was trapped now, Nicki managed to smile while she withdrew her hand. "I wouldn't miss it, Antonio. I'm sorry I had a schedule conflict for your first lecture." Which was basically a polite way to say she'd completely forgotten about it.

"Oh? Rob told me you had a flat tire on the way to campus that night."

Making a mental note to talk to Rob about his habit of making up fake excuses, she shook her head and laughed. "Well, I certainly didn't schedule that. Can you tell me what the focus is for your lecture tonight? I might need to get it straight for my blog, or possibly an article in the magazine?"

Antonio's smile was back in place and he puffed his chest out a little. "I'll be discussing the various uses for wine barrels. I'm sure you'll enjoy it."

"Oh, I'm sure I will," Nicki said. She glanced over at the double doors that an unknown maintenance person had just opened. "Shall we go in?"

Thirty minutes later, Nicki was doing her best to stay awake. She'd tried to take notes, but now was only listening with half an ear as she played with an outline on how to write a wildflower article that would *really* get Matt's attention. Something Antonio said made her hand freeze in place. She looked up and stared at him, concentrating to catch the fleeting thought.

"Oak has been used to age wine for over two thousand years," Antonio droned on, reading directly from his notes.

Nicki was tuning him out again when she caught the tail end of "different grains." Before she realized it, her hand shot up. When he didn't notice her, she called out his name.

"Antonio? Excuse me, Antonio?"

In the row of seats behind her, Shane leaned forward and poked her in the back. "I thought you said you didn't know the guy."

Nicki ignored him and continued to wave her hand at Antonio, who finally stopped and shook his head at her.

"I said I'd take questions at the end of the lecture, Miss Connors, but go ahead."

"Can you please repeat what you said about the grains being different?"

"It's simple enough." He pointed to the enlarged pictures projected onto the big screen in back of him. "French oak is a slower growing tree and has a tighter grain than its faster growing cousin, the American oak."

Nicki studied the pictures as an image from the crime scene flashed through her mind. A smile formed on her lips. "Of course."

She got up from her seat and left the lecture hall, flipping through the contacts on her phone as she did a fast walk out to her car. She found the number she wanted and touched the *dial* button, crossing her fingers it would be picked up.

"Hello?"

"Hi, Stella? It's Nicki Connors."

---

LESS THAN AN HOUR later Nicki flew into her townhouse, tossing her purse in the general direction of the hall table, and yelling for Alex as she ran toward her office.

"What?" Alex popped her head around the wall separating the living room from the hallway. "What are you yelling about?"

"Is Ty with you?"

"Present," he called out. "And watching the game."

"That's too bad," Nicki called back. "Because I need you to bring your cell phone and come into my office." She tossed a look back at Alex. "You too."

Within thirty seconds the three of them were standing in Nicki's office. Alex and her fiancé uncovered the murder board while Nicki frantically scribbled on a full-size sheet of paper. When she was done, she neatly folded the sheet and then ripped it into thirds, handing a piece to Alex and Tyler.

"What's this?" Alex asked, frowning at the phone number on her piece.

"I need you each to call your number and tell them to get here right away."

"Mine says Jenna." Tyler walked over to the far wall and gave it a series of solid pounds. "Jenna," he yelled. "Get over here. Nicki needs to talk to you right now."

An answering pound came from the other side and Tyler turned and grinned at his future wife. "Can I go back to the game now?"

"It depends," Alex said, giving Nicki a stern-eyed look. "On why we need to get these people here?"

Nicki walked over to the murder board, picked up a marker and circled a name.

"Because I know who murdered George Lancer."

## 26

J
ust before eleven the next morning, Nicki, Jenna, Alex and Maxie walked into Holland Winery. The women were smiling and chatting away as they approached the long bar at the far end of the tasting room. Geri was behind the bar, rearranging bottles along the glass shelves. As the group approached, she looked up and nodded at Nicki.

"You're the first customers today."

"Quiet day," Nicki observed. "Where's Kurt?"

Geri picked up a dish towel and started wiping down the top of the bar. "He called in sick. Jim asked me to cover until he could get someone else to come in."

"If you're out here, and there isn't a replacement for poor George yet, who's making the wine?" Jenna asked.

"I'm sure we can get by for one day. What can I get all of you? We have some nice whites today and are featuring a merlot as well."

"Nothing right away," Nicki answered the assistant. Geri was dressed in her usual uniform of black and white. "We're waiting for the rest of our party."

"I believe they've just arrived," Maxie waved at the four men coming through the tall, double doors.

Nicki smiled at the big man bringing up the rear of the newly arrived group. "Hello, Chief. I see you managed to corral all of them."

Chief Turnlow gave a brief nod before pointing to a table close to the bar. "Why don't you gentlemen have a seat?"

"I can't stay long enough to have a seat," Jeremy Brennan crossed his arms over his chest. "I have work I need to get back to. Why are we here, anyway?"

"I'd be happy to sit down and listen to whatever you have to say to us, Chief." Bill Stacy pulled out a chair, sat, and plopped one ankle on top of the opposite knee. "And that's a stupid question, Brennan. Since he's got the three winery owners who either did, or in your case wanted to, employ Lancer, then we're obviously here because of his murder." He looked over at the chief. "Is that right, Turnlow? Have you solved the murder yet?"

The chief shook his head. "No, I haven't."

"So why are we here?" Jim Holland asked.

"I haven't solved the murder, but Nicki Connors has."

Loud indrawn breaths raced around the room as every eye turned to Nicki. She cleared her throat.

"Very dramatic, Chief. Thank you."

Chief Turnlow smiled at her. "Don't mention it, Ms. Connors."

"Believe me, she won't," Jenna said under her breath just before Alex poked an elbow into her ribs.

Not entirely comfortable with everyone staring at her, Nicki leaned back against the bar, angling her body so she could include Geri.

"It was the barrels that told the story," she began.

"The barrels?" Jeremy shrugged. "What barrels?"

"You just keep quiet now, Jeremy Brennan, and let Nicki talk," Maxie said. "Go on, dear."

"Everyone here knows that Geri and I found George's body,

but I spent the most time in that room, since Geri was too upset to stay until the ambulance arrived. Do you remember what I told you about being in that room, Chief?"

The chief nodded. "Sure do. Instead of staring at a dead body, you counted all the rings in the barrelhead and moved on to the stones in the wall."

"That's right. I counted all the rings in the barrelhead."

"And so?" Jeremy demanded, his foot tapping rapidly against the stone floor. "All barrelheads have rings showing on the lids. They're made from trees."

"Yes, they are," Nicki agreed. "And wine barrels are made from very specific trees. Oak trees. While Holland buys both French oak barrels and American oak barrels, George preferred French oak so much that no one ever saw him use anything else when he made his personal blends."

"Common knowledge," Jim Holland said. "We even talked about it at the tasting event."

"Yes, we did," Nicki said. "But I learned yesterday that French and American oaks aren't alike, and it isn't just the flavors they impart into the wine. French oak is a slower growing tree, with a much tighter grain in the wood, much tighter than the grain found in most American oak. When I was in that private room George always kept locked, and staring at the heads of those wine barrels, I saw something I didn't realize at the time was important. The rings exposed on the barrelheads were much further apart then they would be for a slow-growing tree. Those barrels were not French oak."

The chief cleared his throat. "I asked Victor, the warehouse foreman here, to verify that. We both went in and took a look. He verified that the barrels in George's private room are American oak. He also looked up the distribution records from the warehouse and confirmed that George Lancer only signed for American oak barrels in the last year for his personal use, and most of those within a month of each other. Altogether he signed for ten of them. And paid for them because his contract only allowed for French oak barrels."

Nicki looked over at Jeremy. "Ten barrels. The same number you told me was the entire production of George's special blend."

"So? That's what George told me," the young winery owner said.

"He told me the same thing," Jim put in. "His production was ten barrels."

"When the chief told me the results of the lab tests on the wine barrels in George's room, he said all *eight* barrels had tested negative. Eight barrels, not ten. We seem to be missing two barrels."

"Maybe he hadn't used them yet and had them stashed somewhere else, or he could have given some away," Bill Stacy said.

"George Lancer wasn't the kind of man to give anything away, much less whole barrels of his precious creation. But he did give away some secret tastings of his new blend, didn't he, Jim?" Nicki turned to look at the winery owner. "Wasn't that the price you demanded before you would agree to cover the cost for George's tasting event? He was going to give you a barrel of the wine in return, but you wanted to taste it first."

"Hey," Jeremy instantly protested. "He promised me the whole production."

"Quit being a fool, Jeremy. Did you really think Holland was going to put on that event for nothing?" Bill asked. He also turned to look at Jim Holland. "Well, did you get to sample the goods before you agreed to foot the bill?"

Jim slowly nodded. "He let me have a glass. It was worth the price of the event."

"And I'm sure you also had a preview tasting, Jeremy," Nicki said. "To give up a twenty percent stake in your winery, you'd want to know you were getting something of equal value in return."

Jeremy threw up his hands. "Okay, you've got me. Yes, I got to taste his precious blend. And like Jim said, it was worth the price. Fine, we all had a sample. So what?"

"Not me," Bill Stacy said. "I didn't get an advance taste."

"Oh, but you did, Bill." Nicki smiled at his sudden frown.

"There's a second part to this story, and it has to do with Stella. You remember her, don't you Jim? She was your assistant winemaker along with George when he came out with that spectacular private blend that helped put Holland Winery on the map."

"I remember her." Jim nodded. "She left right after that. Haven't heard much about her since then."

"She's working at Sandy's diner, if you'd like to stop in and say 'hi'. It's the first job she's had in ten years because George has been sending her monthly payments all this time."

"Why did he do that?" Jim asked.

"Blackmail," Nicki said, then waited again for the gasps to subside. "George didn't make that blend ten years ago. Stella did. They agreed to let George put his name on it for a price, and then she demanded monthly payments to keep her mouth shut. Which he paid her until three months ago, when he told her he was coming out with a new blend."

Jim Holland slowly stood up. "George didn't make that wine ten years ago? And we've been paying him top wages with all kinds of extra perks this whole time?"

"What are you getting steamed about Jim? He put The White Crown under because of that lie," Bill Stacy growled.

Nicki held up a hand. "He hurt a lot of people because of that lie. And he was going to repeat it."

"What?" Now Jeremy Brennan looked stunned. "He didn't make his new blend either? Who did he pay off for it this time?"

"He couldn't. He was broke and up to his neck in gambling debts," Nicki said.

"We confirmed that with his bookie in New York," Chief Turnlow added.

"Then the wine *was* his?" Jeremy asked.

"No. He didn't have the talent to do that kind of blend. But this time instead of paying for it, he stole it." Nicki turned and faced the bar. "Isn't that right, Geri?"

"How... how would I know? George never confided in me. I had no idea he put his name on someone else's blend," Geri said.

"Oh? When I asked Stella who she told about her bargain with George all those years ago, she said hardly anyone. Just her mother, Victor and one of the interns she was friendly with."

"Victor knew all this time?" Jim snorted, his eyes flashing fire before he pursed his lips and looked at the floor. After a few seconds, he glanced at Geri. "*You* were the intern when Stella worked here."

"Jim mentioned that when I went to interview him a few days after the murder," Nicki said, her gaze on Geri. "You must have realized your wine was being switched and remembered the story Stella had told you ten years ago. All you had to do was take the key Jim kept on a hook in his office and let yourself into George's private room while he was off at one of the other wineries. You must have found your personal mark on some of those barrels in that room and figured out he was gradually switching his wine for yours."

Geri kept her eyes down and her hand swiping the dishtowel back and forth across the bar. "I didn't do anything wrong."

"When you gave us a sample of your personal blend, I thought it was odd that someone with so much experience in the industry would create such a mediocre quality and not recognize it. It was also a strange coincidence when Victor said you'd signed and paid for ten American oak barrels,"

The assistant winemaker looked up. "That's not unusual. A lot of winemakers sign out ten barrels at a time."

"Maybe," Nicki conceded. "But when the chief and I went to check your stacked barrels, we counted twelve, not ten. And two of them didn't have your mark on the bottom. One of those was the same barrel you drew the tasting sample from for Alex and me. They were the only barrels in your area of the storage room that had no mark on them, just like the ones in George's locked area. Those had no mark on them either. Because you, Victor and Stella came up with the idea and never shared it with George. So he never knew to check. After you discovered what George was doing, you must have started switching the barrels back. You know how to operate a forklift. Victor told me almost everyone working here could, including you."

When Geri retreated into silence, Nicki tried another approach. "Since Jim and Jeremy are already familiar with the taste of George's wine, I suppose we could ask them to take a sample from one of his barrels, and then one of yours. They can tell us which matches the special blend George gave them to taste. And Bill can also verify the wine is the same as the sample you brought to him so he'd take you on as his head winemaker." Nicki glanced over at Bill Stacy. "Isn't that right?"

Without a word, the owner of Todos nodded.

Nicki shifted her gaze back to Geri. "That's why you were at Todos the day we passed you coming out of the parking lot. You were there talking to your new boss. It just hadn't been formally announced yet."

"You're ruining everything!" Geri's hands clasped in front of her chest, her wild gaze darting from face to face until it finally settled on Nicki. "You have no idea how hard it was. All those years, working, trying to prove myself, and doing personal blend after blend until I finally got it right." She looked at Jim. "I knew you'd never give me a chance to be head winemaker. Not a woman. Oh no, that would never happen. So I took my blend to someone who would." She smiled at Bill Stacy. "Someone who cared more for my talent than my gender."

Her gaze came back to Nicki. "I let George sample it when it wasn't ready. I thought that would be okay, and was so excited when he said it was good. The man who never had an encouraging word for me said my blend was good, and I should put up as much as I could. I used all my savings, and even borrowed from Victor so I could buy those ten barrels and the crush vari- etals I needed to make the blend. But George must have recog- nized how great my blend was going to be after the proper aging time, and he stole it. That horrid little man replaced my barrels with ones he'd filled with some inferior, cast-off blend. I only found out when I offered to let Victor sample mine after he'd loaned me some money. He, Stella and I were all friends back when I first started. We knew each other's secrets, and we kept them, too." She looked back down at the bar. "Victor and I are still friends. He would never tell anyone about my blend. But when I took a sample from one of the barrels in the back of my stack rather than opening the usual one in front, it wasn't my blend. And my mark was missing. So I went looking for my wine."

Geri glared at Chief Turnlow and raised her chin a notch. "I didn't do anything wrong. It was *my* wine I poisoned, and if George had asked if he could have a glass of *my* wine after he'd made four bottles of it, I wouldn't have allowed him to drink it. But he didn't ask. Because he stole it."

No one said a word when the chief stepped forward. "Geri, you need to come with me."

## 27

"How did you zero in on Geri Gant, of all people?"

Jenna put the question to Nicki, but the whole group nodded and gave her expectant looks.

It was the day after the assistant winemaker had been arrested for the murder of George Lancer. During the last hour, everyone had decided on a spontaneous drop-in to see how she was doing, and to share their astonishment at how it had all turned out.

They were gathered in her kitchen, enjoying the spread of cheeses, crackers, dips and veggie trays Nicki had thrown together for her unexpected, but very welcome, guests. As a special thank you to her friends and fellow amateur detectives, she'd also made a large platter of gourmet sliders for Jenna, a bowl of zucchini fries for Alex and a dish piled high with chocolate candy with cream centers for Maxie.

Her three cohorts sat on the stools at the kitchen counter, while Tyler, myMason and Chief Turnlow crowded behind them. Everyone was relaxed as they enjoyed their favorite munchie and a glass of premium wine, except for the chief, who declared he was still on duty, so he stuck to bubbly water.

Nicki beamed as she chopped more vegetables. Nothing was better than spending time with family and friends. And she included Chief Turnlow in that definition of "friend", although she suspected it would be a long while before he acknowledged it as well.

She dumped the pile of vegetables onto the depleted plate and moved the candy dish closer to Maxie with a huge wink. But not before she stole a piece and popped it into her mouth.

"I'd like to know that myself," the chief spoke up. "Before you came to me with your suspicion on who killed Lancer, I have to admit that Geri wasn't even on my radar. So how did she get on yours? What gave her away?"

Nicki smiled. "Just as I said, it was the barrels that told the story. Only my first clue wasn't in the appearance, but in the size."

"Size?" Jenna adjusted her large glasses on the bridge of her nose. "French or American oak, the barrels are all the same size."

"Yes. Sixty gallon barrels." Nicki nodded and grinned at Alex. "Remember the day we went to see Bill Stacy at Todos? And we saw Geri there that morning?"

"We passed her when we pulled into the parking lot and she was pulling out onto the road," Alex said.

"That's right." Nicki looked at the rest of the group. "And I asked Bill what she was doing there, and he said she was swapping out barrels. Then later I asked Geri the same question, and she said she was delivering barrels because Holland had extra and Todos needed them."

"They told different stories," the chief grunted.

"What does that have to do with the barrel size, dear?" Maxie asked.

"Geri was driving a small compact with faded blue paint. I remembered it clearly. It wasn't any bigger than my Toyota. You couldn't fit one barrel in that car, much less several."

"She lied," Jenna said.

"They both lied," the chief corrected.

Nicki leaned her elbows on the counter. "Exactly. Why would they both lie? At the memorial service, Geri told me how difficult it is for a woman to do well in the wine industry. Even I could tell that neither George nor Jim Holland were going to give her an opportunity. And she also said that she looked for a long time for a helping hand. Past tense. She didn't say she *is* looking or *still* looking, she said it as though she wasn't looking any more. At the time I thought she meant she'd finally given up and was resigned to being an assistant."

"Until Matt told you Bill Stacy and Jim Holland were searching for a head winemaker to replace George, except Bill had stopped his search," Jenna proclaimed.

"Bill wouldn't have any problem promoting a woman," Alex said. "His sister is a doctor and his mother was the winemaker at his parents' winery. He was raised with accomplished women."

"Right," Nicki agreed. "Besides, he told us he'd found his new head winemaker. I'm sure all Geri had to do was produce a sample of her special blend. Since Bill didn't get a sneak taste from George, like Jim and Jeremy did, he had no idea it was the same wine."

Chief Turnlow smiled. "So you were right when you said it was about the wine."

"And a winemaker who couldn't repeat history and buy someone else's creation because he was paying blackmail and had a gambling habit. He was broke." Nicki sighed. "Once Geri discovered he was stealing her wine, she started switching the barrels back. But she didn't have enough time to get them all switched before George died. She ended up with two of his barrels still in her stack. She was counting on the death being treated as a simple heart attack, at least long enough for her to get all the barrels switched back."

"But that's not what happened, thanks to you," the chief said. "You were sure it was murder right from the start."

"And you weren't," Nicki laughed. "But you still sealed off the room until you knew for sure one way or the other. It made all the difference."

"I really stopped by to let you know that our search of Geri's house turned up the missing key, and several bottles of what looks and smells like the nicotine used to kill George, and to scare you off. They're at the lab now. It seems she was making the stuff herself. Had a 'how to' printout she probably got off the Internet."

"That's too bad, really," Nicki sighed. "None of this would have happened if it hadn't been for George's greed for money and fame."

"Geri had other choices. She didn't have to kill him," the chief pointed out. "Don't waste your time feeling sorry for her. You did an excellent job putting it all together and figuring it out."

"*We* did an excellent job," Nicki insisted.

Tyler reached over his fiancée's shoulder for another slider. When she gave him a frown, he just grinned and moved the platter of vegetables closer to her.

"You two make a good team," he said before popping the mini-hamburger into his mouth.

"A one-time experience," Chief Turnlow declared firmly. "Isn't that right, Nicki?"

Nicki smiled. "Absolutely."

"I'm sure you can find something less dangerous to stick your nose into," the chief nodded.

"Uh huh," Jenna and Alex said in unison.

There was a loud knock on the front door. Tyler grabbed another slider and quickly backed away from Alex. "I'll go see who it is."

A minute later he returned to the kitchen, a huge grin on his face. He glanced over at Nicki. "I just met him, but I'm assuming you already know this guy?"

Matt stepped through the doorway and stopped short when he saw the large crowd gathered in Nicki's kitchen.

"Um. Well, I just came to talk with Nicki. And. Well, um..." he trailed off as his cheeks glowed a bright red.

Tyler raised an eyebrow. "Talk? With that I'm-ready-to-grovel bouquet in your hands? Looks more like an apology to me."

While the women raised hands to their mouths to hide their smiles, the chief gave Tyler a stern look.

"No use acting like you haven't been in that same position yourself, son." He walked over and stood in front of the embarrassed editor. "I'm Chief Turnlow. We spoke on the phone."

Matt shook the chief's hand. "Um, yeah. We did."

Her eyes dancing with amusement, Nicki came around the island. She walked right up to Matt and gave him a warm hug. "I'm so glad to see you." She stepped back and looked at the bright mix of daisies he was holding. "Are those for me? A house warming gift for my new kitchen?"

Nicki intended to give the poor guy a graceful way out of the teasing he was sure to get from Ty, but might have known Matt wouldn't take it. He had an incredibly wide honest streak.

"No. Tyler's right. They're an apology." Matt smiled at her. "I got your article."

Nicki tilted her head to one side. "Which one?"

"The one on the wildflowers, where you wrote about them not flourishing and finding another home if the grapevines got too bossy, judgmental and nasty. Even a pissed-off, clueless editor can pick up on the meaning in that."

Behind Nicki, Jenna chuckled. "Subtle, Connors. Very subtle."

"Sometimes it doesn't pay to be subtle," Nicki told him before turning her head and grinning at her friends. "What do you think?"

"He got on a plane and brought flowers. He can stay," Alex declared.

Jenna and Maxie nodded their agreement.

Matt laughed. "Thanks. So, what are we talking about?"

"How Nicki very cleverly solved the murder," Jenna said.

"I know. The chief called me just before I boarded the plane," Matt admitted, smiling at Nicki. "Pretty impressive, Sherlock."

"Okay. Then we moved on to what it feels like to know you're toast," Tyler declared.

"A feeling you're certainly acquainted with." Alex nodded, slapping his hand when he tried to grab another slider.

"Toast?" Matt sounded as confused as he looked.

"Yeah," Tyler grinned. "When you screw up so badly you have to spring for a plane ticket so you can apologize in person."

"And don't forget the flowers," Matt said, holding them out to Nicki.

Tyler shrugged. "Hey man, they're daisies, not roses."

Matt's eyes narrowed. "I happen to know she likes daisies."

"Well if you know so much about her, why did you act like such a jerk?" Jenna demanded.

The tall dark-haired editor sighed and ran his free hand through his hair. "That's what I came to apologize for. I was a jerk. A really worried one, but still a jerk."

"Never mind." Nicki laughed and reached for the flowers Matt was holding out to her. "We'll talk about it later."

# READER'S CORNER

**To My Readers:**

Thank you for spending time to read *A Special Blend of Murder*. As you know, the book takes place in the wine country located in Northern California. Some of the best wines in the world are produced in the Sonoma and Napa Valley regions. In October of 2017, deadly fires broke out across the two valleys and up into the northern coastal region. Forty-two people lost their lives, and almost nine thousand homes and businesses burned to the ground. I live in Northern California, about forty miles southeast of our wonderful wine country, and know how resilient this State is in the face of disasters. But if you happen to be living or visiting near the San Francisco area, our wine country could really use your support. So please visit, if you get the chance. It's still beautiful country, and the vast majority of the wineries are open and always happy to have visitors. There are so many wonderful wineries and restaurants and places to stay, it would be nearly impossible to list them all. But I have to admit, I do have some favorites that I am happy to recommend in this and future books in the series. I'm sure Nicki and all her friends would give them a "thumbs up".

Sincerely,
**Cat Chandler**
I have no affiliation with these two wineries, which rank among my favorites. I simply enjoy visiting them.

## CLINE WINERY

Located on Arnold Drive (Hwy 121/116), about fifteen minutes outside of Sonoma, I can honestly say that I have never had anything but a great glass, or bottle, of wine from Cline. Whenever a Cline Winery wine shows up in the "Wine & Spirits" section of my local grocery store, I buy it. Cline uses a combination of grapes from their own winery and from the Russian River region near the Pacific coastline. The wine tasting facility is always busy, and the staff there is always friendly. I'd suggest arriving near opening time. Cline is so popular, that parking can get a bit tight at times.

## LEDSON WINERY

Ledson has a real visual impact. Built to look like either a small castle, or very large mansion, it's all black and set off the road by itself. It's on Hwy 12, between the town of Sonoma and Santa Rosa, and worth the stop just to see the place. The grounds are beautiful, and inside there is a large wine + shop, as well as very elegantly appointed, multiple tasting rooms. And—they produce good wine. So it's a win all the way around.

## AUTHOR'S NOTE:

I really do appreciate all my readers. Time is precious, and it means a lot that you would spend some of yours reading my book. If you'd like to follow more adventures of Nicki and her friends, please sign up for my reading list:

http://eepurl.com/dhGQYr

New subscribers will receive a link to download a PDF file containing a full chapter that was not used in the book. This is a backstory about how Nicki, Jenna and Alex met in The Big Apple, New York City.

You'll be notified of new releases in my mystery series, and I never share email addresses with any other author or organization. What goes on my list, stays only on my list. I also do not inundate my subscribers with emails of weekly or even monthly newsletters. This is for new release announcements only, and occasionally (very occasionally) a notice of something coming up concerning my books. I will also be adding additional free scenes or short stories only to my list subscribers, with the link appearing in the email.

Also, if you enjoyed the book, please consider leaving a review on Amazon. Good reviews make an author's day, and writing is a lonely business. Hearing a word of praise every now and again really gives a lift to those of us hunched over a keyboard for a good part of our day. If you have any suggestions you think would help improve the book, or find typos or other errors, please feel free to contact me at: cathrynchandler-author@gmail.com. I'm also always open to story ideas. Or if there is a particular character you'd like to see more of, please let me know.

And as always—Happy Reading!

*Cat*

www.CathrynChandler.com

## ALSO BY CAT CHANDLER

**A Food & Wine Club Cozy Mystery:**

A Special Blend of Murder (Revision Feb 2018)

Dinner, Drinks & Murder (Revision Feb 2018)

A Burger, Fries & Murder (March 2018)

Made in the USA
Monee, IL
09 September 2020